Sign up to my newsletter, and you will be notified when I release my next book!

Join my Patreon (patreon.com/jackbryce) to get early access to my work!

ISBN-13: TBD

D1519846

A SLICE OF LIFE FANTASY ADVENTURE

JACK BRYCE

To skinny jeans.

Frontier Summoner 5

David's Character Sheet

Below is David's character sheet at the end of book 4.

Name: David Wilson

Class: Frontier Summoner

Level: 8

Health: 90/90

Mana: 45/45 (+10 from Hearth Treasures)

Skills:

Summon Minor Spirit — Level 17 (3 mana)

Summon Domesticant — Level 16 (5 mana)

Summon Guardian — Level 15 (7 mana)

Summon Aquana's Avatar — Level 11 (10 mana)

Summon Storm Elemental — Level 9 (10 mana)

Bind Familiar — Level 3 (15 mana)

Aura of Protection — Level 1 (4 mana)

Banish — Level 1 (6 mana)

Identify Plants — Level 14 (1 mana)

Foraging — Level 15 (1 mana)

Trapping — Level 16 (1 mana)

Alchemy — Level 17 (1 mana)

Farming — Level 6 (1 mana)

Ranching — Level 1 (1 mana)

Chapter 1

I took a deep breath, taking in the cold air mixed with the smell of wood smoke and fresh bread that always seemed to permeate Gladdenfield Outpost.

It was good to be back here. I always enjoyed my visits to the vibrant community.

Today's work had been a delivery of a batch of

freshly harvested tomatoes and a pickup of some construction supplies I needed to finish work on the homestead.

Now, before I would head back to the homestead, I wanted to check in on Darny at the Wild Outrider. Maybe have a cup of coffee and something to eat before I'd head out. And, of course, while I was in town, I'd pay Celeste a visit.

Whistling a jaunty tune, I made my way down the dusty streets of the lively frontier settlement. Wherever I went, people offered me smiles of recognition, greetings, and friendly nods.

My victories at the Aquana Festival's Gauntlet Run and tournament had laid the foundations of my legend. However, braving Nimos Sedia and returning Clara's party from the maw of a dragon at Hrothgar's Hope had truly cemented my position as a local hero.

Vanity didn't plague me as much as it did some men, but there were lots of advantages to being well-known, not the least of which were discounts and the friendly disposition of most strangers I met. In addition, it was nice to receive some recognition.

After a brisk walk, I arrived at the doors to the Wild Outrider tavern. A few dwarves were loitering outside, smoking pipes and drinking ale. They greeted me warmly, hailing me as Dragon-Slayer, the title Lord Vartlebeck of Ironfast had granted me after I defeated the dragon at Hrothgar's Hope.

I answered their greetings, then headed inside. The tavern was quiet, with just a few of the regular patrons seeking a brief respite from another hard day's work on the frontier.

Darny waved me over before I could take in the small crowd, and I ambled over to him with a casual smile on my lips.

"Howdy, David!" he exclaimed. "Good to see ya! How are things at the homestead?"

"Pretty good," I replied. "Most of the work that came with the expansion is done, and Diane, Leigh, and I are settling into things."

"That sounds mighty fine," Darny said as he poured me a coffee. By now, the burly innkeeper knew exactly how I drank mine. "I'd love to see the place someday!"

"Well, I'll be happy to have you over," I said congenially. "Once we have the place in order, we'll invite you and your wife."

"I appreciate that, David," he said with a warm smile as he placed a steaming mug of strong coffee in front of me.

"So, is Celeste around?" I asked.

Darny shook his head. "She headed out an hour or so ago, but she said she'd be back soon. You're more than welcome to wait for her."

"Yeah," I said. "I think I'll do that. I've been looking forward to seeing her."

He smiled and shot me a wink. "Well, I get the idea that feelin's mutual," he said. "Celeste talks about you a lot."

Admittedly, that was a little flattering. I smiled and nodded my thanks before taking my coffee and turning around. I scanned the tables, trying to find a nice spot when I saw a familiar face.

It took me a moment to place the older elf woman's face, and as I furrowed my brow trying to do so, she noticed me as well. The same light of recognition lit up her expression.

And then I remembered. It was Brynneth, the elderly elf woman I had met at the Aquana Festival.

Brynneth had told me about Aquana and the elven religion and customs. She had seemed very knowledgeable and friendly — if a bit aloof, but many elves were like that.

She sat alone at a table, and recognition dawned on her face as she offered me a broad smile. I suddenly got an idea, and I walked over.

"Hello there, Brynneth," I said. "Remember me? We met at the festival. I am David Wilson. Might I join you?"

The aged elf turned her bright silver eyes upon me, and a smile creased her lined face. "But of course. I remember you well. Please, sit."

I took the seat opposite her with gratitude. "I appreciate you taking the time. How have you been since the festival?"

She smiled. "Ah well, I've been helping a few of the homesteaders around preparing for autumn. It's hard work, but there is plenty of it. Once it gets colder, I will head to the city to winter there. And yourself?"

"Same thing, I suppose," I said with a chuckle. "Getting the homestead ready and improving life one step at a time."

"Ah, such is life on the frontier. What can I help you with?"

I straightened in the chair. "Well," I began, "since we spoke, I have been eager to learn more of elven culture. Who better to ask than you? You were very kind and patient last time. Not to mention knowledgeable."

She waved her hand modestly. "Oh pish. I'm hardly so knowledgeable. But I shall help if I can. What did you wish to know?"

I considered how best to phrase my question. Ever since Celeste and I had kissed for the first time in Ironfast, I had wanted to advance our relationship and take us to the next level. She had made vague mention of courtship, and I knew that Waelin, her uncle, was involved somehow.

I expected I would need Waelin's approval. If she had any other family, I might need theirs too, perhaps. But getting the actual knowledge from an elf firsthand was preferable to guesswork.

"What can you tell me of how elven couples traditionally progress from mutual interest to betrothal? The delicate nuances of courtship among your people are still somewhat mysterious to me."

Brynneth nodded sagely, a twinkle in her silver eyes. "Ah, so it is romance that intrigues you? Worry not, I shall enlighten you."

With that, she sat back and ordered us both something to drink. I accepted her offer graciously, eager to hear more about the rituals of elven courtship.

Chapter 2

Brynneth took a sip of wine before beginning her explanation. "For elves, love is a rare jewel to be treasured, and courtship conducted with care and poetry. As with crafting a fine work of art, there are formal traditions we follow."

I smiled and nodded. "I imagined as much."

She answered my smile with one of her own. "In addition, some of the courtship rituals of elvenkind might prove more difficult for human males. However, things have softened a little since the Upheaval, with humans and elves mixing more often."

"Really?" I inquired. "How so?"

"Well, an important piece of background information is that elven men..." She paused for a moment to consider how to phrase it, and then she just shrugged. "Elven males are not very interested in mating. Most do so only once every twenty to forty, maybe fifty, years."

I nodded slowly, recalling Diane telling me the same thing shortly after we had met.

"Elven women, however," Brynneth continued, "have a drive similar to that of human females. This discrepancy is the origin of what the Coalition has called the Elven Marriage — where females flock to rarer males with more... well, *needs*."

"Yeah, I recall hearing about that."

"Well, humans have such higher needs, and some elven women are attracted to them for those reasons. As such, we see a gradual softening of the cultural barriers that stand in the way of elves and humans mating."

"Alright," I said. "I think I follow."

"Still, some of those barriers remain. However, let's begin at the beginning. In our culture, the courtship ritual is initiated by the man. If the woman wishes to initiate courtship, she will simply ask a man to court her. We are very direct in such things." She raised an eyebrow. "However, I expect you're already past this initial stage."

"Yes," I said, not sure how much to say.

"Where exactly are you?" She waved away any complaint I might have. "Don't worry. I won't tell anyone."

"We kissed," I said.

"Ah!" she hummed. "Then you are dealing with a smitten lady indeed, for it is highly uncommon for elves to even kiss outside of wedlock."

My jaw dropped at kiss. "Wedlock?" I murmured.

"Yes," Brynneth said. "Elves do not engage in physical relations without being married. In your particular case, you have already found an elf maiden willing to take an extra step — the kiss — which you humans exchange more easily. You should consider that a serious concession on her part — a sign that she is really, *really* interested in you and willing to compromise to close any cultural gap."

Brynneth's words elicited a smile from me. I knew Celeste liked me — and the feeling was mutual, alright — but to know that she had gone beyond what was normal in her culture was very flattering. It was also a sign that we should progress things.

Brynneth smiled knowingly. "We may skip the tradition of gift-giving and *tulanei* — the first Tea-Drinking — in this particular case, but the next step would be the *alath-manae*."

"The *alath-manae*?" I asked.

"Yes. It would be 'the Moonlit Walk' in your language. It is a nighttime stroll and officially the first date without chaperones — although you skipped that part entirely. During the *alath-manae*, the suitor must entertain his lady and, at some point, recite a rhyme he himself composed to honor her — the *alath*."

"A rhyme?"

"Just so."

I blinked. False modesty aside, I had been blessed with some talents in life. Poetry was not one of them.

"And what if I'm… well, *not a very good poet*."

"Ah," she hummed. "That is a human limitation. All elves are schooled in the arts. This is a particular phase of courtship where your human culture may hamper you. I suggest getting help. Traditionally, it is frowned upon to get help composing the rhyme. However, there is also *elaethuirne*, which in your language would be 'the Rule of Sisters to Come', which allows the male suitor to enlist the aid of one of his other wives in courting a new wife."

I nodded slowly, my mind immediately turning to Diane.

"If you have wives, which I suppose you do, they may aid you in composing the verse."

"Alright," I said. "So, I compose an *alath*. And

then I invite her along to a Moonlit Walk. How do I extend the invitation?"

"Always in person. And the *alath-manae* must take place between four and seven days after the invitation has been extended. Barring force majeure, failing to do so is a great insult to the prospect and is likely to begin a feud between families."

I chuckled and shook my head. "This is more complex than filing taxes!"

Brynneth gave a pleasant chuckle. "And more deadly, also. Now, during the *alath-manae*, you recite your verse. The *alath-manae* may end in three ways: the first, both parties found the Moonlit Walk satisfactory, and the courtship shall continue. The second, one or both were left unsatisfied by the ritual, and the courtship shall end. The third, one or both were insulted by or during the ritual, and the families shall feud. This feud is most often concluded through a battle to the death by two champions — one of each family."

"This… I had no idea this was so violent."

"The feuds are very rare," Brynneth assured me.

"I haven't heard of more than five such instances in over two centuries. You have nothing to fear."

I nodded, a little reassured. "So, what follows after that?"

"Marriage," Brynneth said. "If the maiden sees in the suitor what her heart desires, the maid will answer with a verse of her own, the *ylath*, which in essence is a veiled invitation to the male to propose to her. Those sweet words seal the beginning of their path as a couple. After hearing the *ylath*, the man may propose, provided the two families have met."

"Families?"

"Hm, yes… Although 'family' isn't exactly the proper translation. It's about the people most deeply involved in the beginnings of the lives of the would-be betrothed. These need not necessarily be parents or even blood. It usually requires the elders who, under elven law, will always remain responsible to an extent for their offspring."

"So… Assuming that my… candidate's parents passed, and an uncle took care of her, it would be that uncle?"

"Just so."

"And since my parents have also passed, and my grandparents took care of me, it would be my grandparents?"

"Just so."

I nodded slowly. It looked like I was going to host a dinner party or something for Waelin and my grandparents, who couldn't have more different personalities.

"This is going to be interesting," I muttered.

"The families must meet in a way that allows them both to prepare food for the other. Baked goods are common, but this is a relatively freeform ritual. If the event passes satisfactorily, the man may propose to the woman at any time thereafter."

"And otherwise, we'll have to fight each other to the death over a selection of elven pies?"

She laughed freely at that before taking a swig from her goblet. "There is indeed a chance for a feud, but I've never heard of such a thing. If everyone is polite and does their best, there is no reason this should go wrong."

I chuckled. "Well, you don't know my

grandpa… So, is there a specific way to propose?"

"Remarkably similar to human custom, we get on one knee. It must, however, be the knee facing the ruins of Iamana that touches the floor. Since we are bereft of the glorious temples of Iamana since the Upheaval, custom demands that it must now be the left knee that touches the ground."

"I should've brought a pen…"

She chuckled again. "Then, you will speak the words, '*Kel-amon, nan-aieseth tara, aes ylmar antara aieser. Vel-ona a vel-mata — ylmë a ylamas faluin.*' This is mandatory."

I swallowed, mouthing the words before turning to her. "What do they mean?"

"It means, '*my love, let not your light fade from me like the starlight fades at dawn. Be at my side and let me linger in your radiance — today and during all the days we may yet be blessed with.*'"

"That… That is very beautiful."

"Those words are so old, that the spoken elven language of today hardly resembles it. To humans, it would be akin to asking someone to marry you in… well, perhaps Latin. Or Sanskrit. We elves care much for tradition."

I smiled. "It's a nice tradition."

She nodded. "I am happy you appreciate it. If the courtship ritual has come this far, it is highly unlikely a woman will refuse. Either way, there are two possible answers. The first is '*Tara uin,*' which means, 'my light is yours'. It constitutes a yes. The second is '*Nan-an tara,*' which could be roughly translated as 'my light is not mine to give' or perhaps 'I cannot give my light free of burden.' That would be a no."

"Alright," I muttered, committing the words to memory.

"Don't worry," she said, offering me a warm smile. "I have never heard of a refusal. Soon afterwards, celebrations may take place, although there are no specific guidelines for how soon this must occur. Different from humans, the bond is made at the acceptance, and the two beloved are married by elven law at that moment."

"Understood," I said.

"And from then on, they are free to share in the deepest pleasures, to wander together, and to further nurture their blossoming bond." Brynneth said. "And once again, while we elves often celebrate the wedding with friends and family, mark that from the moment the words are spoken and the reply in the affirmative is given, you are wed."

"Okay," I said, my head swimming.

She sipped her wine once more. "An elven courtship often lasts a full turning of several years, with many Tea-Drinking ceremonies, exchanging of letters and gifts and many meetings between the families. We do not rush such sacred matters of the heart. But I believe your lady is willing to move faster. This is a necessary compromise."

"How so?" I asked.

"You humans simply don't have centuries, like us elves do."

I nodded thoughtfully. "Of course, that makes sense. What other rituals mark the period of courtship? Do I need a ring like with humans?"

Brynneth pondered for a moment before continuing. "Not necessarily, but it's not forbidden." She offered me a soft smile. "It shouldn't *all* be about elven custom. If you wish to give a ring, then you should do so."

"Alright, and... the wedding celebration?"

"It takes place in a *telhîr*." she replied fondly. "A temporary abode of wood in a place treasured by the couple, often their prospective home. When the time comes, look for me here or in New Springfield, and I will help you construct one."

"Thank you," I said.

She smiled. "Make no mention of it. It warms my heart to see love blossom on the frontier, and I will gladly help."

I thanked Brynneth deeply for indulging my curiosity and for her sage guidance. My mind swirled with the elegant rituals she had illuminated as she returned to her drink.

I would ponder well all she had shared.

Chapter 3

After my enlightening conversation with Brynneth, I lingered in the tavern, lost in thought as I mulled over all she had shared.

The intricate rituals of elven courtship seemed daunting, but my feelings for Celeste made the challenge worthwhile. Celeste was worth any trial, and I wanted to advance our relationship to the next stage.

I nursed my coffee slowly, contemplating how best to broach the subject of courtship with Celeste. Normally not an anxious guy, my palms grew sweaty at the thought of the formalities involved. Though our bond had grown strong, the formal courting rituals still intimidated me.

But then again, I knew her feelings for me were strong. It was as Brynneth had said: she was willing to move faster, and we had even kissed already.

Brynneth's comments had laid bare the strange duality of her attitude towards me, too. On the one hand, she seemed a little shy, while on the other, she had spoken openly of her feelings. Being eloquent, it made sense that elves had no difficulty expressing themselves verbally, while they might be shy in other areas.

Glancing around the rustic tavern interior, I tried to ground myself a little. Doing so, I took comfort in the Wild Outrider's familiarity. How many times had I sat in this very spot, sharing idle conversation or companionable silence with my frontier companions? The tavern had become a second home.

My reverie was interrupted by the creak of the front door. I looked up to see Celeste entering, her lithe frame draped in a gossamer lavender dress. Late afternoon sunlight streaming through the windows enveloped her in a halo, heightening her ethereal beauty, while her pointed ears gave her an exotic charm. My breath caught at the sight.

When her bright eyes met mine, her delicate features blossomed into a radiant smile that made my heart skip a beat. With graceful steps, she approached my table, and I stood to greet her.

"David! What a lovely surprise," she exclaimed, her musical voice imbuing my name with affection.

I took her slender hand in mine, relishing its soft warmth. "The lovely surprise is you. Please, join me."

I pulled out a chair for her, unable to take my eyes off her captivating face. Celeste smoothed her skirts and sat, regarding me keenly.

"You seem contemplative today. Is aught

amiss?" she inquired; her green eyes luminous with concern.

I shook my head, touched by her caring nature. "No, nothing's wrong. I just have a lot on my mind."

She cocked her head slightly, considering me. "Would sharing your thoughts lighten their burden?"

Her gentle prodding almost drew the truth from my lips, but I hesitated, not wanting to spoil the surprise right away. "I'm just feeling cooped up indoors today. Would you like to go for a walk with me?"

Celeste's eyes lit up. "I would be delighted. Some fresh air would do us both good."

I stood and offered her my arm, which she took with a gracious dip of her head. Escorting her outside, I was struck anew by her graceful carriage and the adoring glances it drew. I puffed up a bit in masculine pride at having her on my arm.

We strolled down Gladdenfield's dusty main thoroughfare, exchanging pleasant conversation. The rumble of wagons and amiable shouts of passersby surrounded us, but Celeste's voice was all I heard. Her playful humor and quick wit kept me enthralled.

"So, what brings you to Gladdenfield?" she finally asked.

"Business," I replied. "We had some produce and goods from the homestead to sell, and I also needed to get some building supplies for the expansion."

"I would love to see it soon!" she hummed.

"You will," I assured her, giving her hand a gentle squeeze.

As we spoke, I snuck frequent glances at her lovely profile. The sun gilded her amber hair like a halo, and her eyes shone like emeralds. My heart swelled with emotion. She was without a doubt the most beautiful woman around.

Upon reaching the palisade gates, I turned to her eagerly. "Would you like to head out for a bit? We can go for a short walk in the forest."

She hesitated for a moment. "Isn't it dangerous? I do not have my sword with me."

I waved it away. "We'll stay within sight of the

walls. Besides, I have my spells. No harm will come to us."

"In that case," she beamed. "Yes! I would love a little forest air!" Delight sparked in her emerald gaze as I smiled and led her on.

Together, Celeste and I passed beyond the gates into the woods. The sunlight that pierced the leafy ceiling painted Celeste's fair skin with whorls of gold. A look of blissful contentment graced her features as she turned her face skyward, breathing deeply of the pine-scented air.

Much of the elves remained a mystery to me, but I knew she was a wood elf, and that her love of the forest was deep. I knew the other elves had some sort of dislike of her kind, and her Class — the Stellar Maiden — was even forbidden among them.

"The forest is particularly lovely today," I remarked, wanting to draw her into conversation. "Don't you think?"

"Oh yes," Celeste agreed, closing her eyes briefly as if to better capture the sensory details surrounding us. "It's so peaceful and vibrant. I feel at home in nature here."

"Is it like Tannoris?" I asked softly.

"Indeed," she replied, gifting me with a radiant smile. "And yet… no."

I gave her a confused look, and she laughed freely as she squeezed my hand. "It is a complex question, David," she said. "The forests of Tannoris had more magic in them. And I do not mean the sensation of nature's magic — which is equal in all forests — but *actual* magic. Fantastic vistas and creatures that would not be possible without the palpable energies of mana."

I nodded. "Just like our forests before the Upheaval had no such magic at all."

"Exactly!" she agreed. "Neither Earth nor Tannoris wholly remain. In return, we have been given something new. The other races who live fast and are young — foxkin, catkin, dwarves — they have all adapted so swiftly to this new place. Whereas the ancient elves struggle with such change."

I looked at her sideways. "Do you struggle?"

She turned pensive for a moment. "I try not to," she said at last. "The forest speaks to my soul in its own wordless language. It's like music, or poetry, just beyond my grasp but intuitively understood."

I nodded. "I think I know what you mean. There's a certain rhythm to the forest. The breeze in the leaves, the babbling brook, the birdsong… it all comes together in a natural symphony."

Celeste's eyes lit up at my description. "Yes, exactly! It's so wonderful to find someone who appreciates such things the way I do. And since the Upheaval, the forests still speak. But their voices have changed. It is vital to myself — and to my kin who do not wish to languish in melancholy — that we love this new voice and accept that the old one has gone."

We continued on in awed silence for a time, two kindred spirits finding solace amidst nature's splendor. I snuck admiring glances at Celeste as we walked, and more than once I caught her looking at me as well.

As we passed a sun-dappled glade, Celeste paused and turned to me. She smiled and said, "I've been meaning to ask — how goes the expansion of the homestead? I recall you mentioning ambitious plans to enlarge it."

Her interest delighted me. "It's going very well! We just finished the major structural work. I built an expansion with a whole new floor."

"How marvelous!" Celeste clapped her hands together. "Please, tell me all about it."

Encouraged by her enthusiasm, I described the changes eagerly. "Part of the bottom floor is the original cabin, kept intact, although it's now one big living area. There's a new kitchen, a workshop, dining room, and a storage room as well. I expanded the cellar too."

Celeste nodded along, eyes alight with interest. "It sounds lovely so far. And the top level?"

"The master suite's up there," I explained. "A large bedroom for me and my wives."

At the mention of that, a slight blush vibrantly colored Celeste's cheeks, and she motioned for me to continue.

"There's also a new bathroom and a few bedrooms for guests."

"How industrious of you!" Celeste praised. "Constructing an entire house is no small feat. You must have worked tremendously hard."

I shrugged, pleased by her words. "It was a lot of work, but worth it to make the homestead comfortable for everyone. Though there's still much I want to do to improve it. I'd love to get your impressions on what needs work when you visit."

Her eyes crinkled warmly. "Just say when, and I'll be there."

Our leisurely stroll resumed, but now my resolve to ask about courtship was strengthened, buoyed by her interest in the homestead. Especially the way she had blushed at the mention of the master bedroom had told me many things.

As we looped back toward town, I turned the subject to her singing at the tavern. "How's the singing going?" I asked. "I hear Darny is very happy with having you perform regularly."

Celeste laughed musically. "He is too kind!

Music is such a passion of mine; it's wonderfully validating when it moves others."

"From what I've seen of your talents, I have no doubt your singing can silence the entire tavern," I said. "And that's quite the feat considering the number of bawdy patrons Darny gets."

She laughed at that and nodded. "They are quite the crowd. You know, I was a little intimidated by them at first, but I see now that most of them are kind. They are just… rougher than what I am used to."

I grinned ear to ear. "Frontier folks are generally good people." I agreed.

Ahead, a babbling brook came into view, and I slowed our pace, turning to face her directly. The moment had come, and I could see the question in her eyes.

Pulse racing, I gazed into her emerald eyes as I held her hands. "Celeste, I… have something important I wish to ask you."

She met my gaze unwaveringly. "Yes, of course? Anything, my David."

I steadied my nerves and uttered the formal

invitation: "Would you do me the honor of joining me for an *alath-manae* in four nights' time?"

Celeste's eyes widened, and her cheeks flushed prettily. Then delight crinkled the corners of her eyes. "My beloved," she hummed, squeezing my hands. "Nothing would make me happier. I gladly accept your invitation."

Relief and joy flooded my veins. By elven custom, she had just agreed to an official courtship! Barely resisting the urge to embrace her, I settled for squeezing her hand gently.

"You've made me very happy," I confessed.

"And you me," she murmured, eyes shining. "Happier than I may express! I was hoping for this in the most secret place of my heart. And it flatters me greatly that you have gone to the trouble of learning the customs of my kind."

I smiled. "I want to do things right, Celeste."

She beamed and embraced me, and I reveled in the feeling of her warm and soft body pressed close to me. I was eager to know her more deeply, and by the way she sighed and leaned into me, I could tell the same desire lived in her.

We stood like that for a while before we walked back to town together, fingers interlocked. Anticipation thrummed in the air between us. I could not wait for our Moonlit Walk and the courtship that lay ahead.

Chapter 4

The sun hung low on the horizon, bathing the forest in a warm amber glow as I drove down the winding path back to the homestead in my Jeep.

Tapping my fingers on the steering wheel, I hummed softly, still elated after inviting Celeste to the *alath-manae*. When in a high mood like this, everything about the frontier was even more pleasant to me, and I found myself greatly enjoying the ride.

When the homestead came into view, nestled amidst the trees and wildflowers on the banks of the Silverthread River, my heart swelled with pride and affection. Diane and Leigh would be inside, likely fixing dinner or tending to chores.

I was eager to share the good news with them about my progress with Celeste. While Diane had had her reservations about elves in general, she had warmed up to Celeste on our quest to Hrothgar's Hope to free Clara and her party of adventurers.

Although we still needed to have a deep conversation about the potential new member of my harem, I felt confident that she would accept Celeste as her harem sister. As for Leigh, I had no doubts either.

I pulled up on the dirt road in front of the homestead, put the Jeep in park, and headed up the gravel walkway towards the front porch. Inside, I could hear the lively and vibrant chatter of

Diane and Leigh. To me, those voices were like coming home, and the sound filled me with warmth.

As I stepped through the front door and was greeted by the mouthwatering aroma of Diane's venison stew, my stomach growled eagerly. I hung my jacket on the hook by the door and made my way towards the warm and welcoming clatter.

In the kitchen, Leigh and Diane were chatting amiably near the stove. Diane stood over a large iron pot, her fox tail swishing as she stirred its bubbling contents with a wooden spoon. Leigh leaned back against the counter, sipping a drink and keeping Diane company.

When Leigh's bright blue eyes met mine, her pretty face broke into a grin. "Well hey there, mister! Back from your errands already?"

Diane's head popped up, her fox ears twitching. "David, you're home!"

Before I could react, she rushed over to envelop me in a tight embrace. I held her slender frame against me, breathing in the sweet scent of her hair with its slight hint of lavender. A moment later, her lips had found mine.

"We've missed you today," Diane murmured when she pulled back, nuzzling my neck affectionately. I gave her a little squeeze before releasing her.

"Not as much as I've missed my two favorite ladies," I replied warmly as Leigh took her place and gave me a hug, pressing her delicious body against mine.

"That so?" she hummed. "And you didn't pay a visit to that *third* favorite lady o' yours?" Her words held no bitterness, only gentle teasing, and I grinned as she spoke them.

"Now Leigh, you know good and well there's more than enough room in my heart for all of you." I shot her a playful wink, and she laughed.

"Enough room for a whole busload," she joked before giving me a warm kiss on my cheek.

Diane's blue eyes shone eagerly up at me. "So, how was your day in town? Did you get all your errands done?"

"I sure did," I replied. "It was a very productive trip. I made some good deals selling our produce and got the supplies I needed. What I couldn't offload at the market, I handed over for sale with Randal at the store."

"Well, that's mighty fine," said Leigh. "Good to hear business is boomin' for our little homestead."

Diane nodded her agreement. "Yes, I'm so proud of how hard you work to provide for us." She squeezed my hand affectionately.

"I appreciate you, ladies. Couldn't do it without your support." I gave them both a grateful smile. "But that's not the only news from my trip. I have something else exciting to share."

Leigh's eyes lit up with curiosity. "Oh yeah? Well don't keep us in suspense now!"

"I formally invited Celeste to join me for an *alath-manae* in four nights," I revealed, "and she happily accepted!"

"A what now?" Leigh asked, eyebrow perked.

I chuckled. "An *alath-manae*. It means something like Moonlit Walk. It's a formal elven date, which is an important step in progressing the relationship."

"Progressin' the relationship, huh?" Leigh quipped. "Is that what they call it these days?"

We all shared a laugh at that, and I could see that my women were excited for this upcoming expansion of our little group. Their excitement was sincere, and that made me all the happier.

"It's about time you courted that girl proper," Leigh said, blue eyes dancing merrily. "I bet she's been waiting for it for a while now."

Diane clasped her hands, face glowing. "It's very exciting! I didn't even know elves had such complex names for dates."

I laughed and shook my head. "It's a whole thing," I said. "I ran into Brynneth at the Wild Outrider, an elf I spoke to at the Aquana Festival. She told me all about the elven courtship rituals, and there's a meeting between families in store as well." I grinned. "But we'll manage."

Diane chuckled. "Well, come on! Let's eat, and we can talk some more."

As we sat down to dinner, I recounted asking Celeste, describing her delighted reaction. "She told me I've made her happier than she can express," I shared proudly.

"Aww, that just warms my heart," said Diane.

"She clearly adores you."

Leigh nodded knowingly. "Yup, that elven princess is smitten alright. Your courtship will go smooth as silk."

"The thing is," I began hesitantly, "I'll need to compose and recite a poem during the date."

"A poem?" Leigh hummed. "Well, I'll be… That's quite the fancy date!"

I chuckled. "Well, we'll just be ourselves, but this is one formality that I want to do for her. Truth be told, I'm fairly sure she would forgive me if I skipped all of those formalities, but I want to show her that I'm interested in learning about her culture, and I want to make it feel as right as I can for her."

"That's so sweet," Leigh said, and Diane hummed in agreement.

Our conversation flowed easily as we ate, brainstorming ideas for the poetic verse I'd need to recite to Celeste under the moonlight. Though poetry wasn't my forte, with Diane and Leigh's assistance, I felt optimistic we could craft something heartfelt.

Sitting at the worn wooden table with my two loves, bellies full of the delicious meal the girls had cooked up, laughter and liveliness swirling around me, I was filled with profound contentment. Moments like these made all the hard work worthwhile.

After dinner, Leigh brewed coffee while Diane fetched an apple pie she'd baked, its cinnamon aroma mixing deliciously with the roasted coffee scent. We ate by the fireplace and enjoyed each other's company, while Ghostie and Sir Boozles cleaned up in the new kitchen and dining room.

With her head on my shoulder, Diane traced idle patterns on my arm as we chatted. Leigh sprawled comfortably across from us, nudging my foot playfully with hers now and then.

It was good to be home again.

Chapter 5

After some time relaxing by the crackling fire, Diane asked me if I wanted to slip out into the cool night air for a moonlit stroll together. Leigh wanted to remain in the house, but I got a feeling that she was doing so on purpose.

Maybe there was something Diane wanted to

talk to me about…

The sky overhead was a velvety blanket of darkness, punctured by thousands of glittering stars that seemed close enough to pluck from the heavens. A crescent moon cast its pale silvery light over the surrounding forest. Somewhere in the distance, I spotted the shimmering form of Mr. Drizzles as he patrolled the property.

Hand in hand, we made our way down the gently winding path leading away from the homestead, our boots crunching softly on the fertile soil. All around us, the night sounds of the forest played a natural symphony — the lonesome hoot of an owl calling out from the trees, the whisper of wind through the swaying branches, the gentle burble of the nearby stream tumbling over smooth stones.

The crisp night air was clean and refreshing, scented with pine and honeysuckle. I drew in a deep breath, feeling the chill spread through my lungs. I loved being in Gladdenfield, but this was home. The sounds of the forest and gentle babbling of the Silverthread gave me peace.

Beside me, Diane enjoyed our surroundings in a similar manner, a serene smile gracing her lovely features. Her fox ears swiveled occasionally at noises coming from the moon-bathed woods surrounding us.

We walked leisurely, not in any hurry, simply savoring the peaceful beauty of the night and the comfort of one another's presence. Neither of us spoke, content to communicate through gentle squeezes of our joined hands, small caresses, and the occasional brush of shoulders as we strolled.

After some time, Diane gave a happy, contented sigh and nestled her head against my shoulder as we walked. "I'm so glad we decided to take this walk tonight, my love," she said softly. "It's just perfect out here."

I turned my head to press a tender kiss to the top of her head, right between her soft fox ears. "I agree completely," I said. "It's a beautiful moonlit night."

Diane giggled musically, pushing herself closer to me. We continued to stroll, eventually coming up alongside the gently flowing Silverthread that bordered the homestead property. The water shimmered like liquid silver under the moonlight.

Turning to face me directly, Diane took both of my hands in hers, her expression suddenly serious. Her sapphire eyes seemed to glow ethereally in the pale light as she gazed up at me.

I knew something was coming, and I smiled at her, giving her the space she needed to tell me.

"David, my love," she began, "there is something important I want to tell you." Her voice was hushed but rich with emotion.

My brow furrowed slightly with concern as I searched her features, luminous and lovely in the moonlight. "What is it?" I asked gently.

At my question, Diane's expression transformed, her full lips curving into a radiant, joyful smile. Her eyes shone brighter than any star as she drew in a breath and uttered the incredible news.

"I'm pregnant, David! We're going to have a baby."

Shock and elation swept over me in a dizzying rush. Without conscious thought, I swept Diane into my arms, spinning her slender frame around before setting her back on her feet and capturing her lips in a passionate kiss.

When we finally parted, breathless, Diane let out an amused giggle, silver-blue eyes dancing playfully.

"Well, I take it from your reaction that you're pleased by the news?" she teased.

I cupped her lovely face between my hands, gazing at her adoringly. "Diane, 'pleased' doesn't even begin to cover it," I told her fervently. "I'm absolutely overjoyed and excited beyond words! This is a dream come true." I drew her close again, kissing her tenderly.

When I pulled back, I couldn't keep an enormous grin off my face. "How far along are you? When did you find out?" I asked eagerly, squeezing her hands.

"I suppose just a little under two weeks now," Diane revealed, her own smile radiant as she absently stroked her still-flat belly. "I was feeling some odd nausea lately, so I asked Leigh to get me a test from Gladdenfield last week, and I decided to wait until you were gone today to use it. I wanted time alone to work through the emotions either way." She beamed another grin. "And it was positive."

I shook my head, still struggling to wrap my mind around this incredible turn of events. We were going to be parents!

"A baby," I murmured in amazement. "This is just...beyond anything I could have imagined. What wonderful, amazing news."

Diane's sapphire eyes were luminous with joy and excitement. "I could hardly believe it myself at first. But now, thinking of the future together with our child, I'm just so incredibly happy and excited to start this next chapter with you."

She bit her lip as a new thought occurred to her. "Oh! And if it's alright with you, I was hoping to ask Leigh to be the little one's godmother."

I smiled and nodded at once. "Of course! That's a perfect idea. Leigh will be over the moon."

As the enormity of it all sunk in, my swirling emotions were a tempest — exhilaration, nervousness, protectiveness, pure joy. But gazing at Diane's radiant happiness, I knew without any sliver of doubt that this was meant to be.

Reaching out, I tenderly caressed Diane's cheek, looking deep into her starry eyes. "You're going to be the most amazing mother imaginable," I told her sincerely.

Diane nuzzled her cheek against my palm, placing her hand over mine. "And you're going to be the most wonderful father," she replied softly.

Overcome with emotion, I drew her into my arms once more underneath the glittering blanket of stars, holding her as close to me as I possibly could. The future shone with promise and potential. We stayed locked in that tender embrace for long, blissful moments.

Finally, I drew back just enough to look down into her radiant face. "I suppose we should start thinking of potential names," I mused with a smile.

Diane let out an amused chuckle, her arms still looped loosely around my waist. "Soon enough for that, my love," she assured me. "For right now, let's keep it a surprise for the others. Leigh probably suspects, since she got me the test, but I'd like to be a few more weeks in before we tell everyone."

I nodded my agreement and offered her my arm once more. "Shall we continue on with our walk then? We can think about some names as we walk."

"I'd love nothing more," Diane agreed, threading her arm through mine. And with that, we set off again, strolling leisurely down the winding forest path bathed in moonlight and magic.

Chapter 6

After having received the wonderful news from Diane, sleep was very, very far away. Excitement mastered me, and I decided that I would read for a bit before I'd go to sleep, hoping it would distract me and give me some rest.

I settled into my favorite armchair, eager to delve

into the ancient tome of alchemy recipes I had discovered in Hrothgar's Hope. *Potions and Concoctions* was a thick, leather-bound book filled with obscure potion recipes collected by an eccentric alchemist of Tannoris.

Settling back, I gently opened the gilt-edged pages. The book gave off a musty scent, hinting at the arcane knowledge contained within. I handled the fragile pages with care as I slowly turned each one, scanning the contents.

The opening pages provided background on the book's origins and detailed the various mystical ingredients used in the potions. It was immediately clear that this was a pre-Upheaval tome and not a skill book that would vanish upon reading. As such, it would contain references to Tannorian ingredients only.

The tome began with a treatise on the ingredients referenced within its pages. By the second page, I realized that the author of the work was someone who obsessed over details, for the tome went on endlessly about each little petal, stem, and segment of each ingredient, listing possible pests and everything someone with a botanic mind could come up with.

One chapter featured animal ingredients — such as the blood of an ursagor, basilisk venom, and hippogriff feathers. There were some creatures I was familiar with as well, such as grapplejaws and landcrawlers, which we had battled in the Blighted Land.

Another section focused on elixirs derived from magical plants native to Tannoris. With the merging of worlds, some of these ingredients were likely now extinct. But others may have adapted to our soil and climes and flourished.

After the massive list of ingredients followed the recipes of several potions that the alchemist had devised himself or had learned from others. While overly detailed and extensive, it promised to be a good reference for concocting new potions.

For instance, a recipe for a potion called Breath of Ea allowed underwater breathing by extracting oxygen from the water. Its components were complex — I only recognized a few things, but I carefully transcribed the meticulous brewing instructions.

Then there was Stoutheart Brew, a potion designed to increase damage in combat, and which seemed to be some kind of dwarven ale that also required fermentation. I didn't believe that the ingredients were complex, but the fermentation process would add some serious time to this potion.

I also found a regular healing potion and universal antidote against most poisons and venoms. By their descriptions, they seemed to be very similar — if not the same — as the potions Waelin had furnished us for the expedition to Nimos Sedia.

A staple potion for every adventurer's bag, this was a good one to know. It would sell in much greater numbers than the more complex potions.

The elaborate directions guided the reader through each step — preparing the ingredients, boiling, reducing, and decanting into a vial once cooled. I took meticulous notes and made sure I could easily find the relevant pages in the tome.

I was impressed by the diversity of potions

collected in this ancient book. Once I gathered the necessary ingredients over time, recreating them would provide insight into obscure alchemical arts. It would also train my Alchemy skill and allow us to expand the collection for sale at the general store.

By the time I finished delicately turning each fragile page and meticulously taking notes, my notebook was filled with the details of several new potions. For most of these, acquiring the ingredients would be difficult, but there were perhaps a few I could grow myself. I would have to look into that.

I took a deep breath and closed the book. The clock showed over two hours had passed.

Though there was a way to go before I could try any new recipes, carefully studying *Potions and Concoctions* had already expanded my alchemical knowledge tremendously. The tome's secrets were a valuable addition to my mystical studies.

After returning the aged tome safely to its locked chest, I reflected on the revelations it contained as I tidied my notes. Alchemy had been an unexpected joy to me, especially considering that it was not a skill linked to my Class — I had acquired it through a skill book. But I found the process deeply enjoyable.

There was something magical and spiritual in the deep focus that I appreciated, and the results were simply magical. Besides, mana potions had saved my skin several times over.

My notes securely stored for future reference, I turned down the oil lamps lighting my study and stretched. I had been hunched over the book for hours, and my neck ached slightly.

Heading upstairs, I wondered if Leigh and Diane would still be awake. I could use a massage to loosen up my muscles after spending so long reading. I washed up in the new bathroom, noting the soft glow of light under the door to the new master bedroom, which indicated at least one of my women was still awake.

Entering the bedroom, I smiled to see Diane already peacefully asleep, her breath slow and soft. Leigh sat up reading and put her book aside to kiss me tenderly in greeting as I slipped between the sheets with her.

Soon enough, one thing turned into the other, and we shared our passion in silence, not wanting to wake Diane up. After all, in her condition, she needed her sleep.

Chapter 7

The morning dawned crisp and clear over the homestead, sunlight raining down through the trees to warm the soil. Autumn was here, but the days were still warm.

I awoke refreshed after a peaceful night's sleep, curled up with Diane and Leigh in the spacious bed in our cozy master bedroom. Stretching, I smiled down at Diane's sleeping form nestled against me, her fox ears twitching adorably as she dreamed.

A big advantage of the new master bedroom and second floor was that I could wash up upstairs in the new bathroom. In addition, it was no longer necessary to be so quiet around the house if I wanted to let the girls sleep in.

Freshly washed, I began preparing breakfast in the new kitchen. I lit the stove and made some eggs and fresh strips of bacon I had brought from Gladdenfield. As it simmered, I made some fresh coffee and toast. Soon enough, my girls joined me.

Leigh was her usual chirpy self, but Diane was a little grumpy — something that was bound to happen every now and then with a pregnant woman. Her fox ears drooping, she told me she had thrown up, and the smell of bacon made her nauseous. I opened a window for her, and the fresh air soon revived her, but she settled for just toast this morning.

After a quick breakfast, we headed out to begin

the day's chores. I went to work patching a section of the fence surrounding the farming plot that had been sunk into the soil and tipped over.

Meanwhile, Leigh checked the traps and snares and did a round of the perimeter with her larroling. Diane busied herself in the herb garden, humming softly as she tended to the plants, her mood soon a lot better, lifted by the morning sun and fragrance of the herbs. Ghostie and Sir Boozles drifted around happily, lending assistance where they could.

Around mid-morning, I finished work on the fence and summoned earth and woodland spirits to imbue the soil and our crops, allowing for even faster growth. I also checked on Diane to make sure she was still doing well. Despite the physical exertion and her sickness this morning, she was full of laughter, and we chatted amiably as we worked, our spirits high.

At noon, we ate a lunch of the leftovers from yesterday's dinner. We ate hungrily after the morning's efforts. Bellies full, we returned to finish our tasks — me to patch up the roof as there was still some work to do here and there, Leigh went to the bank of the river to clean and dress the game, and Diane to hang laundry out to dry in the warm autumn breeze.

As the sun dipped low in the sky, we reconvened on the porch to relax and watch the vivid sunset. Leigh headed to bed early this night, and Diane and I lounged by the fire together.

She rested her head contentedly on my shoulder as we unwound from our busy day. We joked and laughed, until our conversation finally lapsed into the quiet comfort that lovers can share.

I then decided that this was the best moment to speak to Diane about Celeste in earnest. After our quest together and the obvious signs of Diane's approval of Celeste, I was more than confident she would welcome the elven maiden as her harem sister.

But I needed to be sure, and I wanted to hear her thoughts to make sure it was all clear as glass between us.

Chapter 8

As Diane and I relaxed comfortably on the hearth rug, gently stroked her silken raven hair as I began delicately, "Diane, there is something I wanted to discuss with you."

She lifted her head from where it rested against my chest to gaze at me attentively, her sapphire eyes meeting mine.

"Yes, of course, my heart. You know you can speak to me about anything." Her voice was warm and open.

I nodded, taking a moment to gather my thoughts and choose my words with care. This was not a conversation to be rushed. "I want to talk about what is happening with Celeste. You've helped me sweetly and selflessly, but before I take things further with Celeste, I want to be completely sure that you're comfortable with Celeste joining our family permanently. I want her to become a member of my harem — of our Elven Marriage."

Diane regarded me thoughtfully, showing no surprise at the subject I had raised. "It's good to talk about this, David," she agreed. "Especially now that your courtship with Celeste progresses. I could sense your feelings for her were continuing to deepen."

"You're right, they certainly have," I affirmed earnestly. "She and I have grown quite close, and I care for her a great deal. I believe she could be a wonderful addition to our family."

Diane drew her knees up, hugging them against her chest as she continued to study me with her intelligent azure gaze. "Bringing another woman into our lives and home is no small matter," she said contemplatively. "But… in foxkin culture, the women are not always consulted for such decisions." She looked at me with big eyes. "It means a lot to me that you do, David."

I reached over to squeeze her hand gently. "Of course. Your feelings are important to me, Diane. I want us to consider this carefully together. To weigh all the implications."

Diane gifted me with a tender smile, squeezing my hand in return. "I appreciate you speaking with me. To be completely honest, when we first met Celeste, I'll admit I had some uncertainties about her."

She paused, and I nodded in understanding. I remembered well Diane's initial wariness around Celeste when we had first encountered her. She had harbored reservations about elves in general.

Diane's expression turned introspective as she continued. "At the time, with my general misgivings towards elves, I was wary of her intentions and did not know what to make of her connection to you. But, after our time together during the quest to Hrothgar's Hope, seeing firsthand her courage and kindness, I realized my judgment of her was too hasty."

I listened intently, gratified to hear Diane voicing openness to the idea of welcoming Celeste into the harem. It seemed spending more time together had softened her original hesitations, just as I had hoped.

"During our travels to free Clara, I was able to get to know Celeste much better," Diane went on thoughtfully. "I saw that she cares for you genuinely, and that she and I share common ground as well, like our mutual love of music." She smiled broadly at that. "I have found great joy in making music with her."

Diane turned her vibrant gaze back to me, her expression earnest. "She seems like a sensitive and good-hearted soul. I believe you and I could come to appreciate her greatly as a harem sister."

I smiled broadly, relieved and gladdened that

Diane seemed receptive to the notion so far. It was a very promising start.

"I'm really glad to hear you say that," I said sincerely. "Getting to know one another appears to have made a big difference."

Diane returned my smile, though her brows furrowed slightly once more in pensive thought. "At the same time, if Celeste were to join us, we would be welcoming our first elf into the harem. That would be new territory."

I angled myself to face Diane directly before the fireplace, giving her my full focus. "You know Celeste and the elven ways far better than I do. Are there any particular concerns on your mind or things we should discuss in advance?"

Diane's lovely features took on a pensive cast as she pondered the question seriously. After a few moments of silent thought, gazing into the flickering flames, she responded.

"One thing that comes to mind is elven custom," she said contemplatively. "I know you've already gotten some information, but as far as I know, elves require marriage before they can join their mate's family."

I nodded. "Yes," I said. "Brynneth explained to me that they do."

Diane's silken tail swished slowly behind her as she kept her eyes on me. There was a thought she did not speak aloud, but I knew her well enough.

I smiled and took her hands in mine, reading plainly her concern. "Diane," I said. "You are my first woman. The simple fact that Celeste's elven customs will require us to marry quickly does not mean that I appreciate you or Leigh less. Don't see this as some kind of hierarchy."

At that, tears wetted her big blue eyes, and she threw herself into my arms. "Oh, David," she hummed. "That makes me so happy to hear. I will admit that I was worried."

I smiled softly, holding her close. "I didn't realize it was this important to you. Otherwise, I would've addressed the issue so much sooner!"

She laughed happily, still hugging me. "Marriage doesn't matter much to foxkin," she hummed in my ear. "But... since you're marrying someone else... I... felt a little strange about that."

I nodded thoughtfully, pulling her a little closer. "I understand," I said. "Don't worry, Diane. No one could ever change how I feel about you. You are my first wife, the mother of my first child, and I will hold you in honor and love always."

She kissed me warmly on the lips before fixing her loving, sapphire eyes on me. "Then all is well, David," she said softly.

My heart swelled with emotion at her open and accepting words. I gazed at her earnestly. "Does this mean you consent to me inviting Celeste to join our family then? To become a member of the harem?"

Diane met my hopeful gaze directly, her eyes clear and resolute. "Yes," she said without hesitation. "If Celeste also consents, I welcome her to join our family." A radiant smile lit her delicate features. "I will be overjoyed to call her my harem sister."

Joy and relief washed over me in a euphoric rush at her wholehearted approval. Unable to contain myself, I drew Diane into a close embrace.

"Thank you, my love," I murmured fervently,

holding her close. "You've made me incredibly happy. I'm so grateful for your blessing in this."

Diane hugged me tightly in return, nestling against my chest. "We will have such a good time together," she hummed.

We remained like that for a while, entwined as we listened to the sounds of Leigh and the domesticants bustling about the kitchen. The future was bright, and tomorrow would be the night of my *alath-manae*.

With Diane's blessings, I hoped that things would progress well.

The next morning, I was up before sunrise to let in the domesticants and prepare a breakfast of toast and cheese. After everyone was awake, we gathered over steaming mugs of coffee to plan the day's work.

Diane would be taking care of the crops today, and Leigh would be fishing to build up the stockpile of smoked fish. With autumn on the way and the smokehouse running, I'd be chopping firewood.

Once Leigh had headed off toward the banks of the Silverthread and Diane was working in the farming plot, checking on our crops of tomatoes, onions, beans, carrots, and lettuce, I made my way into the forest to look for a nice batch of alderwood. Soon enough, I was working up a sweat wielding my axe outside, chopping logs.

Near midday, storm clouds began rolling in. I hurried to finish stacking the firewood in the shed before the downpour arrived. No sooner had I stored the last log than fat raindrops began pelting down. I rushed back to the house just as a loud crack of thunder boomed overhead. Leigh was already coming in from the river.

Safely indoors, I stoked up a fire in the living room hearth while Diane prepared hot cider. We passed a cozy afternoon reading together and listening to the rain patter steadily on the roof. The storm kept up for the rest of the day, and I was happy I'd done the work on the roof yesterday.

When evening came around, we enjoyed a hearty dinner of jacket potato with a delicious stew of hare and a garden salad of homegrown tomatoes and lettuce. The storm continued to rage on outside, thunder rumbling and lightning crackling through the inky sky, but within our snug home, contentment reigned.

As we finished up our meal, I brought up the subject of my upcoming poem recital for Celeste during our *alath-manae*.

"So," I began, "as I said, I need to compose and recite an original poem for Celeste during the *alath-manae*."

Diane's eyes lit up encouragingly. "Yes, very romantic! We should work on it together this evening!" she suggested eagerly.

Leigh let out an amused chuckle and shot me a playful wink. "A love poem, huh? Can't say I ever pictured you as the poetic type, David," she teased. "I mean, you have a lotta skills. Poetry ain't one, I don't think."

I laughed and gave her a playful poke in her soft flank that made her yelp and giggle. "This tongue might not be good at reciting poetry, but it's made you swoon all the same."

"Hm-hm," she hummed. "It sure has, baby."

"But yeah," I admitted, "poetry really isn't my forte. Still, it's an important custom for elven courtship."

"Well, you know I'll help however I can," Diane assured me warmly, reaching over to give my hand an affectionate squeeze. "We'll get you all set to sweep Celeste off her feet with a beautiful verse."

Leigh grinned and stood up, gathering empty dishes. "Y'all go on and work on that poem. I'll tidy up the kitchen here with the domesticants so you can have some peace and quiet."

I shot her a smile before turning to Diane. "I really appreciate you helping me out with this," I said.

Diane smiled; her blue eyes tender. "Anything for you, my love."

Diane and I settled cozily in front of the fireplace in the living room, heads bent over a blank sheet of parchment.

Diane had thoughtfully brought along some

quills and ink for drafting the poem. "First things first — just tell me openly how you feel about Celeste," Diane gently coached. "We'll start from there."

I nodded, a little uncomfortable with speaking so openly, but it would serve a good purpose. With that thought, I began describing the way I saw Celeste.

I took a deep breath and gathered my thoughts.

As I did so, Diane kept her eyes on me, no doubt very interested in what I would say about Celeste.

"Celeste is mystically beautiful," I began slowly. "Everything about her seems touched by magic — her voice, her laughter, her singing, the way she moves. When we're together, it feels like she and I connect on that magical level." I smiled at Diane. "Much like you and me, it feels like the relationship is predestined."

Diane listened intently; her fox ears perked with

interest as she jotted down notes. "That's lovely, keep going," she encouraged. "Tell me more about how she makes you feel."

I nodded, piecing together the truths I'd kept private in my heart. At the same time, I tried to gauge if there was a hint of jealousy in her voice, but there did not seem to be.

"From the moment I first saw her," I continued. "It was like...everything else faded away. She's so elegant and graceful, almost ethereal. Her kindness and wisdom leave me in awe. The sound of her singing is pure magic."

"That's very nice," Diane praised, scribbling furiously. "I can tell how deeply you care for her."

Part of me was surprised at how well she was taking this, but that reasoning still very much came from a foundation of human culture. Diane was a foxkin, and their women often shared a single husband. It must be ingrained into their system to cohabitate with other wives without conflict.

She smiled up at me. "Go on," she gently encouraged me. "I have some great things, but I need some more."

I rubbed the back of my neck and chuckled. "Well," I continued, "our time together has left me walking on air. The world seems more vibrant, and I see beauty everywhere. Her laughter fills me with joy. When we kiss, it's like time stops."

Diane bit her lip, her eyes twinkling. "Oh, this is perfect," she murmured. "Celeste will be so touched. Now, let's shape your thoughts into verse..."

For the next while, we brainstormed rhymes and poetic turns of phrase to capture my feelings for Celeste. Diane wove my words into lyrical stanzas with an instinctive elegance.

As we worked, the crackling fire filled the spaces between scribbling quills and murmured suggestions. Slowly but surely, our combined efforts took shape on the parchment.

I shared more of my private thoughts and feelings, opening up about how Celeste occupied my dreams and thoughts even when we were apart. Diane captured it all, nodding along encouragingly.

After much back and forth, reworking stanzas

and debating rhyme schemes, we had an initial draft of the love poem for Celeste. Diane cleared her throat and read it aloud:

"In the forest's heart, under starlit skies,
Where whispers of ancient trees arise,
There dances Celeste, elfin grace personified,
With hair of amber, where dreams reside.

Her eyes, verdant pools of spring's first glow,
Reflecting the luster of moon's soft throw.
Oh, my heart awaits you, Celeste, my muse,
Your voice, a melody that lovingly infuses.

Apart, the sands of time sluggishly crawl,
But thoughts of you hasten their drawl.
And though the moon may concede to dawn,
My love, undimmed, eternally drawn.

No fairer vision have these eyes beheld,
Than you, with elegance unparalleled.
Your spirit, a harp's sweet symphony,
Resonates with tender harmony.

Kindness, your mantle, sunlight amidst the wood,
Your presence transforms despair to good.
My fair maiden, veiled in mystery's shroud,
Your prowess in battle, silent yet proud.

My world, once dusky, now blazes bright,
For you are the daybreak after the night.
In art, in song, in whispered lore,
Your love, the tide to my barren shore.

Celeste, in you, I've understood,
The heart's sweet bloom, the soul's purest good.
With every note on the harp you play,
In every dulcet tune, you convey...

... A serenade of peace, a canticle of light,
Guiding my spirit through the night.
Celeste, my heart, forever you will hold,
In tales of love until my soul grows old."

I let out a deep sigh, holding the parchment gently. "Diane, this is incredible. You truly worked magic here — I could never compose something so poetic on my own."

Diane tilted her head coyly. "You supplied the feeling; I just helped put it into verse. But I'm so pleased you're happy with how it turned out."

Carefully rolling the parchment, I tied it with a ribbon and set it aside for safekeeping. We had accomplished our goal, and Celeste was sure to appreciate the effort in observing elven custom.

I drew Diane into my arms, nuzzling her affectionately as we relaxed on the plush rug before the hearth. "I'm really proud that you helped me with this," I murmured.

Diane sighed contentedly, nestling closer and laying her head on my chest. "You show me your love every day in so many ways, my love. And soon you'll share these same feelings with Celeste."

I smiled, my heart pleased with her Diane's acceptance of Celeste into her midst, her warm words signaling her true intent. We sat back together, minds wandering and exploring the future.

Chapter 9

The morning dawned crisp and clear, and the early sun bathed the homestead in a warm golden glow. I almost sprang out of bed because today was the day of my *alath-manae* — the Moonlit Walk — with Celeste. Anticipation thrummed through me as I washed and dressed.

Heading downstairs, I was greeted by the mouthwatering aroma of pancakes drifting from the kitchen. The girls had slipped out of bed while I was washing up; Leigh stood at the stove flipping pancakes while Diane set the table.

"Mornin', baby!" Leigh called out cheerily. "We made sure to fix you up a big hearty breakfast before your big date tonight."

Diane hurried over to embrace me. "We want you fortified for the journey and your romantic evening," she said, eyes shining.

I kissed her tenderly. "You ladies spoil me. This looks delicious!"

We settled in for breakfast and lively conversation, enjoying each other's presence and the cozy atmosphere of the house.

Over steaming mugs of coffee, we finalized plans for the day. Diane and Leigh would remain behind to tend to the homestead while I went into town. Since I was going anyway, I would drop off some supplies at the general store so Randal could sell them.

After breakfast, I prepared for the drive into

Gladdenfield. I loaded up the supplies, left some instructions with the domesticants, and said goodbye to Leigh and Diane, promising I'd be back again tomorrow.

The crisp autumn breeze tousled my hair as I took one last look back at the homestead, heart swelling with love and gratitude. Then, I turned over the engine and drove off.

The forest was ablaze with vibrant hues. Already, the crimson and gold of autumn whispered in the branches overhead as I drove down the shaded trail. Birdsong and the gurgle of a winding stream serenaded our passage. The forest would soon turn to autumn, and I was anticipating cozy times by the fire.

Still, as I drove on, the matter of Father still lingered in the back of my mind. The threat of this elder dragon coming to our corner of the world was real, and it would come after me.

My allies were on the lookout, and I believed I would receive ample word ahead of its arrival. Still, it was coming, and I would have to deal with it when it did.

I pushed away my concerns when the palisade of Gladdenfield Outpost dawned on the horizon. There was only a short queue of folks trying to get into town — four vehicles and some people on foot with beasts of burden. The guards waved me through, and I parked close to the general store.

I unloaded the goods I had brought, summoning two domesticants to aid with the hauling. The bell above the door announced my entry as my domesticants zipped past me and toward the counter.

Randal looked up from behind the counter and a broad grin creased his leathery face. "Well, hey there, David! Good to see ya," the older man said. He came around to shake my hand vigorously. "Got more goods to sell from the homestead?"

"Sure do," I confirmed, gesturing at the crates the domesticants were carrying in. "Fresh produce, smoked meat and fish, furs, and more."

Randal nodded approvingly as he inspected the items. "Much obliged! Y'know, stuff from your homestead sells pretty well around here. I've been achin' for some more of them potions o' yours!"

I smiled as I leaned on the counter. "Good, because I've been planning to expand a little and learn some new recipes."

"Perfect," Randal said. As he started tallying it all up in his ledger, he made conversation in his usual gregarious manner. "What else brings ya into town today?"

I leaned casually against the counter. "Oh, I have a date with a certain lady. And..." I hesitated as I remembered what Brynneth had said about rings, then decided to ask, "Say, I don't suppose there's a jeweler around now?"

Randal looked up from his ledger, bushy eyebrows shooting up. "A jeweler?" He studied me curiously, then his expression morphed into one of dawning realization. A broad grin split his bearded face.

"Well, butter my backside!" he exclaimed. "I reckon you're looking to buy a ring for one 'o them pretty gals of yours! Can't say I blame ya, David."

I laughed as he shook my hand again enthusiastically. "Yeah, I might have something in mind."

"Well, your secret's safe with me, son," he said with a big wink. "Which one ya askin', now?"

"All of them," I said. "Celeste, Diane, and Leigh."

He whistled, clearly impressed. "Gonna get expensive, all them rings! But bein' happily married myself, let me tell ya, David: there ain't nothing better than a good wife. And I s'pose it's even better when ya have three!"

I laughed at that and nodded. "I sure think so!"

"Well, lemme know if there's aught I can do! I'd love to help get things ready. We can place orders through the store and whatnot. And, of course, you got them lil' *do-may-dee-cants* or whatever they're called zippin' around to help ya…" At this, he nodded at the domesticants. "But if you need more help, I can round up some fellers from town!"

"That's very nice of you, Randal," I said. "I appreciate that."

He grinned and nodded. "Well, ain't that fantastic!" he boomed. "Happy for you y'all!" His lively eyes twinkled merrily as he leaned in and added in a conspiratorial whisper, "Anyway, you want a jeweler, right?"

I nodded. "Yeah, and a good one, if one's around."

"Well, Ol' Grimfast just set up shop last week. He's a dwarven jeweler, damn fine craftsmanship. Come down all the way from the mines in Bronzehall, Utah. You'll find his place just down the way there."

He pointed helpfully down the bustling main thoroughfare. "Look for the shop with the big glittery gem on the sign. Can't miss it!"

"Thank you, Randal," I said. "And how's the store doing?"

"Oh, pretty fine. We got a tidy profit this month! And we still got reserves from the fine business Leigh did around the Aquana Festival. Things are lookin' even better for fall as lotsa folks will be comin' into the store more often."

"Good," I said. "Listen, I'm gonna find this Grimfast. Thanks so much for your help, Randal."

"Think nothin' of it," he hummed, waving it away. "Go on now!"

Eager excitement kindled in my chest as I headed

out and located Grimfast's shop right where Randal had indicated.

I approached the nondescript storefront located down the dusty thoroughfare from the general store. Above the door hung a wooden sign depicting a large, glittering gemstone, just as Randal had described to identify the dwarven jeweler's shop.

As I drew closer, I noted the shop's name etched into the sign in ornate script: "Grimfast's Fineries."

Pausing outside the entrance, I took in the humble establishment. It was tucked between a leatherworker's shop and a candlemaker's, easy to miss among its larger, more eye-catching neighbors.

Stepping forward, I turned the wrought iron door handle and entered. A tiny bell jingled overhead, announcing my arrival.

The interior was dimly lit and somewhat

cramped. Behind a long glass counter stood a burly dwarf with an enormous red beard braided intricately down his chest. His attire was simple but meticulously cared for.

At my entrance, the dwarf looked up from an eyepiece he had been peering through, no doubt to inspect a piece of jewelry he was crafting. His beady eyes under bushy brows blinked slowly as he took in my appearance.

"Welcome to my shop, lad," he rumbled in a low, gravelly voice. "I'm Grimfast, proprietor of this fine establishment. What can I do for you today?"

I approached the counter. "It's good to meet you, Grimfast. I'm David Wilson," I introduced myself. Up close, the intricate precision of the dwarf's braided beard was even more impressive. It was a three-forked beard, fastened with metal rings adorned with precious stones.

"I was hoping to get some expert advice about commissioning a few special pieces," I explained. "Randal down at the general store recommended your services. He said you do excellent work."

At the mention of Randal, the dwarven jeweler's dour expression cracked into a slight smile. "Randal, eh? He's a fine fellow."

Grimfast leaned forward, planting his thick forearms on the counter as he scrutinized me carefully. "So what is it you're looking to have crafted then, lad?"

"Well, you see, I'll soon be proposing to my girlfriends," I began. "So I was hoping to find an engagement ring worthy of her. Something finely crafted and unique, with an emerald stone ideally."

"*Girlfriends,*" he grunted. "Plural?"

"Indeed."

He grinned broadly. "Takin' after elven customs, eh?" He nodded. "Never been one for it meself. If you'd have ye a dwarven wife, you'd understand why we stick to just one missus most of the time."

I laughed at that, deciding I already liked Grimfast. "I bet," I said. "My girls are a human, an elf, and a foxkin."

As I spoke, Grimfast continued to study me with an inscrutable expression, occasionally stroking his voluminous red beard. "Sounds like an interestin' mash-up… So, engagement rings for your lasses, eh? Well, you've come to the right dwarf for quality jewelry," he affirmed with a nod. Then his brows furrowed worriedly. "Unfortunately, I don't have much on hand currently for taking on special commissions."

I followed his concerned gaze around the shop, taking note of the lack of variety and quantity of pieces on display in the cases. Though excellently crafted, there simply wasn't much available.

"Business been slow since you set up shop here?" I asked carefully, sensing this was a sore subject for the proud craftsman.

"Aye, slower than a lame snail goin' uphill!" Grimfast grumbled. He crossed his burly arms over his barrel chest, his expression stormy. "It's these blasted elves and their Coalition regulation! When I came down from Bronzehall, they refused to let me keep my materials. Had to offload 'em for cheap, and I wasted most me coin on getting' this place. Materials come in from Ironfast, but shipments are few, so the materials are all expensive."

My eyes widened in surprise at this revelation. This was the first I had heard of such harsh restrictions on trade by the Coalition that governed the frontier towns like Gladdenfield.

"On what grounds did they confiscate your things?" I inquired, taken aback and concerned by this news. Such limitations could stifle craftsmen and traders.

At my question, Grimfast's face reddened in anger under his bushy red beard. He spat on the floor bitterly. "Some rot about magical contamination risks, or some such rubbish. It's discrimination against my people — dwarves — that's the truth of it!"

I nodded gravely, privately agreeing that preventing Grimfast from practicing his livelihood seemed unfair. "I had no idea the Coalition was placing such harsh restrictions on dwarven crafters and goods. That seems rather discriminatory."

"Discriminatory doesn't begin to cover it, lad," Grimfast grumbled resentfully. "They claimed too many dwarven objects from Tannoris might somehow upset the 'magical balance' here. Utter troll dung is what it is! I'm just trying to make an honest living as a jeweler."

I nodded sympathetically. The dwarven jeweler had certainly gotten a raw deal, effectively prohibited from fully pursuing his trade and passion. But I only knew half of the story — Grimfast's half. Perhaps there was truth to the Coalition's claim.

"I'm sorry to hear this," I offered sincerely. "Is there any way around these restrictions for you? Anything I could do to help?"

Grimfast tugged his thick beard thoughtfully for a moment, his eyes distant. Then they lit up and he leaned forward excitedly. "Well now, there just might be a way you could help me out," he said in a hushed tone. "And ye'd be helpin' yerself out at the same time!"

"Go on," I urged, intrigued by this shift in his demeanor.

"Before I came down here from Bronzehall, I did some research. A cousin o' mine has the Prospector Class, and he told me there's a very rare deposit o' shimmerstone nearby — a rare Tannorian precious stone," Grimfast whispered. "Problem is, it's in a troll cave, and I can't afford to send a party of adventurers."

I raised my eyebrows at this news. A troll cave trove would certainly contain some treasure besides just the deposit of shimmerstone. It might be interesting for us to explore.

I considered this revelation and its implications. "Have any other dwarves searched for this hoard themselves?" I asked. I was surprised this mythical treasure had not already been recovered if real.

The dwarf shook his head grimly, braided beard swaying. "Nay, I don't think anyone else knows of it. My cousin — he knows from his travels here, but he never told no one around Gladdenfield or Ironfast. Besides, most folks don't tangle with trolls. It's a level 9 challenge, I'd say…"

Grimfast watched me closely, perhaps gauging my reaction. "With access to that deposit, my store would be saved," he added fervently. "I'll make ye your rings at no cost 'xcept what little gold I'd need to add, and if ever you need more of 'em, I'll make 'em free of charge."

I stood quietly for a minute; arms crossed as I contemplated everything Grimfast had shared. If the legendary treasure did indeed exist, this would be a mutually beneficial endeavor.

After all, whatever the troll hoarded would be mine, and I'd get engagement rings from Grimfast. Not only that, but his business would be off to a good start, winning me another friend and ally.

Having weighed the risks and potential gains, I met Grimfast's mossy green eyes steadily. "I tell you what, Grimfast — I'll see what I can do to help you try and find this deposit."

At my words, the dwarf's dour expression transformed into one of awe and gratitude. "You mean it, lad? You would help an old dwarf out?" His voice grew thin with emotion.

"I'll do my best to find it," I promised sincerely. "I'll have to plan the expedition, but it sounds like a challenge I could face."

Impulsively, Grimfast reached out to grasp my hand, his weathered grip surprisingly strong. "Bless you, lad. Thank you for yer kindness! For even considering this, ye've given me hope again."

His eyes glistened.

"Of course," I said. "No promises, but I'll look into this and see if there's a way we can get you set up!"

Grimfast patted my hand gratefully before letting it go. Clearing his throat gruffly, he nodded. "Right, you're a proper lad, David..."

At that, he began explaining where I should find this troll cave. I soon enough understood that it was underground, which made it difficult for roaming or errant adventurers to find it. Apparently, Grimfast's cousin's Prospector Class allowed him to magically sense the deposit, which had led to the discovery of the cave.

Using my map, I learned that the cave was less than a day from Gladdenfield. When Grimfast had told me all he knew, we said our goodbyes for now. My errand to find jewelry had taken an unexpected turn, but I did not regret offering aid to the disheartened dwarven craftsman.

Chapter 10

After leaving Grimfast's shop, I decided to stop by the florist and pick up a bouquet for Celeste before our date that evening.

The florist's outdoor stall overflowed with vibrant blooms, and I selected a mix of purple irises and white lilies artfully arranged by the shopkeeper. Their sweet fragrance filled my senses, and I imagined how beautifully they would complement Celeste's fair complexion.

I wasn't sure if elven culture had the same custom of giving flowers like ours, but as Brynneth had said, it didn't have to be all about elven culture, and I wanted to share a custom of my kind with Celeste as well — other than the ring, which would follow later down the line.

Bouquet in hand, I headed to the apartment above the general store where Leigh used to live and where we now stayed whenever we were in town. She had given me a key so I could use her place.

Letting myself in, I set the flowers down and glanced around the cozy space. It was sparsely but tastefully decorated in Leigh's rustic style.

I spent the remainder of the day there, reading and relaxing. While I loved the homestead, it was nice to have some time off during which I had to do absolutely nothing. And Leigh was an avid reader, so her bookcases were well supplied. In between reading and going for an afternoon stroll,

I even managed to get a nap in — a rare luxury!

When evening came, I freshened up in the bathroom, splashing cold water on my face and running a comb through my hair. As I toweled off, my thoughts turned to the unexpected conversation with Grimfast. His tale of the rare gen deposit hidden away in a troll's cave had sparked my curiosity.

If the deposit of rare Tannorian shimmerstone truly existed, it would be quite the valuable find. The treasure would allow Grimfast to properly establish his business in town and craft the engagement rings I sought. But there was a joy in helping him, too, especially considering the rough deal he had starting out.

However, mounting an expedition to reclaim the treasure from a troll's cave would be no simple feat. Trolls were formidable foes and notoriously possessive of their lairs and loot. It wouldn't let go of its treasures while it lived. We would need to plan and equip ourselves well for the delve.

My Class, Frontier Summoner, afforded me some advantages in this endeavor. With my stable of summonable creatures, we would have a formidable force.

As I changed into a fresh shirt, I considered who might join me on the quest. Naturally, I would ask Leigh and Diane first. Their combat skills and wilderness know-how would prove invaluable. I might also extend an invitation to Celeste, to further include her in our adventures.

Still, I'd have to keep the true purpose of the quest hidden and tell them only that we were out to get the troll's hoard. I wanted the shimmerstone rings to be a surprise. Luckily, Grimfast had told me that he didn't need us to mine the deposit. He had a Mining skill, so he would do that himself the moment the place was clear.

Donning my jacket, I glanced at my reflection in the mirror. I looked sharp but not overdone. I deemed myself ready for the intimate stroll with Celeste ahead. My pulse quickened at the thought.

Satisfied with my preparations, I gave myself a final approving nod in the mirror. I gathered up the bouquet as I made for the door. My heart beat faster, thoughts turning to the romantic evening ahead under the stars with Celeste.

Before all that, I would grab something to eat at the Wild Outrider. I had a secret hope that Celeste would perform tonight so I could see her in action once more.

Stepping outside into the bustling frontier town, I blinked against the afternoon sunlight. Citizens went about their daily business up and down the packed dirt road, waving friendly greetings when they recognized me.

With the bouquet tucked securely under one arm, I set off towards the inn at an eager stride. Though my mind still lingered on preparations for the troll cave delve, tonight my focus rested solely on charming the fair elf maiden during our Moonlit Walk.

Adrenaline and anticipation quickened my steps through town. Oblivious to the passersby around me, my imagination wandered to the magical night ahead. Under the moon's gentle glow, I would recite the verse to Celeste and further strengthen the blossoming bond between us.

As the sign for the Wild Outrider came into view

down the road, I patted my pocket, feeling the reassuring crinkle of parchment containing the poem Diane had helped me craft. Its loving words had come straight from my heart. I hoped they would touch Celeste deeply.

Nearing the inn, I slowed my pace to a measured stride and took a deep breath. Although my path was set, a hint of nerves churned within me. I was an easy guy around women, but something about all the formality and unexplored terrain made dating an elf just a little more exciting.

At the threshold, the sounds of the inn's patrons beginning their evening feast already drifting out, I paused and glanced upward, glimpsing the upper floor window I knew belonged to Celeste's room. Somewhere within, she was likely preparing herself, equally eager for the night ahead. The thought warmed me against the evening chill.

Turning the door handle, I stepped into the Wild Outrider.

Chapter 11

I stepped into the warmth and lively chatter of the Wild Outrider. The lantern-lit interior was bustling with patrons settled in for dinner. I glanced around, taking in the familiar tables and decor.

Spotting an empty table near the corner, I weaved my way through the crowded room. I set the bouquet of flowers down and took a seat, eager for a hearty meal to fortify me before my moonlit walk with Celeste.

Before long, a barmaid stopped by my table. I ordered roast chicken, potatoes, and an ale. The barmaid hurried off, and I settled in to wait.

My eyes drifted over to the small stage along the back wall as I wondered if Celeste would be performing tonight. It was empty for now, but Celeste often sang in the evenings to entertain the inn's guests — it was her deal with Darny. Hearing her lovely voice always lifted my spirits.

Just then, the innkeeper Darny spotted me from across the room. He put aside what he had been doing and hustled over with a broad grin.

"David! Good to see you, my friend," he exclaimed, clapping me on the shoulder.

"Hey there, Darny," I said. "How are things?"

"Oh, pretty good," he said. "Shapin' up to be a busy night, I'd say!"

"Great," I said. "Will Celeste be performing tonight?"

He grinned and gave me a wink. "She sure will

be!"

Satisfied with his answer, we chatted amiably about business at the inn and life out on my homestead. I didn't mention my courtship with Celeste, wanting to remain discreet, although I was sure the perceptive proprietor of the Wild Outrider had his suspicions.

Darny kept me company until the food came, relating humorous anecdotes about recent happenings around town. I always enjoyed his lively spirit and good humor. Finally, when my meal arrived steaming hot, he headed off to help his other patrons, and I dug into the meal.

Between bites, I glanced towards the stage again, but it remained empty aside from a vacant stool and Celeste's gilded harp. I wondered what was keeping her this evening, hoping she hadn't fallen ill.

Just then, the mutterings of the crowd faded to an anticipatory hush. I looked up to see Celeste stepping gracefully onto the stage, looking resplendent in a flowing lilac gown. My breath caught at the sight of her.

Celeste settled gracefully onto the stool, arranging her skirts demurely before taking up her harp. Her fingers plucked the opening notes of a haunting elven ballad. Then her mellifluous voice joined in, imbuing the words with profound emotion.

"O radiant dawn, where have you gone?
The woods lie cold in the gloaming.
The stars are bright, moonbeams alight,
On hilltops old, their glow softly streaming.

Come back, o sweet sun, and end the night!
Let your rays through the clouds come bursting.
Awake the birds, stir the herds,
Paint the sky in morning light blushing.

These darkened days, I walk alone,
Longing for your warmth and brightness.
The icy chill makes me stand still,
My heart awaiting your lightness.

Upon the meadow, dewdrops glisten,
In the silent woods, shadows listen,
For your indigo to fade into crimson,
For night to cede as day comes rushing in.

Dress the hills in emerald hues,

Send the clouds high aloft flying.
Awake the earth, bring rebirth,
Forests, fields, in life be vying.

 Come radiant dawn, night is gone!
Spread your rays far, wide, and yonder.
Let spheres ring, voices upspring,
In dawn's torch, our spirits wander."

Enraptured, I watched Celeste perform, oblivious to my cooling meal. She was spellbinding, utterly in her element. Her voice soared through intricate melodies while her nimble fingers danced across the harp strings.

The inn's patrons were just as captivated. Work-worn faces gazed up at Celeste, visibly moved by her otherworldly performance. Even the most raucous individuals sat silent, hanging on each note.

As I listened, enchanted, my heart swelled with admiration and affection. Celeste's prodigious talent and grace were a soothing sight, furthering only my desire to make her mine.

Shortly before she began her next song, her emerald eyes roamed over the audience, and she found me almost instantly — as if we were drawn together by forces not of this world. She smiled softly and gave me a gentle wave before continuing.

Too soon, Celeste's set drew to a close. The applause was thunderous; I clapped hardest of all. With a gracious curtsy, she glided offstage; her work done for the night. My eyes lingered on her until she disappeared upstairs. She watched me too, shooting a meaningful look that invited me as she headed up the stairs.

"Quite the voice on that one, eh?" Darny commented beside me, also clearly impressed.

I hadn't even seen him coming. I nodded and smiled. Darny gave me a knowing look before excusing himself to tend to his patrons again.

As the inn's din resumed, I finished my drink, eager to join Celeste upstairs. My anticipation for our Moonlit Walk later tonight now thrummed stronger than ever.

After I finished, I summoned a domesticant and had it carefully take the bouquet upstairs to hand it to Celeste. I didn't want to disturb her rest before our date, but I wanted to give her a little sign. I also attached a note to the bouquet, with nothing but my name and a heart.

While waiting for the domestican to return, I caught Darny's eye and ordered an ale. I would linger a bit longer in the cozy atmosphere of the inn before I would knock on Celeste's door to pick her up for our Moonlit Walk.

Nursing my ale slowly, I chatted some more with Darny. He was one of the first folks to befriend me when I arrived here green as grass. Our easy flow reminded me of those early days, and I had found the bartender a good contact — he always knew what was going on.

Soon enough, my domestican zipped back down to me, its spectral form darting between tables. Its return told me Celeste had received my gifts. I hoped the flowers conveyed my affection and that she had found them a nice surprise.

By now, the common room started to empty out as patrons headed off to bed for the night. Only the staunch drinkers remained, ready to empty Darny's kegs of ale and make it another lucrative night for my friend. Taking it as my cue, I finished up my drink and settled my tab with Darny.

He gave me a knowing smile as I headed upstairs.

Chapter 12

Excitement churned within me as I ascended the creaky wooden staircase leading to the upper floor of rooms. In my pocket, I clutched the rolled parchment containing the romantic verse Diane had helped me craft to recite to Celeste tonight.

At the top of the stairs, I paused outside the plain

door that belonged to Celeste. I was looking forward to seeing her, to holding her in my arms again, and this whole thing had me giddy as a high schooler to see her again.

I rapped my knuckles gently against the worn wood. After a moment, I heard the click of a lock disengaging before the door swung open.

Celeste stood framed in the doorway, looking as radiant as ever. She had changed from her stage attire into a flowing gown of shimmering azure that complemented her fair complexion beautifully. Her long amber hair tumbled freely down her back in gentle waves.

Seeing her took my breath away. She had obviously done her utmost to appear even more beautiful than she normally did. The image of her was hauntingly compelling, and the way her gown clung to her supple body roused all kinds of need within me.

I smiled at her. "You look beautiful," I said.

She gave a slightly demure smile, her gaze lowering for an instant before meeting mine again. "Good evening, David," she hummed, her musical voice sweet and warm. Her verdant eyes shone happily. "You look beautiful, too... And I'm so pleased you've come. Please, do come in!"

She stepped back, gesturing for me to enter. I did so, my pulse quickening. Her cozy room was tidy and feminine, with a vase of fresh wildflowers on the table. The bouquet I had sent up earlier now rested beside it in a graceful vase.

Turning to face me, Celeste clasped her hands before her. "Thank you for the lovely flowers," she said sincerely. "You are too kind."

I smiled, relieved she had appreciated the gifts. "I wanted you to know I was thinking of you," I replied. Unable to resist, I reached out to caress her smooth cheek with the backs of my fingers. "I've been looking forward to tonight!"

Celeste's eyes fluttered shut, and she leaned into my touch. When she looked at me again, an impish smile curved her lips. "Such a charmer," she teased.

Taking my hand, she gave it an affectionate squeeze. "Shall we be off then?"

I nodded, a big smile on my face. We headed

downstairs, and Darny shot us a broad smile and gave me a nod as we headed outside. Together we exited the inn hand in hand and stepped out into the cool night.

The velvet sky was adorned with a smattering of twinkling stars. Celeste tipped her head back, breathing deeply. "What a glorious night for a stroll," she remarked appreciatively.

I had to agree. The weather was perfect — crisp but not cold. Together we set off down the quiet dirt road leading out of town.

We chatted amiably as we walked, simply enjoying each other's company.

"Your singing tonight was breathtaking as always," I remarked. "The ballad you opened with was very moving. Did you write it yourself?"

Celeste smiled, pleased by the compliment. "Thank you. I did not write it. It is a song passed down through oral tradition, and I learned it in Thilduirne where I dwelled with Uncle Waelin."

She went on to explain how music was deeply ingrained in elven culture, used to convey stories and preserve ancient tales. I listened, fascinated by this glimpse into her people's customs, which were similar to ours.

"And what about you?" Celeste asked, turning the conversation. "How was your trip into town today? I hope it wasn't too much of a burden to come here only to meet with me?"

I chuckled. "I'd hardly call that a burden, Celeste. But yeah, I delivered some supplies and... took care of a few errands. I spoke with Randal as well. The store seems to be doing well thanks to all the hard work."

"It sounds like you've done so much in such a short time to build and expand it," Celeste marveled. "You're so industrious, David. I do hope I will see your homestead soon."

"You will! Me and the girls would love to have you visit. We're always improving things, trying to make it as comfortable as we can. But I want to do things the right way for you, Celeste. I will show you my house someday soon, perhaps when our families meet."

She smiled warmly. "I appreciate that, David. And your patience. I know these things are different among your kind, and you flatter me with your respect for my people's ways." She shot me a warm look and squeezed my hand gently. "Now, tell me more of your home!"

I went on to describe how some of the latest additions I had told her about previously were working out and what kind of work remained before we were ready for fall. Celeste asked thoughtful questions, hanging on every detail.

"It sounds perfectly idyllic." She sighed wistfully when I had finished. "A little oasis of peace out there beyond the frontier."

I smiled, gratified by her delight in my descriptions. The homestead was my pride and joy, and her appreciation of my efforts meant the world to me. If things went as I wanted them to, she would live there with us soon, and it was important to me that she would love the place.

Finally, we came to the gate. The guards offered us the usual warning, but they knew by now that I was one of the higher-level adventurers in Gladdenfield — I knew what I was doing.

At the edge of town, we left the road, following a

worn footpath into the surrounding forest. The trees rose up around us like silent sentinels as we ventured deeper into nature's domain.

Gently, I guided Celeste along the winding trail, keeping her close against my side. She seemed relaxed and at ease here among the whispering trees and night birds calling softly from above.

In time we emerged in a moonlit glade, the perfect spot for us to rest and reflect. I squeezed Celeste's hand and led her to an old fallen log worn smooth by the elements.

We sat together, our shoulders touching as we gazed up at the stars and the moon. I longed to pull her closer, but I didn't want to rush. For now, I simply savored her nearness and the intimacy of this time alone together under the stars.

"The forest is especially captivating at night," Celeste murmured. "Everything seems bathed in an aura of magic and mystery." She turned her bright eyes to me then. "Being here with you like this feels magical too."

My breath caught at the open affection in her voice and gaze. Unable to resist, I raised my hand to her cheek once more, caressing it tenderly.

Celeste sighed softly and nuzzled against my palm, igniting my passion. But I reined my ardor in, not wanting to push too fast and ruin this special night. Reluctantly, I lowered my hand.

As we sat there, I decided to gently encourage Celeste to open up about herself. "What was it like for you, growing up among the elves?" I asked.

Celeste's expression turned thoughtful. "In some ways idyllic, being surrounded by nature's beauty. But also… lonely." She gazed up at the stars. "Our kind are slow to trust. I often felt isolated. We are wood elves — Waelin and I — and we never fit in in Thilduirne… or anywhere else we went."

My heart ached for the sadness in her voice. "Their loss for not giving you a chance."

"You're too kind," Celeste demurred, though she seemed pleased. "Truthfully, I never felt like I fully belonged. My talents and temperament were… different."

I sensed this was difficult for her to confide. I took her hand reassuringly. "Different isn't bad. It makes you who you are."

Celeste gave my hand a grateful squeeze. "You've helped me see that. I hid part of myself for so long, but with you..." Her voice faltered with emotion. "With you, I feel free to be me."

I felt honored she trusted me enough to be vulnerable. "Good," I said earnestly. "That's how I want you to feel around me."

Celeste gazed at me for a long moment before shyly averting her eyes. "You truly are special, David. With you, I feel...complete."

Her admission made my pulse race, and I realized the time had come for my verse. I pushed away any anxiety in my chest and almost reached for the piece of paper in my pocket.

Taking a deep, steadying breath, I turned to face Celeste fully under the gentle moonlight. Her eyes were luminous as they met mine, her expression soft and open. This was the moment.

"Celeste," I began, gently taking her delicate hands in mine. "I have composed something special that I want to share with you tonight."

Surprise and curiosity lit her fair features. "Oh, David," she hummed, her musical voice warm with affection. "You really have thought of everything." I could practically see her melt at the effort I had put into this evening.

I gave her hands a tender squeeze, gathering my courage. Though usually bold, laying bare the contents of my heart — through the medium of poetry, no less! – made me a little nervous.

"It's a poem," I revealed. "In keeping with elven tradition, I wished to craft a special poem to recite to you this night."

Celeste's emerald eyes went wide, and she raised one hand to her lips in visible astonishment. "David... this *alath-manae* is perfect." Her voice was hushed, tinged with awe. "You composed a poem?"

I nodded, smiling softly. "With some help from Diane. But yes, from the heart."

"I don't know what to say," Celeste breathed. "What a tremendously meaningful gesture. Please, I can't wait to hear it!" Her eyes shone brighter than the stars overhead.

Bolstered by her reaction, I gathered myself and began reciting the verses I had long since committed to memory. As the loving words poured forth, Celeste listened raptly, hanging on each syllable.

It turned out to be easier than I had expected, and perhaps that was because the words were sincere. But as I spoke the words, my heart hungered to learn how she would respond to them.

Chapter 13

When I concluded my poem, Celeste was silent for several heartbeats, clearly deeply moved. At last, she whispered, "That was exquisite. I have never heard anything so beautiful." A single glistening tear traced down her cheek.

I reached out to gently brush it away, my heart

pounding. "So, it pleased you?" I asked hopefully.

"*Pleased* me?" Celeste echoed with a musical laugh. "David, I am utterly overwhelmed. The beauty of your words, your willingness to honor elven rituals… It all touches me profoundly."

Relief washed over me at her words. I had accomplished my goal in crafting something meaningful just for her.

Celeste seemed to glow in the soft moonglow, her eyes aglow with some inner light. Slowly, almost ceremoniously, she clasped my hands once more. "Now, I have a gift to share with you as well, my dearest one."

I gazed at her, intrigued. "Oh?"

Celeste smiled, gave a small nod, and began to recite her *ylath* — the answering poem that was, in fact, an invitation to take things further — in a flawless tongue, her melodious voice ringing with passion:

"My heart flies high as a moon-kissed moth,
Your hand its guiding light through night launched.
No longer lost midst gloom of ancient trees,
For you, sweet love, have set my spirit free.

Recite again the verse conceived by your hand.
Let loving lines like healing balm expand.
For only you my weary soul understand,
And only you can shape our fate so grand.

Your kindness overflows like springtide stream,
Each selfless act no fleeting dream.
With you I'll tread on mossy banks upstream,
Our linked hearts many joys shall gleam.

No longer shall I wade through moonlit mere,
When your strong hand stretches out sincere.
For now I see our destiny shine clear —
To walk as one, dispelling fear."

I sat stunned, scarcely daring to believe what I had heard. Celeste gazed at me expectantly, cheeks endearingly flushed.

"Was that... your *ylath*?" I finally managed to ask.

Celeste nodded, suddenly shy. "It just came to me, listening to your beautiful words. I... I actually prepared something else, but it... Well, inspiration took me, and I spoke these words instead. I hope I have not overstepped?"

"Overstepped?" I echoed in amazement. A broad

smile spread across my face as the meaning sunk in. She had just invited me to propose! Even if she had done it in a limerick, I would have been happy. "No," I said softly. "You did not overstep. It was beautiful."

Unable to contain my elation, I pulled Celeste into a joyful embrace. She melted against me with a happy sigh, and in that perfect moment, nothing else existed but the two of us.

At last, I drew back to gaze earnestly into her shimmering eyes. "You've made me the happiest man alive tonight, Celeste," I told her fervently.

She smiled, framing my face between her soft hands. "As have you me, my love."

My heart near bursting, I slowly leaned in. Celeste's eyelids fluttered shut as she tilted her face up to mine.

When our lips met, the kiss was infinitely tender, conveying all the love and promise held in our joined future. There was also a passion, a great fire roused between us that spoke of what would come once we had finally made our way through the formalities of elven courting.

We remained entwined beneath the benevolent moon for some time, words unnecessary as we conveyed our passion with kisses. The night breeze whispered through the surrounding trees, seeming to share in our joy.

When finally, the time came to return, I pulled her to her feet, and our eyes met once more.

"You know," I said, "I'm happy this didn't end in a duel."

She laughed at that, giving me a playful poke before she flung her pale, moonlit arms around my neck. Smoldering eyes rested on mine, stirring everything within me that was male.

"Perhaps, David," she hummed in a voice that made me come undone, "a duel with me would be quite enjoyable…"

I licked my lips and chuckled, shaking my head. "My patience is being tried…"

She laughed, gave me a playful nudge with her ample hips, then pulled me along by the hand.

"Come," she said. "There will be a time and place for everything. For now, we must return!"

Hand in hand, Celeste and I made our way back through the moonlit forest towards Gladdenfield. A contented silence lay between us, both still awash in the magical emotions of the evening.

I glanced over at Celeste as we walked, her profile elegant and lovely in the silvery light. Her eyes were bright, lips curved in a soft smile. Everything had gone even better than I could have dreamed.

Before long, the torch-lit palisade walls of Gladdenfield came into view ahead through the trees. We followed the winding path leading to the main gates, which stood open at this hour for late-night travelers.

The guards nodded in greeting as we passed through. I bid them a good night as Celeste and I made our way into the sleepy frontier town. Only a few souls were still out and about on the streets.

We walked hand in hand down the main road

toward the Wild Outrider inn. Above us, the inky sky was freckled with glittering stars. Our footsteps seemed unusually loud in the hushed night air.

At the door to the inn, I paused and turned to Celeste. "I had an amazing time tonight," I told her sincerely, giving her hand a squeeze.

Celeste's eyes shone. "As did I, my beloved. It was perfect." She rested a hand lightly on my chest. "Thank you again for putting such thought into elven custom. It means the world to me."

I smiled, pleased that my efforts to honor her heritage had touched her so. "Of course, Celeste. I want to show you how much I care."

We stood there a moment, neither of us eager for the night to end. I still held her hand, loosely entwined with mine. Overhead, the waning crescent moon kept a diligent watch.

The time to say goodbye had come, but since all had gone so well, I knew the time would soon come for rings, but not yet. In my mind, I had resolved that I wanted my women with me on the quest to the troll's cave, and it was another opportunity to let the girls all grow a little closer.

"Well," I began slowly, "I should let you get back to your room and rest. But before I do, there was another thing I wanted to ask you."

Curiosity sparked in Celeste's emerald gaze. "Yes?"

I cleared my throat. "I've come upon a promising opportunity for a bit of adventure. There's a troll cave close to Gladdenfield that likely contains some valuable treasure."

Celeste's elegant eyebrows lifted in surprise. "A troll cave?"

I nodded. "Yes, apparently this troll has been making its lair close to Gladdenfield. It's likely responsible for some of the robberies in the area. I want to mount an expedition to clear it out and claim the loot."

I met her eyes to drive the next point home. "It would be dangerous, but with my abilities and summons, plus your skills and those of Leigh and Diane, I think the four of us could manage it. So, I wanted to extend an invitation to join me if you're interested."

Celeste pursed her lips thoughtfully, mulling over my proposal for a moment. Then she smiled and gave a resolute nod. "It sounds like quite the quest! I would be happy to join you, David." Her eyes glimmered eagerly at the prospect of an adventure. "Despite the hardships, I greatly enjoyed our quest to Hrothgar's Hope. I would be honored to join you once more."

I gave a satisfied nod. Having her skills along would improve our odds tremendously. "That's wonderful news," I said enthusiastically. "With the four of us, I'm sure we'll return victorious. We make a great team."

"I quite agree." Celeste laughed. She gave my hands an affectionate squeeze. "I look forward to fighting by your side again, dear one."

Her lyrical voice was warm with anticipation, reminding me of the competence she had demonstrated against the goblins, kobolds, and of course the dragon on our quest to free Clara and her companions from Hrothgar's Hope. Though gentle, Celeste was a formidable warrior.

"Excellent. Once I work out more of the details,

I'll let you know the plan," I told her.

Celeste nodded. For a moment, we simply smiled at one another, thrilled to have another adventure in store. The troll cave's treasures would help raise our levels, letting us tackle future conflicts.

At last, I knew I couldn't delay any longer. "I should really let you get to bed now," I said regretfully. "We both need rest."

"You're right, it is getting late," Celeste agreed.

Unable to resist, I drew her into my arms once more. Celeste melted against me with a contented sigh, returning my embrace. I breathed in her sweet scent, savoring these last moments together tonight.

When at last we parted, Celeste gazed up at me tenderly. "Good night, my beloved," she whispered. "Parting is such sweet sorrow."

I smiled softly. "Good night, Celeste. And thank you. I had a wonderful time."

Unable to resist, I captured her lips in one final, lingering kiss. Then, reluctantly, we slowly separated, parting ways for now.

I watched until Celeste had disappeared safely inside before turning away, my heart light as a feather. Our moonlit stroll had been pure magic.

Chapter 14

With a lingering smile, I turned and began the short walk back to the apartment above the general store, reflecting happily on the enchanting *alath-manae* I had just shared with Celeste. The night air was cool and crisp, filled with the hushed silence of the sleeping frontier town.

As I strolled along the deserted main thoroughfare, hands tucked into my pockets, my mind replayed each cherished moment spent with Celeste under the moonlight. Her acceptance of my invitation to the formal elven courtship ritual had been the first hurdle, and her reaction of pure delight had relieved my soul.

Reciting the heartfelt poem Diane had helped me craft had been the next test. Though laying my feelings so bare made me anxious, the look of wonder and emotion on Celeste's lovely face as she listened washed away any lingering uncertainty.

When Celeste had then shared her answering *ylath*, the sheer joy I felt in that moment was indescribable. Her willingness to advance our relationship meant everything to me and showed how deeply her feelings for me ran.

As I passed by darkened houses, their occupants long asleep, I smiled up at the crescent moon overhead. It had borne witness to the blossoming love between me and the fair elf maiden tonight. Everything about the evening had been perfect.

The time we had spent relaxing in each other's

company beneath the stars had only strengthened the bond developing between us. Learning more of Celeste's past and her struggles to feel accepted among other elves had made me want to shower her with affection.

My heart swelled with protectiveness and care just thinking about her. In the short time I'd known Celeste, my feelings had grown so much deeper than mere attraction. She occupied my thoughts often — as I did hers — and I longed for the day we never need to part again.

At the same time, my mind turned to the conversation I'd had with the dwarven jeweler Grimfast. If the rare deposit of shimmerstone in the troll cave truly existed, it would be quite a valuable find.

As I turned onto the street housing the general store, smiling absently to myself, I let my thoughts meander to imagining the troll cave quest. A troll was a formidable foe, so we would need to prepare and equip ourselves well for the delve into its lair.

My summonable creatures would be indispensable. And if we managed to lay low the beast, we would probably gain significant experience, perhaps even level up. I was level 8 now — significantly more powerful than most people in Gladdenfield. So far, the prognosis was that my Bloodline — the dragon at Hrothgar's Hope had called me 'Goldblood' – allowed me and my companions to progress faster.

If true, that was a great boon. Perhaps it was also the greatest weapon in the battle against Father.

As I approached the store, my thoughts turned back to the troll, and I reflected that we also needed an ample supply of healing and mana potions on hand. My alchemy skills had improved steadily, but creating potions still required deep focus. I looked forward to further honing my mystical abilities.

My mind was full of recipes and ingredients as I went up the stairs. Upstairs, I sank down by the hearth, stirring the embers absently. There was much on my shoulders, but I had risen to every challenge so far. With determination and courage, I would continue to do so, no matter what hardships lay ahead.

My Class, Frontier Summoner, was part of that. I had been gifted with great power, and I aimed to use it to help others. Vanquishing the troll and aiding Grimfast would be the next steps on that path.

Tomorrow I would speak to Diane and Leigh, sharing the news about the *alath-manae* and inviting them on the cave quest. Their enthusiasm was sure to match my own. After all, Leigh loved adventure, and while Diane was a little more cautious, she might want to join us as well — depending on how well she felt in her current state.

As the night deepened around me, I pictured the four of us delving into caverns dark and deep, my summoned creatures flanking us. The troll would put up a vicious fight, but I could control it with my summons, having the guardians tank it, while Celeste dished out the damage, aided by my other women.

And whatever treasure we retrieved would be a boon to us. We could secure the homestead, perhaps expand a little more, and we could get a greater stockpile of supplies.

As I prepared for bed, I was already making plans in my mind to prepare for the expedition. The journey itself, at least, would be easier than the one to Hrothgar's Hope as we didn't have to brave the rough terrain of the Shimmering Peaks or cross through the Blighted Land. The fight itself would likely be harder, but would it be much more difficult than the battle with the juvenile dragon?

But further speculation about the dangers could wait until tomorrow. Tonight, I would rest, refocus, and restore my energy. Tomorrow, I would return to the homestead and speak with Leigh and Diane.

With these reflections sustaining me, I finally headed to bed, though images of the challenges and adventures ahead still lingered in my mind. But I did not fear what tomorrow might bring.

As such, I lay down calmly, enjoying the scent of Leigh that still lingered in the house and the linen before drifting off into a quiet sleep.

Chapter 15

The morning sun shining through the curtains woke me gradually. Stretching, I rose from the bed, eager to return home and share the events of last night with Diane and Leigh.

After washing up and having a light breakfast, I gathered my things, said goodbye to Randal at the store, and headed out to where my Jeep was parked. I loaded up the stuff I had brought before paying a quick visit to the market.

People were just setting up their stalls, but I managed to find several packets of seeds for the ingredients I'd need to grow to make healing potions. They were Blackheart, the juice of the heart-shaped berries of which would form the base; Simmerstalk, which would need to be boiled, and Thulaemos, a sweet-scenting herb, the leaves of which would need to be dried and powdered.

After purchasing all these supplies, I left Gladdenfield, eager to return home. The drive home along the winding forest trail was peaceful. Squirrels chattered from the branches overhead, and birdsong filled the air. It was still early when the homestead came into view, smoke drifting up lazily from the chimney.

Parking the Jeep, I greeted Mr. Drizzles and the larroling before I strode up to the front door with a spring in my step. I found Diane and Leigh seated at the kitchen table, enjoying hot mugs of coffee. Their faces lit up when they saw me enter.

"David, you're back!" Diane exclaimed, rising swiftly to embrace me. I held her slender frame close, breathing in her sweet lavender scent. It had been only a day, but still, I had missed her and Leigh.

Leigh was right behind her, engulfing me in a warm hug. "We've missed ya 'round here, baby," she said, blue eyes twinkling merrily. "How'd it go with Celeste last night?"

I couldn't keep the grin off my face, recalling the magical evening I had shared with Celeste. "It was amazing," I said. "We had a lovely time. Let me tell you all about it."

As we enjoyed some coffee together, I recounted every detail of the *alath-manae*, from the romantic forest stroll to reciting my love poem, to Celeste responding with her own verse — the *ylath* — signifying she wished to advance our relationship and invited me to propose to her.

Leigh and Diane listened raptly, hanging on my every word. "That's beautiful!" Leigh exclaimed when I had finished. "She must be head over heels for you."

Diane smiled knowingly, her tail swishing behind her. "So, this means you two are officially courting now, right?" Diane asked.

When I nodded, her smile broadened. "I'm so happy for you, David."

Leigh winked and nudged my arm playfully. "Looks like we'll be needin' that big bed after all!"

I chuckled. "It's still early stages, but yes, we've begun the formal elven courtship ritual," I explained. "There are more steps to come, but this was a very promising start. I appreciate you two supporting me in this. It means a lot."

Leigh waved her hand airily. "Shoot, we just want you to be happy, baby."

Diane nodded her agreement. Their encouragement filled me with gratitude and love.

Over more coffee, I also told them about my encounter with the dwarven jeweler, Grimfast, and his intriguing tale the nearby troll cave.

Leigh's blue eyes lit up at the prospect of adventure and plunder. "A troll cave?" she echoed excitedly. "Count me in!"

Diane looked a little more hesitant. "A troll could

be very dangerous," she said worriedly, one hand drifting to rest protectively over her belly. I reached out to squeeze her arm reassuringly.

"Don't worry, we'll be well prepared. And you know I'd never let any harm come to you." Diane relaxed at my words, nodding slowly. "I suppose one more adventure before I take things easier wouldn't hurt, as long as we're careful."

"With my summons, your skills, and Celeste's magic, we'll be a force to be reckoned with," I said confidently. "Speaking of which, Celeste has already agreed to join us. You two will get to know her a little better."

"Well, ain't that just perfect," Leigh said happily. "The more the merrier!" Diane looked pleased too; I knew she had warmed up to Celeste during our previous quest.

The three of us spent the rest of the morning planning out the troll cave expedition, poring over maps of the surrounding wilderness. I described Grimfast's instructions to locate the hidden cavern entrance. It was less than a day's walk southwest from Gladdenfield.

Diane pored over the map with me, her Scout skills helping trace the best route there. Meanwhile, Leigh jotted down ideas for provisions and equipment we would need to pack. I smiled, watching my two capable loves eagerly tackle the preparations.

By the time for dinner, we had outlined a solid plan. Over a simple meal of bread, eggs, meats, cheese, and apple cider from the cellar, we discussed our strategy for confronting the troll and retrieving its loot.

"We'll have Diane scout the location," I said. "That will give us a layout of the lair. Our strategy depends on that, but I would say our best chance is to have my summons take the lead — say two or three guardians. They will take most of the punishment while the rest of us — aided perhaps by Aquana's avatar — deal damage.

Diane nodded thoughtfully. "If we can control it with your summons, peppering it with ranged attacks would be best."

Leigh smacked the table decisively. "I like it! That beast won't know what hit him." I grinned at their enthusiasm.

Over the next few days, we would gather supplies, work on the homestead, and make final preparations for the delve into the troll's cave. With adventure and honest work ahead, the days were looking bright.

Chapter 16

The next three days at the homestead were filled with preparations for our upcoming troll cave expedition. While Leigh and Diane focused on gathering provisions and readying our equipment, I decided to spend the time productively by planting the alchemy seeds I had bought in town and brewing up more mana potions.

After breakfast on the first day, I headed out to the plot where I grew ingredients for alchemy, my shovel in hand. I had already prepared three sections for the new seeds the day before. Kneeling in the soft soil, I carefully planted the Blackheart seeds, patting down the earth gently over each one. I repeated the process for the Simmerstalk and Thulaemos.

Satisfied with my work, I summoned my spirits to imbue soil and crop. I still had a free slot to bind a familiar, and I had considered doing so to permanently bind an earth or woodland spirit, but I wasn't yet sure — especially with the threat of Father looming, we might need something more combat-able.

After washing up from the gardening work, I decided to spend the rest of the morning brewing up some mana potions. Over the past weeks, I had honed my Alchemy skill considerably through regular practice. Inside my laboratory, I gathered my alchemical equipment and the necessary ingredients — thauma root pulp, dried wispstalk leaves, and essence of magebread.

Following the now familiar recipe carefully, I combined, distilled, reduced, and decanted the potion into several vials over the course of a few hours. The finished product gave off the telltale azure shimmer of a mana-restoring draught.

I already had a good stockpile thanks to many hours of practice, but more never hurt. Our upcoming adventure would surely test our mystical reserves. The healing potions would not be finished before we would embark on our adventure, so I would purchase those in town.

That evening after dinner, Leigh, Diane, and I sat by the fireplace playing cards and discussing more plans for the troll cave. Leigh's enthusiasm was infectious, putting a sparkle in Diane's eyes despite her natural caution. I shared in her enthusiasm, looking forward to another adventure.

The next day I rose early, invigorated. While my ladies continued preparations, I decided to spend the morning focused on essential chores around the farmstead. After breakfast, I gathered my tools and ventured out into the crisp morning air to check the snares and traps.

Methodically, I made my way through the woods, resetting traps as needed. Several had been triggered, yielding two plump rabbits and a squirrel. Pleased with the catches, I reset the snares carefully using new bait. After that, I cleaned and dressed the kills, leaving some meat for consumption and preparing the rest for treatment in the smokehouse.

With the traps seen to, I spent the late morning hours chopping and stacking firewood. The rhythmic thwack of my axe splitting logs echoed through the quiet forest. I worked up a good sweat hauling and stacking the cut timber in the shed to dry. Keeping our hearth well-stocked was vital.

Around midday, drawn by my growling stomach, I set aside my axe and wiped the sweat from my brow. The woodshed was filled with neatly stacked cords of oak, maple, and birch. Satisfied with my productive morning of essential chores, I headed inside to wash up before lunch.

Over our meal, we discussed my potion brewing progress. Diane's eyes shone with pride in my developing talents. "Someday your potions will be renowned across the frontier!" she said confidently.

I laughed. "Well, we'll need a much bigger garden if we want to achieve that."

In the afternoon, with my alchemy pursuits and woodcutting concluded for the day, I decided to spend some time working on minor homestead repairs and upkeep. I patched a few lingering holes in the old roof, oiled squeaky door hinges, and reinforced the smokehouse. The mundane chores brought a sense of satisfaction as I cared for our home.

As dusk neared, I noticed the first tiny sprouts poking up from the freshly planted alchemy plots. The seeds were already starting to germinate thanks to my nurturing spirits. I watched with a sense of pride as the domesticants watered gently before I headed inside to wash up before dinner.

That evening we enjoyed a delicious meal of small game made with an abundance of vegetables freshly picked from our garden. Over the meal, our conversation turned again to the troll quest.

Jack Bryce

Anticipation and excitement were palpable. Though we would be ready when the day came to set out, I knew we would remember to appreciate our time at the homestead as well.

After dinner, Leigh challenged me to a few rounds of cards by the fire, while Diane read peacefully on the sofa. Soon enough, the card game escalated, and Leigh and I got into a wrestling match instead. Diane joined in, and before I knew it, we were all panting on the floor, naked and satisfied.

The next morning dawned clear and mild after a night of gentle rain. The grass glittered with dewdrops in the warm sunrise. Birds twittered cheerily from the branches overhead, their chorus a natural fanfare welcoming the new day.

It was a perfect morning for patrolling the homestead environs and making sure that everything was safe before we would set out for Gladdenfield tomorrow.

After breakfast, I readied my equipment and stepped outside, eager to roam the forest. I began by summoning Mr. Drizzles, my storm elemental

156

familiar. With a crackle, his amorphous cloud-like form materialized before me, energy arcing across his misty body.

Together, we ventured into the surrounding woods to patrol the perimeter, remaining alert for any signs of intruders or threats. Cautiously, I attuned my senses, listening for unnatural sounds amidst the forest's natural rhythm. Mr. Drizzles floated beside me, lightning occasionally rippling outward to scan the area.

By late morning, after thoroughly combing the western and northern section of the woods, I felt satisfied that there were no immediate dangers in that area or traces or trails we should be mindful of. I would take a break and continue later.

As Mr. Drizzles continued his tireless patrol, I headed back inside for a break, breathing deep the crisp autumn air redolent of woodsmoke. The patrolling contributed to the peace of our simple homestead life.

After washing up, I joined Diane and Leigh to catch up, recounting the uneventful but productive patrol. We enjoyed a simple but hearty meal together, talking lightly before I headed back out with Mr. Drizzles.

The rest of the day passed swiftly as I walked the bounds of our land, keeping vigilant watch. Though no threats emerged, patrolling strengthened my woodcraft skills, attuning me to the wilderness. Before long, dusk fell, and I turned my feet homeward for dinner and rest. Tomorrow's adventure awaited.

The next day, I spent some time assisting Leigh with various chores around the farm before we broke for lunch. Together with Diane, we talked and laughed as we ate. Of course, we were excited as well, knowing that we would head out there again tomorrow.

Before long, evening had fallen once more. After dinner, Leigh, Diane, and I relaxed by the fire with music, books, and card games. Tomorrow we would head to Gladdenfield to finalize plans with Celeste before setting out on our subterranean adventure. But tonight, we simply enjoyed the gift of a peaceful evening together.

As we prepared for a little time in the bedroom

together, I felt contentment and readiness in equal measure. We had used these three days wisely, preparing both practically and spiritually. Though challenges awaited, our shared strength and devotion would surely carry us through. What lay ahead, we would face together.

Cleansed by restful sleep, the dawn of our adventure greeted us with crisp, invigorating air. Today our fellowship would venture forth, spirits united against whatever darkness awaited beneath the earth. But come what may in the caverns ahead, our homestead would be waiting for our return, safely guarded by my storm elemental.

Chapter 17

Morning light stirred me from a deep sleep guided by the gentle babble of the Silverthread nearby. Dreams had been pleasant and abundant, and the crisp scent of my sheets, mixed with the delicious scent of my women, made its way into my nostrils.

I blinked awake, immediately filled with

anticipation. My girls were already up and — judging by the sounds — bustling about downstairs. I understood their excitement; today was the day Leigh, Diane, and I would journey to Gladdenfield to prepare for our expedition to the troll cave.

I rose and dressed swiftly before heading downstairs. In the kitchen, Diane was packing our provisions into rucksacks while Leigh double-checked our equipment. Their efficiency brought a proud smile to my face.

Diane's face lit up when she saw me. "Good morning, my love. Ready for our adventure?" Her eyes shone with excitement. Beside her, Leigh grinned at me, hefting her pack.

"You know I am," I chuckled, giving Diane a quick kiss. "How are the preparations coming along?"

"We're just about finished," Diane said happily, cinching a bag closed.

Leigh hoisted another stuffed rucksack over her shoulder. "All set here too. That troll had better watch out 'cause we're coming!"

I laughed, thrilled to be embarking on this quest with my two capable partners. "Then let's have a quick breakfast, and we'll be on our way."

Over a breakfast of porridge, we did a final review of the journey ahead. Our first stop would be Gladdenfield to meet up with Celeste and finalize plans. Afterwards, we'd venture into the wilderness and locate the hidden troll cave, which we would be able to find thanks to Grimfast's instructions and Diane's skills as a Scout.

Bellies full, we carried our gear outside and loaded up my Jeep. After a final check that all was in order around the homestead, we set off down the forest trail leading towards town.

The larroling was hanging on the back; it didn't like it, but it was the fastest way for us to travel right now so we wouldn't lose too much daylight. After all, it was our plan to set out immediately after we met up with Celeste.

Diane rolled down her window, sighing happily as the morning breeze ruffled her raven hair. Leigh whistled a cheerful tune from the backseat. Their high spirits were contagious.

The vivid emerald and gold of the changing leaves rushed by outside as we drove. The crisp air of early autumn invigorated me. We had had some good days at the homestead, and it was nice to now be on our way again.

We joined on the main road at the old cottonwood. There were several other vehicles and beasts of burden heading into town. Travelers greeted each other and us with friendly words.

Before long, the timber palisade walls of Gladdenfield came into view. I steered us through the open gates as we entered the lively frontier town. We parked and left the larroling in the stables as required. Then, we made our way to the Wild Outrider Citizens waved in greeting as we passed, but we did not stop to chat. I knew that if we hurried, we would make it to the site of the troll cave by evening.

We made straight for the Wild Outrider Inn where Celeste awaited us. Soon, I would look upon her graceful form and intelligent emerald eyes again. It pleased me that we would venture forth together into peril, because it would strengthen our bond even more. Moreover, it would strengthen the bond between her and her future harem sisters as well.

The interior of the tavern was dim and smoky, crowded with patrons getting their breakfast before labor in town called. My eyes scanned the rustic taproom and quickly alighted on Celeste seated alone at a corner table.

She looked up, and her delicate features blossomed into a radiant smile when she saw me. My heart quickened as I strode over to greet her.

"David, you've arrived!" Celeste exclaimed, rising swiftly to embrace me. Her lithe form pressed close, igniting my desire.

"Good to see you too," I said, holding her tight.

Diane and Leigh greeted Celeste warmly, clearly pleased to have her along. Together we sat and discussed final details over mugs of coffee that Darny cheerily brought us.

I unfurled my map, tapping the marked location. "This is where we'll find the cave entrance. We should be able to reach it by nightfall if we leave soon. However, I'd rather not enter the place at night. We should camp at a safe distance and enter in the morning with renewed energy."

Diane traced possible routes with her finger. "I can take point and scout the path ahead once we near the area. I should be able to find us a sheltered location to camp. The area is heavily forested, which will shield us from hostile eyes." Her abilities would be vital.

"Sounds perfect, ladies," I said decisively. "We've got a solid plan, it seems. We should gather any final supplies and be on our way while there's still ample daylight."

They nodded, finishing their drinks before rising to gather their things. Together we headed back out into the crisp morning air, spirits united in common cause. The future teemed with promise and peril.

Our first quest together had culminated in victory against the dragon at Hrothgar's Hope. Now, with our expanded fellowship, I was confident we could vanquish this troll and claim its legendary treasure.

As we made final preparations and purchases —

including health potions — before heading out to the gate, gathering up the larroling, Darny came after us to present us a packet of chocolate chip cookies, compliments of his wife, as well as a bottle of honeyed mead to drink by the fire. We thanked him profusely for his support and kindness.

At last, all was ready. We performed a final check if all our packs were comfortable and all the gear stowed away securely. It would be quite the march, so making sure we were off to a good start was vital. The larroling carried a pack as well, although it did so with an annoyed snort.

And with that, the time had come. With a grin, I led my women through the gates, and we immediately turned off the path — no roads led to where we were headed. Our adventure into the unknown began now.

Chapter 18

The palisade wall of Gladdenfield faded behind us as we set off into the surrounding forest, leaving the frontier town behind. Our journey to the hidden troll cave had begun. For now, I took point, leading us southwest, following Diane's directions.

As we moved, we brushed aside low-hanging

pine branches. The crisp afternoon air carried the scent of woodsmoke from the town, but that faded soon enough. The woods were thick here. Only overgrown stumps hinted at human activity.

Our boots crunched on the carpet of dried leaves and needles blanketing the forest floor. Diane walked beside me, one hand resting lightly on the hilt of her crossbow, her sapphire eyes alert as she scanned our surroundings. Leigh and Celeste followed several paces back, engrossed in lively conversation, their laughter drifting up to us occasionally, with the larroling bringing up the rear.

Overhead, birds flitted from tree to tree, singing out cheerful calls to one another. Squirrels chittered as they darted around, busy gathering nuts for the coming winter months. The woods seemed peaceful, showing no signs of threats, but we remained watchful nonetheless.

"How are you feeling?" I asked Diane in a low voice as we hiked over the gently rolling land, keeping a brisk pace. "Looking forward to this adventure?"

Diane gifted me with a radiant smile, her fox ears twitching. "I feel wonderful," she assured me, giving my hand a grateful squeeze. "The fresh air and exercise will do me good."

I returned her smile, cheered by her energy and positive attitude. My earlier worries about bringing her along in her condition had vanished. Diane was resilient and more capable than most. It gladdened my heart that she was with child, and it reinforced my desire to protect her and shield her from harm.

A little past noon, we took a brief break, eating some of our rations. Normally, I would have stopped a little longer, but we were on a tight schedule, wanting to scout the troll's location and find a safe place to camp before nightfall.

As the afternoon wore on, the sun sank towards the horizon at our backs, casting long shadows before us. The larroling trailed behind, its huge form casting an especially elongated shadow. Its snuffling grunts and heavy footfalls followed our passage.

Gradually, the landscape began to change as we

journeyed deeper into unsettled lands. The terrain grew rockier, and the trees thinner. Craggy outcroppings broke up the forest floor, tangling exposed roots. The going slowed as we picked our way over the uneven ground.

The sun continued its way as we pushed on, the shadows around us deepening. The tiredness in my limbs reminded me we would need to stop and make camp soon, but I wanted to cover as much ground as we could before night fell.

Ahead, the land sloped upward, blanketed in places by great boulders and outcroppings. Diane led the way nimbly up the incline, the larroling huffing behind her. Its bulky frame made the ascent more laborious.

At the crest, we paused to catch our breath and take stock of our surroundings as the light bathed the rugged wilderness. The towering pines and jagged rocks took on an almost sinister cast in the gathering dusk. Somewhere ahead, amid this trackless land, lay the hidden entrance to the troll's lair.

Pressing forward once more, our voices dropped

to hushed tones. Our eyes scanned warily for any sign of threats as we picked our way down the far side of the ridge. Then I spotted it — a massive print sunk deep into the muddy earth lining a tiny stream.

Kneeling to inspect it, I splayed my hand over the track. The print was easily twice the size of my palm. Unease prickled my spine. Our quarry was nearby.

"Troll," Diane confirmed grimly when I waved her over. Leigh and Celeste gathered round, peering down at the discovery.

"And not long ago, either," Diane added. She pointed out indentations still brimming with water. This beast was close, though likely now safely in its lair. It would emerge when darkness fell, which was the reason we needed to find a safe place to camp.

Pressing on with heightened caution, we came across more signs over the next hour — trampled vegetation, claw marks gouged into tree bark, remains of local wildlife that had been cruelly eviscerated, and of course, copious heaps of stinking troll dung.

Each grim discovery affirmed we closed in on our destination. The troll's territory was now all around us. We needed to find a suitable place to shelter before full darkness set in. But first, it made sense to send out a scout while we still had a little daylight left.

"Diane, can you scout ahead quietly and try to locate the cave entrance?" I asked. "Don't get too close but see if you can spot it from a hidden vantage point before it gets fully dark."

Diane nodded, sapphire eyes glinting with determination. "You got it," she said before melting silently into the shadows, her lithe form disappearing swiftly between the trees thanks to her high Scout skill.

While we awaited Diane's return, the rest of us located an ideal secluded spot to make camp, a tiny cave tucked into a rocky bluff and screened by thorny brush. Leigh and I swiftly camouflaged the entrance with dead branches and pine boughs while Celeste began preparing a cold campfire-less meal. We wouldn't make a fire tonight to avoid drawing the troll to us. The larroling hunkered down moodily at the cave mouth.

Before long, Diane returned from her little scouting foray. She materialized out of the darkness as I kept watch at the perimeter of our camp with the flashlight while Leigh and Celeste were busy preparing the food.

"Find anything?" I asked quietly as she slipped back into camp.

"I did," Diane confirmed, her eyes bright. "I found a sheer rock face at the base of a hill up ahead. It's concealed by a thick wall of undergrowth and tangled vines, easy to miss if you didn't know what to look for."

She went on animatedly, "There are narrow cracks and openings in the stone that definitely lead into some kind of cave system. And that's not all — animal bones and carcasses were strewn about all around the entrance. Looked like the leftovers from meals."

Diane wrinkled her nose in distaste. "The whole area reeked of troll, too. You couldn't miss that stench once you got close. So, I'm feeling very confident that's where the beast makes its lair."

I nodded along as she described her findings. "That does sound exactly like what we're looking for. Excellent scouting, Diane!" I said approvingly.

Diane smiled happily at the praise. "Just doing my part," she said modestly.

We gathered close and spoke in hushed voices. Our cautious whispers echoed faintly off the cave walls in the deepening gloom. Our quest's objective was now within reach.

With Diane's valuable intel secured, we quickly finished up our cold camp rations before settling down to try and rest. No fire would be lit tonight, so we huddled close for warmth as we attempted to build our strength for the confrontation ahead.

Taking the first watch, I listened intently to the night sounds, ready to raise the alarm at any sign of approaching danger. But all remained quiet. As I stood watch, I summoned a guardian and bound it as a familiar. Doing so would save mana for tomorrow, and I could dismiss it when the encounter was completed.

Tomorrow, we would venture into the heart of

the troll's domain and face the beast on its own turf. But for now, we had done all we could to prepare. Sleep would be elusive, but resting as best we could was vital. The decisive battle was nearly upon us.

As night deepened around our hidden cave camp, I alone kept vigil while my companions tried to rest. We had pushed hard to reach the troll's lair before dusk, guided unerringly by Diane's peerless scouting. Now, beneath the star-studded sky, we sheltered but a stone's throw from our foe's domain.

Perched atop a flat boulder at the edge of our camp, I strained my senses and listened, relying on a little moonlight and keeping my flashlight close in case I heard something. We had spread dry twigs and branches and anything that would make sound when stepped on by a troll around the camp, although Leigh and Diane had assured me that trolls were bad at sneaking anyway; we would hear it coming.

My eyes scanned the dark forest ceaselessly, probing the shadows for any glimmer of movement. One finger rested on the trigger guard of my rifle, and I was ready to rouse the others at the first sign of approaching peril. We were anxious to confront the beast, but the troll held the advantage at night as it was active and hunting.

My sharp ears picked up the occasional snap of a breaking branch or rustle of disturbed foliage as small creatures went about their nocturnal business. Once, faint but unmistakable, a distant howl echoed through the woods — likely a prowling wolf or wild dog. But nothing indicated the troll stirred abroad. Not yet.

When the moon at last peaked overhead, that quiet period where night seems to hold its breath, I climbed carefully down from my rocky vantage point. Moving stealthily, I made my way over to rouse Leigh for the next watch. She lay curled on her side, blonde hair mussed. I almost hated to wake her, but we all needed to share the burden tonight.

At my gentle shaking, Leigh woke with the instant alertness of one used to wilderness living. When she saw it was only me, she relaxed and nodded, rising without complaint to take over the watch. I flashed her a grateful smile before settling down to claim what rest I could. I left the guardian with her.

Despite my bone-weariness, sleep eluded me. I shifted endlessly atop the hard ground, mind churning with thoughts of the day ahead. Would we be able to field the might needed to vanquish the troll? So much depended on my mystical abilities, but I had a deep reserve of confidence thanks to our ample experience as adventurers.

Seeking to calm my racing thoughts, I did my best to match my breathing to the slow rhythms of slumbering Diane and Celeste. In and out, deep and steady. Gradually, some of the tension gripping me unwound. My eyelids grew heavy, my head pillowed on my pack.

Just as sleep was finally claiming me, a faint but chilling sound in the distance jarred me awake. I bolted upright, senses straining. Had that been a roar? Straining my ears, I caught the faint echoes of... *something*. An unearthly cry, twisted with rage.

Moving swiftly, I scrambled from my bedroll and hurried to where Leigh kept watch. She turned sharply at my approach; her revolver already drawn. From her expression, I knew she had heard it too. The guardian stood beside her, shield raised and ready to defend her.

"The troll," I whispered urgently. "It must be leaving its lair to hunt."

Leigh's face was grim, her jaw set stubbornly. "Reckon you're right. Whatever that was, sure weren't no night critter." Her knuckles whitened on the grip of her revolver. Any beast that crossed our path tonight would regret it.

Together, we listened intently as the strange wailing faded, moving farther into the distance. The troll was on the prowl, but its objective seemed elsewhere tonight. Likely it was already well past our position.

With the larroling and Leigh on guard, I returned to bed, where I slept uneasily until the pale light of dawn at last filtered through the trees.

The morning chorus of birdsong was a welcome relief after the unsettling howls that had shattered the night's tranquility. But we could not relax entirely. The coming battle waited.

Rousing the others, we ate a quick, cold breakfast before finalizing plans to assault the troll's lair. Everyone showed signs of weariness, but an undercurrent of determination charged the air. This was the purpose of our quest: not just treasure but putting an end to the beast's depredations.

Gathering our weapons and gear, we set off in single file. Moving stealthily, we circled wide around to approach the cave entrance from the west. The concealing screen of underbrush came into view ahead.

Gesturing for the others to hold back, I crept forward alone through the brush. Holding my breath, I eased slowly up to the wall of stone Diane had discovered last night on her scouting foray.

Ancient, weathered granite rose steeply before me, disappearing into vine-shrouded overhangs overhead. The heavy scent of brine and mold emanated from fissures in the rock. Unsavory stains surrounded the openings — reminders of the gruesome means by which the troll sustained itself. Bones lay scattered about, cracked and gnawed.

I took a step closer, and the overwhelming stink of troll dung hit my nose. I almost gagged, but I remained there in silence, letting my senses adapt. The interior of the cave would smell no better, and we would need to fight in there.

As I waited, I saw clearly a trail of fresh blood and prints. The monster had feasted last night, and it would now be slumbering in its lair, waiting for night again.

I withdrew quietly to rejoin my companions. Diane's information had been accurate. Hopefully that boded well for our success today. Together, we would see this horror wiped from the land.

Beckoning the others close, we moved a safe distance away and formed a tight huddle to finalize our strategy; voices hushed. We all readied our weapons — Celeste her two-handed sword, Diane her crossbow, and Leigh her revolver. Taking a deep breath, I steadied the grip on my rifle. The larroling and the guardian stood ready, too.

Our fellowship was prepared for combat, silent and focused beneath the sheltering trees. For a moment, we simply looked at one another, taking solace in each other's presence before the coming trial. Then, as one, we turned and began creeping back toward the lair. My pulse thundered; senses heightened. Our assault was moments away.

When the cave entrance came back into view through the concealing brush, I motioned my allies to halt and hang back. Steeling myself, I edged forward and peered into the gloom-shrouded aperture. The foul air rushing out made me recoil, but the effect was less than it had been the first time around.

Beckoning the others forward, we agreed that Diane would go in first stealthily and get the lay of the place while the rest of us waited outside. As always, I disliked sending her ahead alone, but I knew by now my Diane was stealthier than any of us and always managed to stay out of trouble.

Soon enough, she returned from the shadows,

announcing that the cave was small — just one chamber at the end of a long tunnel. The chamber was large enough to let us all fight, and by the heavy breathing she had heard, the troll had to be inside. She doubted it was sleeping because it was grunting to itself.

"Trolls rarely sleep," Leigh said. "Their nature doesn't require it. But they hate the daylight, and they will wait it out."

"No sense hanging around until it falls asleep, then," I said. "We follow the plan. I take the lead with the guardian, and it will tank for us. I'll summon another if necessary. The moment combat is joined, Celeste and the larroling move up to join the melee, while Diane, Leigh, and I will lay down fire."

Firm nods from the others. Weapons ready, we moved. This was it. Side by side, we strode resolutely into the cavern entrance, our footsteps echoing on the damp stone floor despite our best attempts to remain silent.

Ahead waited the looming confrontation we'd come here seeking. Together, we faced the darkness.

Chapter 19

Grim purpose propelling our steps, we ventured into the yawning cavern mouth. The tainted air rushing out was like a physical blow, fetid and rank. I summoned my willpower, forcing myself not to retch. We had to push forward.

The rough-hewn passage sloped gently

downward; the way ahead lost in inky gloom. Diane took point, picking her way over the uneven floor with preternatural grace. We kept our flashlights low, trying not to alert the troll to our presence prematurely, our senses primed to have the advantage of the first strike.

The trickle of unseen moisture dripping echoed around us, underscoring the oppressive silence. The fetor thickened with each step as we descended into the dank warren of the beast's domain. Ahead, the tunnel opened into a larger cavern as Diane had described it would.

At the threshold, Diane halted, raising a clenched fist. We froze, scarcely daring to breathe. Her fox ears swiveled, testing the stagnant air before she beckoned us onward.

We crept into a vast chamber, pillars of natural stone soaring up into shadowed recesses overhead. Scattered bones lay underfoot, and we avoided them to the best of our ability, not wanting to make a sound. Across the room hulked a mound of boulders and deadwood — the troll's crude nest.

A guttural snort issued from the piled debris,

followed by the scrape of claws.

Muscles tensing, I moved to summon another guardian for 7 mana, leaving me with 48, when an earsplitting roar shattered the silence.

Lumbering upright from its nest stood the troll, a hulking abomination. Crusted with filth, its slab-like head swiveled toward us, piggish eyes smoldering with malice. Nostrils flaring, it inhaled our scent and bellowed fury.

"Steady..." I cautioned as the troll stomped closer, each thunderous footfall reverberating through the stone floor.

My allies arrayed in formation — guardians fore, spellcasters and ranged behind. The beast's fetid breath washed over us as it loomed near.

When the troll lurched within striking distance, massive fists swinging, the dual guardians surged to meet its charge. Their shield absorbed the first blow as they pushed back, driving the monster back a pace with a surprised grunt.

"Aquana's avatar!" I called out, expending 10 mana to summon my most powerful minion to join Celeste and the larroling when they would engage the troll in melee. I quickly followed up with my Aura of Protection spell, and a shimmering glow surrounded my summons, the larroling, and Celeste.

And just in time! Snarling, the troll lashed out again, but the guardians held firm thanks to the aura, denying it entry to our ranks.

As Celeste and the larroling moved in to engage the troll up close alongside my summons, I quickly summoned a storm elemental to join them. I was now at 24 mana, with a significant force of summons afield.

Aquana's avatar called down blasts of water to smite the fiend, while the storm elemental unleashed jagged forks of lightning. The troll reeled under their mystical barrage. At the same time, the guardians, Celeste, and the larroling distracted it, landing blows and avoiding its lumbering counterattacks.

From behind this frontline, Diane marked the troll as her foe with her ability, then began picking it off with expertly aimed piercing shots from her crossbow. Each bolt found a vulnerable joint or gap in the beast's hide, eliciting howls of outrage.

Meanwhile, Leigh circled at a distance, unleashing precise revolver rounds at the fiend. Wherever she spotted an opening in its defenses, a blast of fire would explode against its thick skin. As she did so, she commanded and bolstered the larroling, increasing its power and inciting it to great combat skill!

Under our coordinated assault from all sides, the troll grew increasingly frantic, its attacks losing precision. Still, its constitution was formidable. The beast refused to fall, continuing its relentless efforts to smash through my creatures' guard.

A maddened swipe from the troll disintegrated one guardian, but I called forth a replacement without missing a beat, leaving me at 17 mana. Even as Celeste's blade whirled into the troll's side, drawing a deep gash, the creature bellowed with fury as it smashed Aquana's avatar into a puddle with a rock.

Grimly, I re-summoned the avatar. Sure, the mana cost was staggering, but my summons were doing just what they needed to — they were keeping the beast away from the allies that could actually perish from its strikes. I quickly drank a mana potion after the water elemental joined the melee.

Leigh and Diane kept up their withering ranged fire, coordinating smoothly to exploit every opportunity. Bolts and bullets peppered the troll's body in a nonstop barrage, but incredibly, it continued its assault without faltering.

Despite its numerous grievous wounds, the fiend seemed energized by little more than furious determination and innate violence. It crashed against our formation like a battering ram, heedless of its own torn flesh or shattered bones.

But so too did we press on, resolute in our shared purpose. My summons, though flagging, continued their valiant resistance against the beast's onslaught. Together with my allies, we would see our grim work through to the end.

And gradually, the furious exchanges began taking their toll. Though the troll still stood, its movements turned sluggish and clumsy because of the blood it had lost. Sensing a possible turning point, my comrades and I redoubled their efforts, determined to capitalize.

"Keep it up!" I called out after firing a round with my rifle. "It's going down!"

Leigh's revolver clicked empty, and she was out for a bit as she reloaded the weapon. Beside her, Diane continued peppering the fiend with a nonstop stream of bolts, using all of her Scout combat abilities to drive each quarrel home.

But then, the troll let out a mighty bellow, and red fire raged in its eyes. With a sweep of its fists, it destroyed two guardians and smashed my storm elemental. Celeste only just managed to dodge the mighty attack in time, with Aquana's avatar absorbing the remainder of the attack.

And as we stood there, the red fire in the troll's eyes seemed to light up the cave. It grew, muscles bulging as it increased in size, wounds closing even as we stood there. From its neck, forearms, and knuckles grew deadly spines.

I blinked, surprised.

"It's a two-stage enemy!" Leigh, most experienced of us in adventuring, called out.

"Brace yourselves for the second stage! It will be even more powerful!"

I swallowed, then quickly downed a potion as the troll completed its stage evolution, putting me at 27 mana. My women braced themselves as well, with Leigh snapping the chamber of her revolver shut, Diane placing another bolt in the groove of her crossbow, and Celeste flourishing her two-handed blade.

It was time for the true test!

The troll let loose another ear-splitting roar as it completed its transformation, emerging larger and more fearsome than before. Spiked protrusions jutted from its limbs and head, and a red glow like flames licked around its body.

"Steady, it's just another beast to be slain!" I rallied my companions, summoning two fresh guardians to flank the monstrosity.

Together with Celeste, the larroling, and

Aquana's avatar, they surged forward to re-engage the troll as it roared defiance. I instructed them to guard Celeste's flanks and keep her safe from harm.

The beast swung its spiked arms in wide arcs, forcing my summons to raise their shields. Celeste nimbly rolled beneath the attacks, bringing her sword up in an uppercut that drew a steaming line across the troll's thigh.

As the melee recommenced, I quickly downed another mana potion. The second phase of this fight would be brutal. Behind the frontline, Leigh and Diane took aim once more.

With a squeeze of the trigger, Diane sent a bolt sailing straight into the troll's left eye. It reared back with a scream of agony, clawed hands clutching its face. In that moment of distraction, the larroling lunged forward and clamped its powerful jaws around the troll's ankle.

Howling, the beast slammed its spiked forearms down toward the tenacious pet. It slammed into the larroling, and the wild beast howled with pain as the furious attack drew blood.

Sensing the impending defeat of her pet, Leigh called out, "Disengage!"

Her command made the larroling release its grip and limp back just in time. It drew a trail of blood as it moved, and I could tell that it was seriously wounded.

"Feed it a healing potion!" I called out to Leigh before focusing my fire on the troll again.

Enraged beyond reason, the severely wounded troll swept its arms in a wide arc, shattering one guardian completely. I quickly summoned a replacement, keeping our frontline intact. It was vital that we fielded enough guardians to keep the troll away from Celeste and ourselves.

Aquana's avatar peppered the fiend with punches that packed the power of the sea while Celeste's sword sang its song of blood and death. Though slowed, the frenzied troll was far from finished. A red glow still suffused it as it raged and roared with fury.

It stomped forward, spikes bristling, and unleashed a furious barrage of pounding blows against the surviving guardian. The stalwart summon barely weathered the assault, but the troll's attack left its flanks open. I popped another potion and summoned a storm elemental to reinforce the melee.

"Keep it up!" Diane called.

Meanwhile, Leigh had fed the larroling a potion, and it rejoined the melee as Leigh fired her revolver at the troll again. The troll cried out in pain as claw, bullet, and blade rent its skin.

Sensing victory close at hand, we pushed harder. A hail of bullets and bolts pelted the severely wounded troll. It staggered under the relentless assault, movements slowing.

With a wild cry, Celeste ducked beneath the troll's reach and hamstrung it from behind with a mighty sweep of her blade. The beast's leg gave way, and it toppled forward with a ground-shaking crash.

In a flash, all my summons piled on top of the fallen monster, hammering it relentlessly with fists, water, and even the guardians' shield. Leigh circled closer, revolver leveled unwaveringly, still commanding the larroling into the fray.

From her hidden vantage, Diane continued sniping the prone troll's most vulnerable spots with ruthless precision. Each bolt found its mark unerringly, guided by her preternatural Scout senses.

Thrashing in violent death throes, the gravely wounded troll managed to throw off my creatures with its spasming bulk, destroying Aquana's avatar and one guardian in the process.

But they did not need replacing. The troll struggled to rise, and the red glow that had surrounded it was fading.

Seeing it mustering its last defiant stand, Celeste pointed her blade tip-down and uttered a fierce cry. Before the troll could regain its footing, she lunged forward and plunged her sword straight through its skull up to the hilt.

A violent tremor shook the beast's body. Then, slowly, it toppled back to the cavern floor and lay still, impaled by Celeste's blade. A final sparkle of its second-stage red glow flickered and died.

For several heartbeats, we simply stood catching our breath, eyes fixed on the fallen foe as if expecting it to rise again. But the troll remained motionless. As we waited, a notification flashed at me, informing me that I had attained level 9.

At last, Leigh loosed a whoop of victory that echoed off the soaring cavern walls.

Lowering my rifle, I approached to inspect the gigantic carcass. "Incredible work, all of you," I declared, meeting each of their exhilarated gazes in turn.

Though taxed, none seemed seriously wounded. The larroling had suffered a wound, but the health potion had helped. Still, it would need some tending.

"Any of you girls level too?" I asked.

"Sure did, baby!" Leigh hummed. "Level 6! Never would've thought I'd get *that* high!"

"I've reached level 6 too," Diane said, beaming with pride.

"Level 4 for me," Celeste confirmed, obviously somewhat surprised. "I... I didn't think such swift advancement was possible! If this is truly the effect of your Bloodline, David, then it is nothing short of miraculous!"

I smiled broadly. "I hope it is," I said. "We'll find out more about that later, though. Let's have a look around..."

Kneeling, I carefully searched the troll's crude nest. Scattered amid gnawed bones and grisly remains lay items the fiend had pilfered from past victims and had kept because it liked shiny things. Coins of gold and silver lay there, as well as a few items of jewelry that might fetch a good price. I stowed away everything of value in my pack.

While I searched, Leigh moved to stand beside Celeste. "That was some mighty fine swordsmanship back there," she said admiringly, shooting the elven maiden an appreciative look. "Remind me not to get on your bad side!"

Diane laughed in agreement. "No beast stands a chance against the four of us together!" Her fox ears were held high, tail swishing proudly.

I was excited to hear those words, realizing that through the hardships of adventure, we had all grown even closer still. Their high spirits lifted my heart. Working in unison, we had felled a formidable foe.

And of course, there was now the deposit of shimmerstone. I couldn't see it — likely, it lay under the rock and would need some digging to reach. But I wasn't going to tell my women about that. After all, the rings that Grimfast would craft for me would be a surprise.

"Let's keep searching this chamber," I suggested, rising and scooping up my pack. "We'll make sure we have everything of value before we leave."

"After that," Leigh said, "we gotta get rid of the remains. Trolls are territorial, and the stink of a troll corpse is likely to draw in another, thinking it can claim its territory."

I nodded. "That sounds wise. It'll take some time, though, to drag this thing outside and burn it."

"Perhaps afterwards, we might spend the rest of the day at the camp back at the cave?" Celeste suggested. "To unwind and recover our strength."

"That's a good idea," I said. "We can travel back tomorrow as we have plenty of supplies." I glanced at Diane. "But maybe Diane can find us a location to camp that's a little more charming?"

She chuckled and nodded. "Plenty of time for that!"

I nodded. "Alright," I said. "First things first. Let's make sure we have everything."

Reenergized by our victory, we fanned out through the expansive cavern to make sure the cave was clear.

Chapter 20

After thoroughly searching the troll's lair and gathering anything of value, we turned our attention to the gruesome task of disposing of the massive corpse. While a new troll could roam into the territory at any time, disposing of this corpse would at least make that a little less likely.

Working together and with a few summoned domesticants, we managed to haul and drag the enormous carcass out of the cave and a good distance away. The troll had been over ten feet tall, so transporting it was no easy feat even with magical aid. By the time we reached a suitable clearing, we were sweating.

Gathering dry brush, twigs, and any burnable material we could find, we piled it high over and around the troll's body. I then used a small amount of lamp oil from our supplies to accelerate the blaze once it caught. Stepping back, we watched the pyre.

Within moments, flames sprang up and began rapidly engulfing the grisly remains. A pillar of greasy black smoke billowed up through the trees as the fire grew. Of course, such a pyre risked drawing attention, so we would make our new camp at some distance from this location.

But before we left, we watched in satisfaction as the roaring blaze consumed all traces of the vile beast we had slain. The clearing reeked of burning hair, flesh, and fat, but it was a smell of victory.

Before long, all that remained were ashes and charred bones.

"Well, that's the last we'll see of that ugly brute," Leigh proclaimed with satisfaction. "Good riddance!"

We all nodded our agreement before making sure that the remains of the pyre wouldn't reignite and light up the forest in our absence. When we were sure that the fire was thoroughly extinguished, we left the site of the pyre.

With the gory remains disposed of, finding an idyllic site to make camp and recuperate was next on the agenda. Diane set out to scout the surrounding wilderness, eager to locate an ideal sheltered spot near fresh water where we could recover our strength in comfort and solitude.

While we awaited Diane's return, I decided to forage for wild edible plants, herbs, nuts, and berries that might supplement our rations, while Leigh set about tending to the larroling's wounds. I asked Celeste if she would join me, thinking it would be a good opportunity for her to learn more about identifying edibles in the wilderness. She readily agreed.

Of course, I had an ulterior motive. During our previous battles, it had appeared that Celeste relived some of the traumatic experiences induced when her uncle, who had a Changeling Class, attacked her in an attempt to absorb her powers. The attack had been her first real combat, and although she had defeated him, she had fallen into the comatose slumber from which her other uncle, Waelin, would save her with my assistance.

I wanted to know how she was doing because I saw the same troubled look in her eyes now as I had back then. But we would ease into the conversation, and I decided to show her a little bit of wilderness lore first.

As we searched, I began pointing out which plants were safe to harvest. "See these leaves here with the purple veins? That's called miner's lettuce. And these little ruffled greens are wild arugula, also edible."

Celeste listened intently, committed to expanding her knowledge. As we slowly amassed ingredients for a wilderness salad, I glanced over at her. Despite her graceful composure, there was a shadow in her emerald eyes that gave me pause.

"Is everything alright?" I probed gently. "You seem very quiet since the battle."

Celeste turned to me; her expression conflicted. "I suppose I have a lot on my mind. That fight — it brought back some difficult memories."

I halted our foraging and guided Celeste to sit beside me on a fallen log. Taking her hand in mine, I prompted softly, "Talk to me, please. I want to know what you're feeling."

She took a steadying breath. "Seeing that troll's madness and violence... it reminded me of the evil I saw in my uncle's eyes when he attacked me. I've tried not to dwell on that traumatic time, but the old fear rose up again unbidden."

I gave her hand a supportive squeeze. "That's completely understandable. You faced real darkness that day. But you summoned incredible courage and strength to defeat him."

Celeste managed a small smile at the reassurance, but melancholy still lingered in her expression. "Afterwards, I never wanted to take up arms again," she confessed. "The violence sickened me. But now..."

She trailed off uncertainly. I nodded encouragement for her to continue unburdening her heart.

"Continue," I said. "Please. I want to hear more."

"Something has changed in me," she admitted with a smile. "Your presence... I'm not so sickened or scared by it anymore. And... well, I feel it is thanks to you."

I squeezed her soft hand. "That sounds like a breakthrough," I said.

She nodded. "With you, fighting side by side against that troll, I felt no fear or hesitation," Celeste said, wonder dawning in her eyes. "Only resolve. With you near, the darkness cannot touch me."

Her admission brought a rush of emotion. "I'm honored you feel that way," I said earnestly. "And I swear to you, I will never let any harm come to you. And don't feel ashamed if those feelings resurface, Celeste. We all have wounds — no one gets through life unharmed. The true art is learning to live with the scars, rather than trying to hide them."

Celeste squeezed my hand, her features softening. "I know, my love. I will try." She turned her face up to the sunlight through the leaves, some inner burden lifted.

After that, her emerald eyes fell on me again, and she smiled, the burden slipping away. I could not resist, and so I kissed her, drinking of her sweet lips once more.

If it had been any other woman, I would have begun undressing her then and there, but I knew Celeste needed to wait until she was bound to me by marriage. Such were the customs of her people, and I would respect them.

After our talk, I showed her that the forest teemed with bounty if you knew where to look. Soon enough, we were joking around and laughing as squirrels peeked at us curiously from the branches.

Before long, we had gathered a respectable haul of nourishment. But more importantly, Celeste and I had spoken of her trauma. Hand in hand, we returned to Leigh closer than ever.

Leigh had bound the larroling's wounds by now, and the creature seemed happy once again. Leigh shot Celeste and me an appreciative look as we showcased our findings, which made Celeste beam with pride.

"That'll help with the stew I'm planning to make," Leigh said.

Eventually, Diane emerged from the leafy undergrowth, an excited smile on her lovely face. "I've found the perfect spot!" she announced. "Follow me, it's not far."

Grabbing our gear, we eagerly trailed after her, hungry for rest and refuge. Diane led us along a winding deer trail to a secluded glen nestled between towering pines. A sparkling stream babbled through, spanned by a fallen mossy log. The clearing was carpeted with soft grass and clover, sprinkled with wildflowers. Soft sunlight spoked down through the fragrant needled branches overhead.

"Oh, it's absolutely perfect!" Celeste exclaimed, turning slowly to take in the woodland sanctuary

Diane had discovered for us. Leigh gave an approving whistle.

"You've outdone yourself, Diane," I said, pulling her into an appreciative one-armed hug. Her fox ears twitched happily at the praise. This glen appeared custom-made for resting and recovery.

We quickly set about establishing camp, unfurling bedrolls and unpacking cooking utensils. Leigh started a fire and soon had her stew bubbling merrily. The boughs of surrounding evergreens provided shelter should rain fall, although the skies were very blue with just a few snow-white clouds.

While Leigh tended to the food, I made sure to gather plenty of firewood to last us through the rest of the day and the night. As the stew bubbled, Diane returned from refilling our waterskins in the stream.

Celeste and I worked together to pitch the tents.

After that, we ate a light lunch of our provisions and lounged comfortably on our bedrolls, reflecting on the harrowing fight and reveling in our victory.

Leigh regaled us with colorful retellings of past exploits from her adventuring days. Eventually, the conversation lapsed into tranquil silence, accompanied only by the soft babble of the brook and the bubbling of the stew. The afternoon drew on, but we would relax here for the remainder of the day.

Taking the moment as it came, I focused on leveling up. Having reached level 9 awarded me with another familiar slot, as well as 10 health and 5 mana. In addition, I would be allowed to choose one spell from three.

The selection was hardly interesting, because a single spell took the stage — an Evolve Summon spell. That spell allowed me to upgrade any summon in the field — including a familiar — for a limited amount of time. Upgraded summons would be much more powerful and efficient, dealing up to twice as much damage and having up to twice as much health. Utility minions like the domesticants would work faster and quicker. At a cost of 5 mana, it was a pretty good deal.

The other two spells were Summon Frakay, which was a wispy fire elemental, and Call Lightning. Sure, they were useful, but I did not focus on direct-damage spells, and I already had a damage-dealing elemental — two, in fact. Reasoning thus, I chose the Evolve Summon spell.

Satisfied with my choices, I reviewed my character sheet.

Name: David Wilson

Class: Frontier Summoner

Level: 9

Health: 100/100

Mana: 50/50 (+10 from Hearth Treasures)

Skills:

Summon Minor Spirit — Level 21 (3 mana)

Summon Domesticant — Level 20 (5 mana)

Summon Guardian — Level 21 (7 mana)

Summon Aquana's Avatar — Level 15 (9 mana)

Summon Storm Elemental — Level 13 (10 mana)

Bind Familiar — Level 5 (15 mana)

Aura of Protection — Level 3 (4 mana)

Banish — Level 1 (6 mana)

Evolve Summon — Level 1 (4 mana)

Identify Plants — Level 16 (1 mana)

Foraging — Level 18 (1 mana)

Trapping — Level 18 (1 mana)

Alchemy — Level 22 (1 mana)

Farming — Level 9 (1 mana)

Ranching — Level 1 (1 mana)

Things were looking good! And through achieving level 15 in my Summon Aquana's Avatar spell, the mana cost had also been lowered by 1. This was good, as I used Aquana's avatar fairly often.

Drowsy from physical exertion and satisfied, I lay back on the plush grass and watched cottony clouds drift lazily across the azure sky overhead. Nearby, Celeste leaned silently against the trunk of a mighty pine, eyes closed as she listened to the whisper of the breeze stirring the needled branches.

The fair elf maiden seemed utterly at peace here amidst the ancient trees. Seeing her serene expression, I felt a powerful swell of emotion. I longed to always provide her sanctuary and respite from whatever storms she had weathered. Soon, with the engagement ring from Grimfast, I could make that dream reality.

As I began drifting into a comfortable nap, Diane rested with her head pillowed comfortably in my lap. Leigh, seeing we were all resting, rose and began patrolling the camp so we could rest. The blonde frontierswoman was an image of beauty and strength as she rolled her shoulders and began her patrol.

Drowsiness overtook me, and I drifted into a light slumber lulled by birdsong and the gentle gurgle of the stream.

Chapter 21

I was gently roused from my nap by the smell of simmering stew wafting through camp. Blinking awake, I sat up carefully so as not to disturb Diane, who was still dozing with her head in my lap.

Across the campfire, Leigh bent over a bubbling pot suspended over the flames, wooden spoon in hand. She looked up and flashed me a grin when she saw I was awake.

"Rise and shine, sleepyhead!" she said. "Stew's just about ready. Why don't you go wake the other two?"

I nodded and blinked myself a little more awake. We were still in the beautiful glade, but the sun had proceeded along its path. At the edge of our camp, the larroling was patrolling. I looked down, savoring Diane's beauty as she idly napped in my lap for a moment before I gently shook her shoulder.

She stirred, yawning, her fox ears twitching. "Something smells delicious," she murmured appreciatively.

Together we went over to rouse Celeste, who had drifted off beneath the pine tree, arms wrapped around her knees. She looked so peaceful that I almost hated to disturb her, but the scent of the hearty stew beckoned.

Celeste's emerald eyes fluttered open, and she gifted me with a sleepy smile. "Is it time to eat?" she inquired. When I nodded, she allowed me to help her gracefully to her feet.

The four of us gathered around the flickering campfire as Leigh ladled out generous portions of chunky stew into our bowls. She had crafted it from the meat we had brought with us, and the wild vegetables Celeste and I had foraged earlier, producing a mouthwatering wilderness meal.

We ate hungrily, exclaiming over the delicious flavor. We opened the bottle that Darny had gifted us before we departed from Gladdenfield Outpost, and it was a fine mead indeed!

Life was good as we sat there, ate, and drank. The sun had begun its descent, bathing the forest in warm amber light. A peacefulness descended over the sheltered glen as we enjoyed the meal together. We all ate our fill, happy to be together and well and enjoy another great meal.

Bellies full, we lounged contentedly around the fire, watching the flames dance and snap. Somewhere nearby, an owl began calling out its lonesome nightly serenade. The larroling snuffled and grunted in its sleep. It would nap now, Leigh had said, and patrol later.

As twilight deepened, a chill crept into the night air. By unspoken consent, we shifted closer together seeking warmth and comfort. I slipped an arm around Diane, and she nestled against me contentedly. Celeste had her head in my lap.

Leigh poked at the fire, sending sparks swirling upward. "Can't believe we actually took down that ugly troll," she remarked with a satisfied grin. "We're a force to be reckoned with."

Diane and Celeste voiced their agreement. I smiled, reflecting that it was not only their formidable combat skills that made them so valuable but their indomitable spirits. Each was remarkable in her own way.

We enjoyed a comfortable silence for a time, lulled by the hypnotic dance of the flames. An occasional pop or crackle punctuated the stillness. Overhead, the emerging stars glittered like diamonds against velvet.

Leigh sidled a little closer to me, nudging my foot playfully with hers. "With you leadin' us, that beast didn't stand a chance," she said, blue eyes dancing. "Gotta say, you takin' charge like that gets my heart racin', sugar."

The naughty blaze in her eyes lit up the fire in me, and it sure didn't help that Celeste's delicious and soft body pushed up against mine. The elven maiden gave a coy little giggle at Leigh's remark, her cheeks flushing.

Diane hummed in agreement, lightly tracing her fingers along my arm. "Watching David in action is the best thing there is," she purred, fox ears twitching.

I chuckled at their antics, giving Leigh's delicious, soft thigh a light squeeze in return. She gave a playful yelp and licked her lips in a way that told me she wanted more.

"Well, I can't take all the credit. You ladies leave me speechless with your skills."

"Now don't go gettin' shy on us," Leigh teased. "You know we love showerin' our big strong man with a little admiration." She nuzzled against my shoulder affectionately. "Plus, I don't mind you speechless… If you ain't talking, that tongue of yours is free for… other stuff."

Celeste turned red at that and covered her

mouth, but I couldn't help but chuckle.

Diane giggled, nestling closer on my other side. Her hand traced delicate circles on my chest.

I slipped an arm around each of their waists, drawing them near. "This tongue is always at your service, ladies," I joked, planting a tender kiss on Leigh's golden head.

As I did so, Celeste squirmed in my lap, feeling something harden. I could see a light haze of lust in those big green eyes. Part of me supposed it was a little unfair that Diane and Leigh were teasing me so.

"Why don't the two of us go wash up, hm?" Leigh purred at Diane. "Girls gotta be clean before they get dirty."

Diane giggled and followed her harem sister. Leigh shot me a meaningful look before she sashayed off, those hips sending my mind straight to the gutter.

I felt Celeste stir slightly, her slender frame pressing a shade closer as she shifted her weight. Turning my head, I realized she was studying my face quietly, an unreadable expression in her luminous eyes.

"What is it?" I asked softly, intrigued by her pensive mood.

Celeste hesitated, glancing down almost shyly before meeting my gaze again. "I… I feel a little… Well…" A blush tinted her fair cheeks.

I sensed this was an important moment. Gently, I ran my hand through her amber locks, giving her my full attention. "You can speak your mind," I said. "Just like we discussed."

Celeste took a small breath before continuing quietly. "I… I care deeply for you, David. But there are certain... *needs*. I've been trying to push them back. But…" Her blush deepened, but her eyes never left mine. "There's nothing we can do about it, I guess. Not until we complete our… our courtship."

It didn't take a genius to figure out what she wanted. The gentle glow on her cheeks, the hazy bedroom quality of her eyes, the way she squirmed in my lap. Of course, elven custom required that we wouldn't make love until we were married.

But there had to be *something* we could do.

"There's really nothing?" I asked. "I mean, I'm patient, but if I can help you, Celeste, I will."

She looked a little confused. "I'm… Is there… I have little experience…"

I grinned, enjoying the way her full bosom heaved as her breath quickened. "Come on, Celeste," I said. "I know you watched us."

"W-watched you?"

"Yes," I said. "On our way to Hrothgar's Hope at night. You watched me and Diane."

She bit her bottom lip and shot me the cutest look, although I could tell the shame just made her want to disappear. "I'm… I'm so sorry… I'll apologize to Diane, too… I never meant to… Maybe I should just leave."

I grabbed her hand and smiled at her. "Leave? Why would you leave? We like you. You have needs too, Celeste. What point is there in denying those? And we don't mind it when you watch. Soon enough, you'll be a member of our family."

"You… You don't mind?"

"Of course not."

She took a deep breath and smiled at me, her

chest still heaving. "It's all so exciting to me," she purred. "I... I just never... Well..."

I shushed her. In the distance, I could hear the soft laughter of Diane and Leigh, and my eyes were burning when they rested on Celeste again. "I know we cannot share the deepest pleasure until we are wed," I said. "But if I know my girls, Diane and Leigh are in the mood for a little tumble tonight."

Celeste giggled and bit her lip again, looking at me with those big, green eyes full of expectation.

"So, what do you say you watch us again?" I suggested, letting my hungry gaze roam down her elegant curves. "Only this time, you don't hide..."

Chapter 22

The crackling of the fire accompanied the soft giggles of Diane and Leigh as they joined us and turned to Celeste, excited by my suggestion they'd overheard. Celeste's gaze lingered on them before returning to me, and a blush spread across her cheeks.

"Come, sit with us, Celeste," Leigh beckoned, her tone light and teasing as she settled onto a thick bed of moss, patting the space beside her.

Diane joined her as she spoke, their bodies close. The heat between them was palpable even from a distance, and my lust to claim them stirred.

Celeste hesitated, her eyes flitting between the two women and me. The air was thick with anticipation, a palpable electricity that seemed to draw her in despite her shyness.

I stood, extending my hand to her. "It's okay," I reassured, my voice low and steady. "We want you here with us." She placed her trembling hand in mine, and I led her to the inviting spot beside the fire.

Diane and Leigh began teasingly undressing one another, their eyes always on me, full of desire and need as their hands roamed each other's bodies, deftly unbuttoning shirts and unlacing bodices. The sound of their deepening breaths mixed with the rustle of fabric falling to the ground.

Celeste watched, her breathing shallow, as Diane's and Leigh's bare skin was revealed to the flickering flames. Diane's athletic curves and the soft swell of her breasts contrasted with Leigh's voluptuous form, her ample bosom and the freckles dusting her skin like a constellation of desire.

Standing over them, I, too, undressed, baring myself to Celeste for the first time. I felt the weight of Celeste's gaze upon me, lustful despite her shyness. My muscles flexed and relaxed with each movement, and I could feel her eyes tracing the contours of my body as my clothes joined the growing pile on the forest floor.

Diane and Leigh turned their attention to me and came over on their knees. Soft hands explored my bare chest, tracing the lines of my body before venturing lower. Their touches were like fire on my skin, igniting a primal need within me.

"Your turn to undress, Celeste," Leigh whispered, her voice thick with lust as she and Diane, now completely naked, beckoned to the elven maiden.

Celeste's hands trembled as she began to shed her clothing, but she did not hesitate as she revealed to my lustful eye the perfection of her own body. Her amber hair cascaded over her pale shoulders, framing full breasts that rose and fell with each nervous breath, the perky nipples hard. Her waist tapered into the curve of her hips, and the sight of her green eyes, wide and filled with a mix of fear and longing, captivated my soul.

As Celeste's last garment fell away, the beauty of her nakedness was laid bare before us. Her skin glowed in the firelight, a spectacle of smooth curves and delicate lines that spoke of her elven heritage. Her pussy was soft and pink, with a cute little tuft of amber pubic hair, and I felt almost physical pain at the desire to enter her and claim her as my own.

But not yet…

"She's beautiful," Leigh purred as she studied the elven maiden.

"Truly," Diane agreed.

Celeste blushed and bit her plump lip as she turned her gaze to the ground for a moment. But soon enough, she raised her gaze once more and watched us as she sat down to look at us, her hand idly tracing her own body.

With Celeste now as bare as the rest of us, Diane lay back, parting her thighs in a silent invitation. I knelt between them; my gaze locked with hers as I lowered my mouth to the warmth of her sex, needing to taste her and show Celeste how I pleased her future harem sisters.

Diane gasped, her hands finding their way to my hair, guiding me closer. I tasted her, the sweetness of her arousal mingling with the smoky air. My tongue danced over her delicate folds, eliciting moans that echoed through the glen.

Leigh and Celeste watched with rapt attention, their own hands wandering over their bodies. Leigh's fingers dipped between her legs, while Celeste, cheeks flushed with a rosy hue, delicately touched her inner thighs, her movements hesitant but filled with curiosity as her slender fingers teased her wet pussy lips.

"Oh, David," Diane moaned.

She writhed beneath me, her breath coming in short gasps as I brought her closer to the edge. Her scent enveloped me, a heady mix of lavender and arousal that drove me to lavish her with more fervent attention.

The sound of Leigh's soft moans intermingled with Diane's as she watched us, her own pleasure building. Celeste's eyes were wide, her hand moving with more purpose as she witnessed the passion unfolding before her, and she mewled with lust as she began teasing her little clit.

"D-David…" Diane purred. "Oh, it's so good… You're… Oh, I'm cumming, David!"

Diane's body tensed, her back arching off the mossy bed as she reached her climax. I gave no quarter, taking great joy in her pleasure as I kept lapping at her little nub. Her cry of release was a sweet symphony to my ears, evidence of the pleasure that coursed through her.

As Diane's shudders subsided, I rose to my knees, her taste still lingering on my lips. Leigh and Celeste's gazes were heated, their bodies flushed with the heat of their own arousal.

"You are both so beautiful," I murmured, my voice husky with desire as I took in the sight of their naked forms, the way the firelight danced over their skin, highlighting each curve and valley.

Leigh chuckled, a sultry sound that sent shivers down my spine. "Come here, you," she said, reaching for me with a glint in her eye.

Celeste still watched, her breath hitching as she realized the night's show was far from over.

I moved to join Leigh, my cock hard and ready. I hovered over her, the heat of her body calling to me, promising untold delights. Celeste's hand stilled between her thighs, her eyes locked on the scene, captivated by the raw passion. Her cheeks were red as she watched how this would unfold.

"I'm going to fuck you," I said to Leigh, my voice a hungry growl. "And Celeste and Diane will watch."

Leigh met my gaze unflinchingly, her own desire unabated. There was a wildness in her eyes that matched mine, a primal need that sought to be sated. "Yes," she purred. "Do it, baby. Show her how you fuck me."

Celeste and Diane looked on, their eyes hazy and full of fire as I stepped up to claim Leigh and show them how I would do it.

Slowly, teasingly, Leigh got down on her hands and knees; her big, freckled ass jiggling invitingly. Diane, still flushed from her orgasm, gave a purr of appreciation, and Celeste turned positively red, spreading her legs to show her delicious pussy as she played with it.

I swallowed hard, the sight of Leigh's curves and Celeste's sweet flower and heaving chest sending a surge of heat straight to my groin.

Moving into position behind Leigh, I ran my hands over the smooth expanse of her back, savoring the warmth of her skin against my palms. She was a delight, as always, pure pleasure and perfection, with her blonde hair spread over her shoulders.

Leigh let out a soft moan, her hips pushing back against me as if urging me to take her right then and there.

"Are you ready for me?" I asked, my voice thick

with arousal.

"God, yes, David," Leigh drawled. "Fuck me hard, make me scream for you."

I positioned my throbbing cock at her entrance, teasing her with the head before sliding in with one smooth thrust. The delicious warmth of Leigh's body enveloped me, her slick walls clenching around me like velvet.

And as I entered her, I kept my eyes on Celeste. The elven maiden gave a yelp of delight, slipping a slender finger into her tight little pussy at the same time as I entered Leigh.

"Oh fuck, yes!" Leigh cried out as I began to move, setting a rhythm that had her soft flesh rippling with each powerful stroke. Her dirty talk only spurred me on, my thrusts growing more fervent.

Diane and Celeste sat close to the fire; their eyes locked on our coupling. Diane's hand had found its way between her thighs as well, despite her earlier orgasm, and her fingers worked in small, deliberate circles over her clit as she watched us with rapt attention.

Celeste, her cheeks flushed with a rosy hue, bit her lip as her own hand mirrored Diane's movements, slipping a finger in and out of her tight womanhood as well. Though she watched us, I could tell she was lost in her own pleasure, exploring the depths of her desire.

The sight of Celeste touching herself while she watched me fuck Leigh only added fuel to the fire raging within me. "Do you like watching us, Celeste?" I grunted, my pace relentless as I drove into Leigh, making our skin slap together.

Celeste's nod was timid, but her arousal was palpable, her hand moving with more conviction as her breaths grew shallow and rapid.

Leigh's voice was a sultry purr that filled the night air. "Tell him how much you love it, Celeste. Tell him how wet watching us makes you."

Celeste's voice was barely a whisper, but it carried clearly to my ears. "It's so... beautiful. I love it, David."

Leigh's moans grew louder, her body quivering with each thrust. "That's it, baby, give it to me. I want you to fill me up! Please cum inside me," she begged, her words dripping with lust.

I felt the familiar coil of pleasure tightening in my lower belly, the pressure building to an almost unbearable intensity. "You're going to get it, Leigh. I'm going to fill you up just like you want," I promised through gritted teeth.

Leigh's cries reached a crescendo, her back arching as her orgasm overtook her. "David! I'm cumming!" she screamed, her pussy clenching around me in powerful spasms.

The sight of Leigh's ecstasy, the tightness of her around me, and the lustful gazes of Diane and Celeste watching us were all it took to send me over the edge.

With a guttural growl, I released deep inside Leigh, my hips bucking as I filled her with my cum. Leigh's body milked me for every last drop, her satisfied moans filling the glen.

Celeste's eyes never left mine as she witnessed the raw, primal act. Her hand moved frantically now, her own climax building at the sight of our union.

"Yes, David... yes..." Celeste panted, her body

tensing as her pleasure peaked. With a sharp cry, she shuddered, her orgasm washing over her as she watched me spill inside Leigh.

Seeing Celeste cum made me growl with need and slam into Leigh again, shooting my last rope of hot cum inside her and making her squeal with pleasure. The sight of Celeste's perfect body shuddering and shaking made my mind spin with the possibilities of the future when I would finally get to claim her and fill her with my seed.

With a growl, I collapsed onto Leigh, both of us panting and slick with sweat. Diane crawled over to us; her own pleasure evident on her flushed face as she kissed me deeply.

Celeste, still trembling from her release, joined our embrace, her arms wrapping around us in a tender gesture that spoke of her deep affection. Their scents filled my nostrils, firing my desire even more, and I doubted that we would be done for the night.

But for now, we lay there together, a tangle of limbs and satisfied sighs, the fire's glow painting us in warm light. The night wrapped around us like a blanket, and for a moment, everything was perfect.

Diane nuzzled against my neck; her breath warm against my skin. "That was incredible," she murmured.

Leigh chuckled, her voice husky. "We put on quite the show, didn't we?"

Celeste's soft voice was the last thing I heard before drifting into a contented doze. "How much I loved watching you..." she said, her words a gentle benediction as we all hugged and collapsed together, her confession sealing the bond between us.

Chapter 23

The next morning, I awoke to beams of golden sunlight filtering through the pine boughs sheltering our camp. Blinking awake, I smiled at the sight of Leigh, Diane, and Celeste still sleeping peacefully.

Last night had been intensely passionate, and I

was really happy that I had finally gotten a deeper glimpse of Celeste's more... well, *carnal* side. Even though she had only watched, I knew she was ready. All that remained was for us to wed, and we would do that after the families had met.

I stretched leisurely beneath the blankets, but then I rose to prepare breakfast. Our little camp in this glade had been a slice of heaven, but we would soon have to return to Gladdenfield. I would turn in the quest with Grimfast, and we would return to the homestead.

Before long, the alluring aroma of freshly brewed coffee roused the others awake. They rubbed the sleep from their eyes and gifted me with soft smiles as their supple bodies joined me around the fire.

Leigh yawned and sidled over next to me, slipping an arm casually around my waist. "Morning, handsome," she purred, nuzzling my neck. "Ready for round two?"

I chuckled at her insatiability, giving her a playful swat on her curvy rear. "Let me get some coffee in me first, you little vixen."

Leigh just laughed, clearly still reveling in the

decadent memories of last night.

Diane laughed along with her harem sister as she wagged her finger. "No round two until we're back home!" she said. "If it were up to Leigh, we'd grow old here doing nothing but making love and sleeping."

"Don't sound like too bad a fate to me," Leigh teased before sticking her tongue out at Diane.

Celeste joined us, blushing, although she giggled a little at the quips of the other girls. She seemed a little abashed, but not ill at ease, and I was happy to see that.

I smiled warmly at her. "Good morning, Celeste. I hope you slept well." A pretty blush graced her cheeks at my words.

"Good morning," she returned softly. "I slept very soundly, thank you." Her luminous gaze lingered on me a beat longer than necessary, no doubt conjuring vivid images of what she had witnessed between us under the stars.

Once we were all up, we gathered around the crackling fire to enjoy breakfast — simple fare of porridge, bread, and sausage.

We ate with vigor, fueling up for the journey back to Gladdenfield ahead of us today. Though yesterday's battle had been taxing, the time recuperating in this tranquil glade had refreshed our spirits. We were ready to return home.

Over breakfast, we happily rehashed highlights from the troll fight, from the initial clash and the surprise of it revealing its second stage to the climactic final moments of its defeat. Though intense in the moment, we were all proud of our achievements.

Leigh playfully elbowed Celeste. "That finisher you pulled off was epic! Burying your sword in the beast's skull like that? Badass."

Celeste laughed, clearly delighted at having impressed the experienced frontierswoman.

As we conversed, I surreptitiously studied Celeste, watching for any hint that she felt awkward around us following last night. But if anything, witnessing our intimacy seemed to have brought her even closer into our circle and increased her desire to fully join us.

When breakfast concluded, we set about

breaking camp and readying our gear to depart this tranquil sanctuary and return to civilization. Though the serene camp had served its purpose, I knew we all looked forward to sleeping in real beds again soon.

While the girls finished up taking down the tents and kicking dirt over the fire, making sure every cinder was doused, I went to refill our waterskins in the creek one last time. The sun was warming the air considerably. It would be a pleasant hike back, but autumn was set to begin.

Waterskins replenished, I returned to find the others waiting expectantly, packs slung over their shoulders. Celeste had brushed out her amber hair and neatly braided it. The larroling snorted happily as we were all united. Seeing them ready to embark, I felt a swell of fondness for my brave and capable companions.

"All set to head out?" I checked. At their confirming nods, I smiled and hoisted my own pack. "Then let's be off. If we keep a good pace, we should reach Gladdenfield before dusk." My words were met with eager agreement. Home beckoned.

Filing out of the serene glade, we took one last lingering look at the idyllic glen that had sheltered us, committing its beauty to memory. Then, spirits high, we struck out along the trail leading back toward civilization. The morning breeze carried the promise of home.

Our journey passed enjoyably, the bonds between us evident in our easy banter and companionable silence. We paused only briefly to eat a light lunch of leftovers from yesterday's stew.

The larroling, too, seemed in good spirits after a full day's rest and followed at an ambling pace, snuffling at the foliage curiously. Leigh kept one hand on its back, communing with her loyal pet through their mystical bond. Its wounds from the troll fight continued to heal.

By late afternoon, familiar landmarks heralding Gladdenfield's outskirts came into view through the trees up ahead. Smoke rose from chimneys, and we could hear the distant sounds of livestock and people busy with evening chores.

Emerging from the forest, we beheld the timber

palisade walls of Gladdenfield directly ahead. The sight made us speed up a little, and we covered the final stretch in good time. There was only a little activity at the gates. The guards hailed us in recognition and allowed us to pass.

Crossing the threshold back into town's hustle and bustle, we were greeted by the open market where local homesteaders and craftsmen were selling their wares. Many a soul offered us a friendly greeting as we stabled the tuckered-out larroling in the livery. Leigh fussed over her pet, making sure it had plenty of feed and a cozy stall bedded with fresh hay.

"What about drinks and dinner at the Wild Outrider?" I asked the girls once the larroling was stabled. "I think we earned ourselves a treat. And besides, there's a certain dwarf I need to talk to."

"Oh?" Leigh hummed, perking an eyebrow. "That sounds mysterious!"

The other girls purred agreement and watched me with big eyes, but I wagged my finger and laughed. "I'll tell you girls later. Come on, let's go!"

With that, we made for the Wild Outrider Inn.

Chapter 24

The warmth and liveliness of the Wild Outrider Inn enveloped us as we stepped through the doors. Lantern light flickered over the familiar rustic interior crowded with frontier folk settling in for dinner and drinks after a long day's work.

Darny's broad grin greeted us from behind the

bar. "Well, look who it is! Back from another successful adventure by the looks of ya," he exclaimed. "Go on and get yourselves a table. I'll send a girl over with menus."

We claimed a table near the back and sank gratefully onto the wooden chairs. It felt good to be back amidst the comforts of civilization.

Before long, a cheery barmaid arrived bearing four leather-bound menus along with a round of complimentary honey mead from Darny. We each took a grateful sip of the sweet, heady beverage before perusing our options.

Everything sounded delicious. In the end, I opted for the burger — Darny's wife made the best in town. Leigh chose the smoked trout, while Diane selected roasted quail. Celeste decided on the vegetable medley. We were ravenous after our long journey.

While we waited for our food, we chatted amiably about nothing in particular, simply enjoying the chance to fully relax. The inn's din of conversation and clatter of dishes enveloped us pleasantly.

It was good to be back at the Wild Outrider among friends. Our adventure with the troll had been a tough one, especially considering the troll's unexpected second stage transformation.

But seeing the good folk of Gladdenfield unwind after a long day of work made me realize that any of them might have been the troll's next victim, should they wander from the road. Perhaps we saved one of them from such a fate, and that was heartening knowledge.

Our heaping plates arrived steaming hot, and we dug in with gusto. Everything was cooked to perfection. Diane even snatched a couple of my fries, which I playfully pretended to guard. Laughter and good-natured bickering flowed freely.

Over the course of the meal, curious patrons and a few new adventurers stopped by our table to ask about the plume of smoke they had spotted in the forest yesterday and if our heading in that direction with laden packs and weapons the morning before might have had something to do with that. Laughing, we gave them a basic rundown of our troll slaying feat, leaving out the finer details.

Leigh eagerly reenacted the killing blow, jabbing her fork dramatically into a piece of smoked trout. Celeste blushed at the attention but looked pleased. It felt good to finally relate the full tale of our harrowing victory against the vile beast.

As we neared the end of our satisfying dinner, I scanned the boisterous taproom but saw no sign yet of the dwarven jeweler, Grimfast. I supposed he must be busy this evening, but like all dwarves, he would finish the day at the tavern.

For now, I was content to relax here with my ladies, full and warm and safe. This inn had been the site of so many memories on the frontier. I leaned back contentedly in my chair and let the convivial atmosphere wash over me.

Leigh ordered us a round of Darny's finest whiskey to cap off our feast. The smooth, smoky spirit tasted like triumph. We tapped our glasses together in a wordless toast, our eyes conveying everything.

Diane nestled against my shoulder. "It's so nice

to be back," she said softly.

I wrapped an arm around her and pressed a kiss to her raven hair. After a couple of days of sleeping rough, the comforts of civilization were a balm.

The whiskey left us all feeling warm, relaxed, and perhaps a little sleepy. But there were still a few hours left until bedtime, so we lingered, enjoying the inn's lively ambiance.

Our table was near the center of the action. All around us, patrons were drinking, gaming, and breaking into lively frontier songs. An atmosphere of camaraderie filled the air.

From across the room, Darny spotted us and came over to chat. "Good to see you folks relaxing after your latest exploit," he said jovially. "Why don't you have the ladies sing us a tune about your victory over the troll?"

His suggestion was met with enthusiastic agreement from the nearby patrons who had overheard. Diane and Celeste looked at each other shyly at first but then nodded.

"Alright, one song coming up!" Diane laughed. She and Celeste made their way up to the stage, heads bent together as they decided what to perform.

A hush fell over the crowd as Celeste's fingers expertly teased out a rollicking melody from the harp. Then she and Diane began to sing in gentle harmony, their voices blending beautifully together.

[Celeste:]
"Come gather close and hear our song,
Of a quest we four set out upon."

[Diane:]
"To find a troll and win renown,
We left our city, ventured out of town."

[Celeste:]
"We journeyed far through the frontier wild,
And so we traveled many a mile.
O'er streams and glens till we drew near,
The distant mountains tall did appear."

[Diane:]
"And in their foothills, overgrown in murk,
A cavern waited filled with riches stark.
Bones lay scattered round its stony girth,
This was the troll's accursed berth."

[Celeste:]

"Steeling our courage, weapons drawn,
Into the gloom ahead we marched on.
There came a roar to shake the stones,
The fiend erupted from its bone-strewn home!"

[Diane:]

"It stomped the earth and flailed its arms,
Each fist a cudgel that could kill or harm.
But arrows flew to pierce its side,
Our brave companions would not hide."

[Celeste:]

"The battle raged, blows hammered down,
Still we did not waver or turn around.
At last, my sword pierced its vile head,
The troll crashed down, defeated."

[Diane:]

"Victorious, treasures claimed in heap,
Of friendship, courage, our ballad will speak!
Our quest ahead has only begun,
Under the stars our tales live on."

[Both:]

"So drink a toast to bonds anew,
Tempered and strengthened brave and true.

Four hearts now bound in fellowship fast,
Destinies entwined to last!"

When the last triumphant note faded, the room erupted into thunderous applause and raucous shouts for an encore. Blushing, Diane and Celeste complied, launching into a lively drinking song that soon had the whole establishment boisterously singing along.

As the rowdy musical number reached its crescendo, I spotted a new arrival pushing his way through the crowded room — none other than Grimfast! The dwarven jeweler had come in unnoticed during Diane and Celeste's performance.

He saw us, and hope shimmered in his eyes, his lips forming into a smile as he realized what our appearance here meant. I gave him a nod, which he answered before beckoning me to follow. I excused myself to Leigh, then followed Grimfast to an empty table near the back.

Chapter 25

I followed Grimfast through the crowded tavern to a small table tucked away in a quiet corner. The sturdy dwarf sank down onto the bench with a weary sigh, looking at me expectantly.

"I take it you bring good tidings, lad?" he asked without preamble, his gravelly voice barely audible over the noise. "You've got a look of success about you since last we spoke."

I slid onto the bench across from him and nodded. "We cleared out the troll's lair as discussed," I confirmed. "It put up a vicious fight, but we emerged triumphant in the end."

Grimfast's craggy face split into a broad grin beneath his fiery beard. He reached across to clasp my hand in his calloused grip. "Well done, laddie! I can't thank you enough for taking on that quest. My livelihood might have been saved by your brave deeds."

"It was our pleasure to help," I said sincerely. "And we did manage to recover some valuables from the creature's hoard." I placed a bulging coin purse on the table and slid it towards him.

The dwarf picked it up almost reverently, his eyes widening as he hefted its considerable weight. "By my great-granddad's braided beard," he muttered in awe. "This is a kingly sum!"

"I'd like to invest it in your business," I said with a smile. We didn't need the money right now, and I expected that a stake in Grimfast's shop might yield more in the long run.

Grimfast quickly tucked the purse away and nodded. "Aye, an investment that shall reap rich rewards, that I promise!" he declared fervently. "I'll draw up the paperwork, but you'll have a stake of one half with a sum like this! It'll allow me to expand my inventory."

"Good," I said with a nod. "I trust you'll invest it well!"

"Oh, I will, laddie!" His expressive brows furrowed slightly in thought before he continued. "Now then, you'll be wanting those rings crafted as swift as can be, I imagine?"

"Yes, that would be ideal," I confirmed.

The dwarf nodded. "I'll need to secure the shimmerstone, but I can do that meself now that the troll is gone. Perhaps a sturdy kinsman or two will help me out. Give me a day or three, laddie, and I'll have three rings for ye. For starters."

I nodded, offering a smile to the earnest craftsman. "That sounds good. Please don't rush the process on my account. I know how seriously dwarves take their craftsmanship. I'd rather wait longer for flawless work."

"Worry not, my friend!" Grimfast exclaimed. "I'll have yer rings, and the stars will envy their shimmering, aye! Rings fit for three queens! We dwarves are stubborn as stone when we put our minds to it, and I'll make ye what ye need!"

I gave him a pleased nod. "Excellent. May your will shape steel, my friend."

"Spoken like a true friend to our folk," Grimfast said approvingly. "Trust that I'll deliver three masterpieces worthy of your bonnie lasses. The shimmerstone deposit holds more than enough. You have me oath on it."

"Thank you for understanding," I said sincerely. "I'll come back to Gladdenfield in a day or three to recover the rings. Might be a day later."

The timing was perfect. By then, I should have been able to take Celeste, Diane, and Leigh with me to New Springfield and arrange a meeting between Waelin and my grandparents in the well-protected warren of Louisville.

Grimfast nodded gratefully. "Worry not, friend," he said. "The rings will be waiting for ye!" With that, Grimfast grinned and gave my shoulder an appreciative pat. He raised his flagon enthusiastically for a toast. "To new friends and business partners, aye?"

I smiled and raised my flagon. "To new friends and business partners," I agreed.

As we drank to our burgeoning alliance, my eyes drifted to my women once more. Their conversation had hushed for a moment, and all three of them were looking over at me, smiling.

"Time to go back to yer bonnie lasses, methinks!" Grimfast joked.

I chuckled, then gave him a nod. "We'll be leaving Gladdenfield tomorrow, but I'll be back in a day or three. Or I'll send someone else to pick up the package."

Bidding the amiable dwarf a good night, I returned to the table where my three lovely companions awaited me. Their eyes lit up as I sank back down onto the bench beside them.

"There you are!" Diane exclaimed. "We were wondering what business called you away so suddenly." Her fox ears twitched curiously. "And to a dwarf, no less!"

"Top secret men's talk," Leigh said knowingly, shooting me a playful wink.

I just laughed. "All I'll say is that it was productive. But that's all you nosy girls need to know for now." I slipped an arm around Leigh and Diane's shoulders, drawing them close as I smiled warmly at Celeste.

"Ooh, so mysterious," Leigh purred, nuzzling against me.

Celeste watched our interplay, her eyes dancing merrily. "I do wonder what you would need a dwarf for," she mused.

"Ale, I'd wager," Diane teased.

I just grinned and tapped my nose ambiguously. We passed a few more minutes in lively banter as I dodged their inquisitive queries with humorous evasiveness.

As the hour grew late, I stifled a yawn and suggested we head upstairs to bed. It had been an eventful day, and I was pleasantly exhausted.

Leigh twined her arm through mine as we stood. "Sleep sounds mighty fine," she agreed, "though I got some other ideas about how we might pass the time first." A suggestive smile curved her lips.

I grinned and shot a look at Celeste. "Would you like to join us tonight?"

"Hm," Leigh hummed. "You might learn a thing or two watching."

Celeste turned beet red, but then she giggled and nodded. Laughing, I gathered my enthusiastic ladies, and together we headed out to Leigh's old place above the general store.

Chapter 26

The next morning, we all woke up refreshed in Leigh's cozy apartment above the general store. After quick breakfast together downstairs, we began preparing for the journey back to the homestead. There was still work to be done securing the place for autumn.

Once breakfast was finished, I said goodbye to Celeste, promising her that I would set up a meeting between our families once I had made my affairs at the homestead in order. She clapped her hands excitedly and gave me a big kiss goodbye before heading back to the Wild Outrider.

Loading up the Jeep, we headed to the livery to pick up Leigh's recuperated larroling. The beast snorted happily at seeing its mistress again. Leigh stroked its snout affectionately before helping it into onto the back for the ride home.

The drive was peaceful, with the sunlight raining down on us through the vibrant canopy overhead. Leaves were already turning color, and the beauty of autumn would soon be upon us.

Chatting amiably, we reached the old cottonwood and turned down the road to the homestead. Soon enough, the homestead came into view on the banks of the Silverthread. Seeing its sturdy log walls nestled amidst the trees filled me with warmth. Mr. Drizzles was patrolling the grounds, and the domesticants were zipping happily about.

Parking in front, we unpacked our gear from the trip. The larroling bounded over to inspect the homestead — which it regarded as its territory — and the domesticants happily bustled about, pleased with our return.

Unloading the supplies, we stepped inside the house. The cozy interior smelled of hearth smoke and lavender. Ghostie and Sir Boozles zipped over to twirl happily around us, chirping endless greetings.

"It's good to be home," Diane sighed contentedly, glancing around our snug abode. I slipped an arm around her shoulders in agreement, breathing deep the familiar, comforting scent.

"Alright, let's talk about what needs doing today," I said briskly. There were always tasks to be seen to after returning from a trip away.

Together we took a walk around outside to inspect the buildings and lands. I decided the smokehouse roof needed patching before the autumn rains set in. The garden plot also required care, and some of the crops would soon be ready for harvest.

Diane would check on the traps and do some foraging. Leigh volunteered to focus on the crops. Meanwhile, I would patch the smokehouse roof and spend any spare time getting some more firewood for the hearth and smokehouse.

I smiled approvingly at my capable companions. "Sounds like we've got a solid plan. Let's get to work."

The early autumn air felt invigorating as we split up to tackle our chosen tasks. Soon I was clambering onto the roof of the smokehouse with my toolkit, ready to seal any gaps. The methodical work absorbed me pleasantly.

Nearby, Leigh was busy working on the crops, caring for them and making sure they had the nutrients they needed as they were slowly ready for harvest. I had summoned and bound a woodland and earth spirit to assist her. Meanwhile, Diane hummed softly to herself as she set off to inspect the traps and forage some extra food for this evening.

We broke for a delicious lunch of vegetable soup with bread prepared by Diane and Leigh using what they had foraged. The hot meal fortified us for the afternoon's tasks ahead. Laughter and conversation flowed easily around the wooden table as we took our repast.

After eating, we continued our work. Having patched up the roof, I shifted to chopping wood so that our supply would be greater. We would go through much as the days grew colder.

By late afternoon, gray clouds rolled in, and a steady rain began pattering down. But we had accomplished much, thanks to our combined efforts. We all reunited at the house before the downpour hit.

As evening came and the rain pattered merrily outside, we gathered around the fire in the living room. The rain drummed soothingly on the roof, and we prepared our evening meal together, laughing and talking, with the girls often singing. Ghostie and Sir Boozles assisted and, before long, we had a delicious meal of quail and potatoes with the leftover soup as the first course.

Once the hot meal was ready, we crowded around the worn wooden table, hungry after our productive day. Hearty conversation and laughter filled the cozy room as we ate and drank. Everyone seemed in high spirits.

As we finished up, I decided the peaceful atmosphere was perfect for sharing my news. Clearing my throat, I began, "So I have something to mention about tomorrow..."

Two pairs of curious eyes settled on me. I smiled mysteriously. "How do you ladies feel about a little trip to New Springfield in the morning?"

Leigh's eyebrows shot up in surprise. "Well dang, you coulda knocked me over with a feather, hun. What's the occasion?"

Diane wore a similar expression of intrigued anticipation. I chuckled at their reactions.

"I have some business to take care of there. And I was hoping you two would join me." I let my words hang tantalizingly. They exchanged excited glances, immediately intrigued.

"A trip to the city sounds wonderful!" Diane exclaimed. "I haven't been to New Springfield yet. What sort of business?"

"All in due time," I said mysteriously. "For now,

just be prepared bright and early tomorrow. It should be a memorable trip."

Chapter 27

The next morning, I rose early, eager to get on the road to New Springfield. Downstairs, I brewed coffee and prepared a quick breakfast.

Soon, I heard Leigh and Diane stirring upstairs. They came down smiling, albeit still sleepy-eyed.

Leigh gave me a peck on the cheek before

pouring some coffee. "Mornin' handsome," she said. "Ready to hit the trail?"

"I am," I admitted with a smile while Diane kissed my other cheek. "Can't wait to spend the day on the road with you two."

Diane giggled and took a piece of toast and nibbled it daintily. "I'm pretty excited," she said. "I've not been to a big city in a long time. Are they... accepting of foxkin?"

"They're pretty rare in the city," I said. "But the Coalition welcomes all. You might get a funny look or two, but that's all."

Over breakfast, I outlined the two-hour drive ahead until we'd hit the city. It was a safe, well-traveled route with few monsters or threats thanks to frequent Coalition patrols. It was still not allowed to travel that stretch unless you had a Class, but it was probably the safest stretch in the entire area.

After eating, we loaded up the Jeep and set off down the long dirt driveway, leaving the homestead in the care of the domesticants, the larroling, and Mr. Drizzles. I didn't expect us to be gone for more than a single night. The morning air was fresh and cool with a hint of autumn.

At the main road, we turned in the direction of the city. More traffic joined as we left the wilderness behind. Merchants, adventurers, and pilgrims traveled to and from the great city, which served as a hub for many of the outposts.

As we bounced along, memories flooded my mind of the first time I'd come this way — the day I left New Springfield to live as a Frontier Summoner on my own homestead. I'd been so full of hope and ambition to make my mark.

While the road was familiar, everything else had changed. Back then, I was alone. Now I journeyed with two amazing women at my side — soon to be three, or so I hoped. My skills had grown tremendously since that moment I left the city with Caldwell. I didn't even have a Class back then.

I looked at the pretty women at my side. Leigh gazed out her window, enjoying the ride, while Diane hummed to herself, fox tail swishing contentedly. I reveled in their presence, feeling profoundly grateful for having these two lovely girls in my life.

As we approached the city, more vehicles appeared. Most of the traffic on the frontier was on foot or with beasts of burden, but closer to the city, one would see more cars and trucks. Many were traders, but several bore the insignia of the Coalition as well.

And there were a lot of fresh faces — people who looked like they did not know the hardships of frontier life. As I studied a few of them, I realized that I must have looked that way as well when I first made my way into Gladdenfield.

Seeing them made me think how much my frontier life had taught me. I could identify plants, track animals, forecast the weather from subtle signs. And my homestead gave me such pride and purpose. It had changed me — from a man just going through the motions to someone in control.

I was thankful for that. Life was better this way.

As New Springfield drew closer, nostalgia washed over me. I had been so naive leaving home that first time. In the wilderness, I'd faced tests of courage and grit I never imagined. But I persevered.

Now I had love, a Class, a home, and resources earned through determination. Adversity had honed me. While I began this path alone, now I had my ladies along with my powers and skills to keep us safe. I felt blessed.

"Penny for your thoughts, baby," Leigh hummed beside me; her big blue eyes fixed on me. Diane listened in as well.

I chuckled. In my deep thoughts, I hadn't even noticed that the girls had been watching me intently.

"Well," I began, "I was thinking about how much has changed since I was last here. A season passed, but it feels like years."

"Good years, I hope?" Diane ventured.

I looked at her. "The very best," I said before turning my attention back to the road.

Both girls smiled at that, and nothing more needed to be said.

Approaching the city, traffic thickened. Wagons and beasts hauled goods destined for frontier shops. New Springfield fed the outposts, yet they provided raw materials in return. A mutually beneficial relationship.

At last, the city wall and guard towers came into view ahead. The scale and grandeur of the city awed me. In the past, it had just seemed normal to me, but now, with the knowledge and experience of a true frontiersman, I understood the momentous effort it took to keep a place like this running in the frontier.

"There it is," Leigh hummed.

I nodded as I joined us in the queue of vehicles and travelers trying to get into the city. "Here we are indeed…"

After waiting in the queue, we finally passed through the imposing gates into New Springfield. The sprawling city unfurled before us, its scale and clamor of activity dizzying after life in the quiet woods.

Crowds of people — mainly humans and elves

— hurried along the cobblestone streets lined with shops and vendors loudly hawking their wares. Omnibuses rumbled past, along with delivery wagons and official vehicles marked with the Coalition's insignia.

After passing through the weathered stone gates, we entered New Springfield proper. Compared to the rustic environs of Gladdenfield Outpost, the orderly streets and multistory buildings felt dizzyingly urban. But despite the greater scale and crowds, New Springfield retained a quaint, provincial charm.

Instead of towering skyscrapers, the city center was comprised of orderly rows of two- and three-story brick buildings with peaked roofs. Flower boxes adorned many windowsills, splashing the streets below with vivid color. The paved roads bustled with wagons, beasts of burden, and pedestrians rather than being crammed with vehicles.

We drove along at a crawl, navigating around handcarts laden with goods and townspeople chatting on corners. The crowds seemed dense after the wide-open frontier, but the pace was unhurried. Up ahead, the central plaza housed the imposing marble edifice of Coalition headquarters.

"Well, don't this beat all," Leigh exclaimed, twisting in her seat to gawk at the orderly streets and quaint buildings scrolling past. "Sure is busier than I'm used to! What do you make of it, Diane?"

Diane's fox ears twitched as she took in the relatively urban environment. "It's all a little overwhelming," she admitted with a shy smile. "But the energy is exhilarating in its own way. And the smells are amazing!"

I had to agree with her as the scent of baked goods and sizzling meats wafted in through the windows. "Just wait until you taste the food here," I told them. "City folks may not have all our wilderness skills, but they've perfected the culinary arts."

Leigh nodded approvingly. "If it tastes half as good as it smells, I reckon I'm in for a treat!"

After locating parking space for the Jeep, we ventured forth on foot to properly explore the city center. The web of narrow streets teemed with activity. Bakers balanced trays of fresh loaves while arranging artful displays. Shop clerks enthusiastically hawked wares from windows decorated with flowering vines. The smells of roasting chestnuts and grilled sausages made my mouth water.

I smiled at my companions' undisguised wonder as we strolled. "Go on, take a look around," I encouraged. "We've got time."

Leigh wasted no time ducking into the nearest mercantile, exclaiming over the colorful bolts of fabric and exotic wares. Meanwhile, the enticing aroma wafting from a bakery lured Diane inside. I followed, chuckling as her fox ears pricked up excitedly while examining the rolls and cakes on display.

When Leigh rejoined us, I bought us all a glazed donut from the friendly baker. After that, I ushered my women back outside and handed each of them one of the treats.

"Oh, it's all so incredible!" Diane hummed enthusiastically as she nibbled on the treat. "I can't wait to explore more."

I gave her delicious hip a pleased squeeze. "Good! It brings me joy to show you and Leigh the city. Back when I still lived here, I could never have hoped to visit the place with company like you two!"

Many locals tipped their hats or nodded as we passed. We paused to observe a trio of street musicians joyfully performing a jaunty folk song on their fiddles and hand drum. An infant giggled and clapped from his mother's arms.

I fished a coin from my pocket and flipped it into the musicians' open instrument case. They nodded thanks without missing a beat. Diane sighed happily.

"Everyone just seems so joyful," she remarked.

"It's a great place for those who feel no need to explore the wild frontier," I explained. "Most people here are happy. There are, however, a few like me who dream of what lies beyond the walls. For those, it can be hard."

Leigh looped her arm through mine, and Diane gave me a kiss as we set off again through the lively streets. Despite New Springfield having never been my favorite place, their enthusiasm unlocked something nostalgic in me, letting me see my old town through fresh eyes.

When we passed a confectioner's shop, the sugary aroma drew us inside. Glass jars brimmed with rainbows of candy, chocolate truffles dusted in cocoa, sugared almonds, and dozens more tantalizing treats. I purchased a mixed sack of sweets, laughing as Leigh and Diane's faces lit up like children's.

We strolled leisurely toward the central plaza, nibbling candies as we drank in the provincial charms. The pale stone facades of the two- and three-story brick buildings were quaint compared to the mammoth structures of true metropolises. Flowering vines scaled many walls, and window boxes burst with blossoms.

The plaza opened up before us, paved in weathered cobblestones surrounding the grand marble edifice of Coalition headquarters. Its imposing colonnaded facade looked slightly incongruous amidst the more modest architecture around it. Pigeons fluttered and cooed around a simple stone fountain.

We took seats on the fountain's edge, enjoying the spray's misty chill. Diane trailed her fingers through the burbling water while Leigh tossed crumbs she had saved from the candies to the delight of the pigeons flocking nearer. Watching my companions, I felt profoundly content.

Soon enough, we began the gradual ascent up the wide marble stairs leading to the imposing bronze doors of the Coalition headquarters.

The stern-faced guard scrutinized us before allowing us to pass into the expansive lobby. Our footsteps echoed off the polished marble floors and towering ceilings arched high overhead. People in fine suits hurried purposefully about, contrasting oddly with the dusty, trail-worn field agents and adventurers also waiting their turn.

I led Leigh and Diane over to the large reception desk at the back of the lobby. Behind it sat a polite elf woman with her golden hair in an elegant twist. Her eyes widened slightly at the sight of Diane's fox ears, but she quickly smoothed her features.

"Welcome to Coalition headquarters. How may I

assist you today?" she inquired pleasantly.

"Yes, hello," I began. "My name is David Wilson. I'm here to request a meeting with Agent Caldwell, if he's available. I'm a former pupil of his."

"Oooh," Diane hummed softly. "So *that's* why we're here…"

The receptionist nodded. "Let me just verify that with him. One moment please." She disappeared through a door behind the desk.

Leigh and Diane shot me intrigued looks. "It's always nice to see Caldwell," Diane said. "But is there any particular reason?"

I grinned. "You'll find out."

Soon the receptionist reappeared. "You're in luck. Agent Caldwell will be right down to greet you himself," she informed me with a smile. "You can have a seat while you wait."

I thanked her before leading Leigh and Diane over to the plush waiting area. Settling onto an embroidered sofa beside them, I let out a breath.

Chapter 28

We did not have to wait long before I saw a familiar figure emerge from a side door and stride across the polished marble floor toward us. Caldwell looked just as I remembered, clad in his neat dark suit with his hair combed precisely into place. His usually serious face broke into a rare broad smile when he saw me.

"David Wilson, as I live and breathe!" he exclaimed, extending his hand which I stood to shake warmly. "What a pleasant surprise. It's good to see you, my friend."

"You too, Caldwell," I replied sincerely, a warm smile surfacing.

Caldwell had been the one to scout me as a potential mage for the Frontier Division of the Coalition. Without him and the resources he had extended to me, my Class might have awakened much later — perhaps not at all. But besides helping me out, he was a stand-up guy, friendly and generous, and I sincerely liked him.

Caldwell's gaze moved to Leigh and Diane, who had also risen respectfully. "And Leigh and Diane — lovely to see you both looking so well." He shook their hands in turn. "Welcome to New Springfield," he finally added.

"We appreciate you taking the time to meet with us," Diane said politely with a dip of her head.

"For David and his friends, anytime," Caldwell assured her. He turned back to me, appraising me keenly. "Frontier living seems to agree with you. You're looking fit."

I grinned. "Can't argue with that. Level 9."

He narrowed his eyes, then blinked and shook his head. "You're joking, right?"

"Most definitely not."

He was silent for another second, then broke out laughing before heartily shaking my hand again. "My friend, you are just full of surprises! You almost have me beat! This *has* to be your Bloodline."

I grinned. "Well, I like to think you had a hand in it, too. If it weren't for you…"

Caldwell waved off my praise modestly. "You have the right spirit for it. I merely gave you a nudge out the door. Your ascension to a Class would have happened anyway." His tone turned more serious. "Now then, to what do I owe the pleasure?"

I glanced around the bustling lobby. "Perhaps we could speak somewhere more private?"

"Of course." He smiled at me and my women. "Just follow me."

We followed as Caldwell led us through the side door and up a flight of marble steps. We emerged in a spacious office decorated in dark wood and emerald green upholstery, with a large oak desk stacked neatly with files and papers.

Caldwell gestured for us to take seats on a leather sofa along the wall as he sank into the chair behind his desk. Lacing his fingers, he regarded me expectantly. "Now then, what's on your mind?"

I cleared my throat, deciding not to mince words. "Well, I'll get right to the point — I'm courting an elf maiden named Celeste, and I'd like to arrange a formal introduction between her uncle and guardian, Waelin, and my grandmother and grandfather. Since Waelin works for you now, I decided you were the best person to approach to establish contact."

"Ah-ha!" Diane and Leigh exclaimed at the same time, exchanging meaningful looks. "So, that's why we're here…"

Caldwell's eyebrows shot up in surprise before his expression morphed into one of dawning comprehension. "I see!" he exclaimed. "Well, indeed, he works for the Frontier Division now, although his job will soon be finished." He thought for a moment. "I suppose we can spare his magical talents for a few days…"

"Thank you, Caldwell," I said sincerely. "There's still much to be done, but Celeste and I both wish to move forward. All that remains is to give my grandparents a call. Since phones don't work out in the frontier, I thought I'd do it here as well."

Caldwell listened attentively. "Of course," he remarked when I had finished. "And if I recall, your grandparents reside primarily in Louisville, correct?"

"That's right," I confirmed.

"Very good. Then I will arrange for permission to use Coalition resources to teleport your grandparents here." Caldwell rose and went to his desk, rifling through some papers.

I blinked, utterly surprised at this. Teleportation was extremely costly as it could only be done by high-level mages, and only of a very restricted number of Classes. To the world's frustration, no magical items existed that could open permanent gateways.

I exchanged a look with my girls, who were basically brimming with excitement, before I turned back to Caldwell. "That is a really grand gesture," I said.

He smiled at me over his shoulder. "Ah, and easily justified. We don't want to waste an asset like Waelin by having him travel for several days. Using teleportation magic, we can have him back to work in no time!" He winked at me. "At times, the Coalition is a stifling bureaucracy, but I've been around for a while, and I know the tunes to play to do a favor to a good friend."

I smiled and nodded. "Thank you, Caldwell. I really appreciate that."

"Make no mention of it," he said. "Now, as luck would have it, Waelin is expected here later today to provide a report. You can meet with him then, if you'd like."

"That would be ideal, thank you," I said.

Beside me, Leigh and Diane exchanged pleased glances at how smoothly this was unfolding.

"I can take my grandparents and Waelin from

here to the homestead," I suggested to Caldwell. "Since that is where I intend to hold the ceremony."

"We'll arrange transportation for both," Caldwell said. "You needn't worry about it or their security. We'll transport them by separate vehicles so as not to accidentally introduce them on the ride in. I don't know too much about elves, but they dislike it when custom is not honored. I will arrange transportation back as well in the following morning, assuming they will lodge at your homestead?"

"Caldwell, that's really great," I said. "I won't forget this. And yes, we'll make bedrooms in order for them."

Caldwell nodded, looking satisfied. "It is my pleasure! And consider it done. I will send word to Waelin as soon as he arrives that David Wilson requests an audience regarding his niece Celeste."

The way he spoke made it clear that Waelin could not refuse such a summons. "Why don't you and your girls go to the Mestoque?" Caldwell continued. "Have them give you the suite. Just mention my name, and all will be arranged. I will send Waelin there. And you may place your call to your grandparents there as well."

"The suite!" Leigh breathed. "Oh wow!"

"Well, a little luxury from time to time for the people doing the hard work out there is more than just," Caldwell said. "You are my friends, and I want you to feel welcome."

I stood and enthusiastically shook Caldwell's hand again. "I can't tell you how much I appreciate this."

Caldwell waved aside my effusive thanks. "Think nothing of it. Your family has done much for the Coalition. It is only right that I return the favor." The warmth in his usually stern gaze spoke volumes.

Diane stood as well, smiling brightly. "We are so grateful for your assistance." Leigh vigorously nodded her agreement.

Caldwell gave a single nod of acknowledgment. "Again, it is my pleasure! Now, why don't you three go enjoy the Mestoque? I will send Waelin your way when he returns."

"We will," I said. "Thank you."

He nodded. "Oh," he quickly added. "I also wanted to send you a letter soon regarding the Bloodline matter."

I perked an eyebrow. "You have news?"

"I have found a Bloodmage who can help divine the properties of your Bloodline. They are quite rare, as you know, and this one is a regular caller at Ironfast."

"Yeska of the Wildclaws?" I asked, remembering Lord Vartlebeck's promise to send her my way when next he met her.

Caldwell blinked. "Indeed… But how…"

I chuckled. "I met Lord Vartlebeck, and he promised he'd send her my way."

Caldwell grinned, shaking his head again. "I swear, David," he muttered, "you're making friends and allies wherever you go." He clapped his hands. "Well, perfect! Then that's settled as well. I've worked with Yeska before. She's a bit feisty, but I'm sure you'll manage. Now, off with you! Go enjoy!"

Thanking him again profusely, I said goodbye to

Caldwell before leading Leigh and Diane back out into the sunlight-washed streets.

A weight fell from my shoulders as we stepped outside. The first necessary step to unite Celeste and me had been accomplished far more smoothly than I could have hoped thanks to Caldwell's intervention.

Chapter 29

Leigh, Diane, and I leisurely strolled down the bustling city streets, spirits high after the productive meeting with Agent Caldwell. His generosity in arranging everything had lifted a huge burden from my shoulders.

"Well, wasn't that just the bee's knees," Leigh

exclaimed, looping her arm through mine happily as we set off down the cobblestone street. "Thanks to Caldwell, this trip's shapin' up even better than I imagined!" She whistled appreciatively. *"The Mestoque*! Now that's luxury!"

Diane nodded eagerly, slipping her arm through my other one. "It was so kind of him to set all this in motion for us. And staying at such a fine place!" Her fox ears twitched excitedly. "I've heard it's the finest inn around."

I smiled at their enthusiasm, giving each of their hands an affectionate squeeze. "Only the best for my ladies. Caldwell's really gone above and beyond. I owe him for this one."

"Nonsense!" Diane hummed. "You've done so much for him, too. Enjoy the favor freely given. It creates no debt."

"I agree with Diane," Leigh said. "You worked hard, baby. Enjoy the little extra!"

Following the directions Caldwell had provided, we made our way along quaint, tree-lined lanes towards the promised luxurious accommodation. Shopkeepers smiled and nodded politely as we passed, and I found myself straightening with pride to have Leigh and Diane on my arms.

Before long, an elegant three-story brick building came into view, with a polished brass sign over the door identifying it as The Mestoque Hotel and Inn. Flowering ivy climbed the pale stone facade, accented by rows of gleaming windows.

Ascending the steps, I held the etched glass door for Leigh and Diane before following them into a lavish lobby decorated in jewel-toned fabrics and dark, gleaming wood. A crystal chandelier cast a warm, inviting glow over the rich furnishings. Soft lute music drifted from concealed speakers.

Leigh let out an impressed whistle as we crossed the plush carpeting to the reception desk. There, an impeccably dressed elf woman stood ready to assist us. She gave our traveling outfits a look before she smiled at me. "May I help you, sir?"

I informed her that Caldwell of the Coalition's Frontier Division had arranged the suite for us. Her eyes widened briefly in surprise before she schooled her features into a polite smile. "But of course, sir," she said smoothly. "May I please have your name?"

"David Wilson," I replied.

The elf woman nodded, glancing down to scan the ledger on the polished reception desk. After a thorough perusal of the registrations, she glanced up again and offered a hospitable smile. "Indeed, Mr. Wilson. The penthouse Grandeluxe Suite is indeed booked under Caldwell's name for your party."

She lifted an ornate brass key from its hook behind the desk. "The Grandeluxe Suite is our finest and comes with much comfort. I will show you myself if you'd like."

I nodded graciously. "Thanks," I said. "We appreciate you accommodating us on such short notice."

The receptionist smiled politely. "Of course, sir. Right this way, please."

She stepped smoothly out from behind the large reception desk and led us toward the sweeping grand staircase in the back of the elegant lobby.

We followed her up the staircase and down a long hallway before stopping at an ornately carved wooden door. Unlocking it with a heavy brass key, she ushered us inside the palatial accommodations.

The suite was even more sumptuous than the lobby, adorned in velvets and silks of deepest emerald green. Floor-to-ceiling windows looked out over the central plaza. Fresh roses sat arranged artfully on an inlaid sideboard.

Leigh let out a low whistle as she ventured farther inside to inspect the plush furnishings. "David, this is fancier than a royal palace!"

"Especially Lord Vartlebeck's palace," I quipped, referring to the crude but defensible stone fort at Ironfast. My joke won a laugh from both of my girls and even a smile from the professional and straight-faced elven receptionist.

"It's beautiful," Diane hummed. Her eyes were round with awe as she trailed a hand over the smooth cherry wood furniture.

I smiled, gratified by their delight. "Only the best for you ladies. Why don't you relax while I go call my grandparents?" With that, I turned to the receptionist. "Is there a phone I can use?"

"Indeed, there is, sir," she replied. "The suite

comes with its own telephone in the bedroom." She gestured at the majestic door that led to the master bedroom. "Before I leave, is there anything else I may do for you?"

"Someone will drop by to visit me," I said. "An elf named Waelin. When he arrives, could you arrange a room for us where we can speak in private?"

"But of course, sir. Anything else?"

"No, that's it," I said. "Thank you very much."

"No trouble at all, sir." With those words, she bowed and turned with a smile.

Diane and Leigh were already exploring the grand suite, talking in excited voices about the luxury and the comfort, throwing big eyes at the Jacuzzi in the middle of the suite. I smiled at that, happy that they were getting a taste of the princess's life.

Of course, they were both women of the frontier, and they'd get bored with luxury like this soon enough. Still, it was nice to revel in it every once in a while.

Leaving them to their antics, I headed into the

bedroom to place a call...

Chapter 30

I entered the lavish master bedroom of the suite, admiring the plush furnishings and tasteful decor. Across the room sat an elegant desk and chair, upon which rested a glossy black telephone.

Crossing over, I sank down into the plush chair and picked up the receiver. After providing the operator with my grandparents' number in Louisville, I leaned back and waited as the call was connected.

Soon enough, I heard my grandfather's gravelly voice on the other end. "Hello, who's calling?" he inquired.

"Hey Grandpa, it's me, David!" I said warmly.

"David!" he exclaimed happily. "How are you, my boy? It's been too long since we talked." In the background, I could hear my grandmother asking excitedly if it was me.

"Yeah, yeah, yeah!" Grandpa replied impatiently, his voice muffled because he had his hand over the receiver. "How's your grand adventure?" he asked me, his voice loud again.

I smiled, picturing their faces. I had missed them. "I'm doing really great, Grandpa. Sorry it's been a while. I've been so busy out on the frontier that I haven't made it back to the city to visit or give you guys a call until today."

"Oh?" Grandpa queried. "Do tell! What have you been up to out there?" My grandmother's voice chimed in, urging him to put me on speakerphone so she could hear.

After some fumbling, Grandma's voice came through clear as well. "David, sweetheart, it's Grandma! Tell us all about life on the frontier. Have you met someone special yet? You mentioned some girls in your letter, now. Tell us about them, sweetie!"

I chuckled. "I sure have, Grandma. Let me tell you all about it." I then launched into describing my homestead by the Silverthread River, the cozy cabin I had built and expanded. I told them about clearing the land, building fences, establishing a garden and smokehouse.

I had sent them two letters over the past few weeks, but those had been pretty succinct. As their only living grandchild, I knew they thought of me daily, and I was happy I could finally give them some details in person.

"It's a great feeling being self-sufficient out here," I said. "Hard work, but very rewarding."

I then started telling them about Diane and how we had met in Gladdenfield when I first arrived. "She's amazing — smart, tough, and very beautiful. I honestly couldn't manage all the homestead tasks without her help. She's been with me since the beginning, and…"

I stopped myself short, not wanting to reveal that she was also pregnant with my child. That would be news I would share in person since I would be seeing them soon. "Well, I can't wait to introduce her to you!" I added.

Grandpa chuckled knowingly. "Sounds like quite the special gal."

"Oh, she is," I agreed. "And there's another wonderful woman in my life too." I proceeded to tell them about meeting Leigh, the sweet frontier girl who I'd fallen for just as hard as Diane. I described her kindness, her positive outlook on life, and her skill as a shopkeeper and Beastmaster.

Grandma sounded amazed. "Two lovely ladies? My oh my!"

Grandpa guffawed. "I always knew you were a charmer, my boy. Following those old elven customs, eh?"

I laughed sheepishly. "I suppose I am. They truly make me happy, Grandpa. I can't imagine life without them now."

"It sounds blissful!" Grandma chimed in.

"There's one more lovely lady I should mention," I continued. "Recently, I met an elf maiden named Celeste. She has the most enchanting musical voice and such a courageous spirit."

Grandma gasped excitedly. "An elf?"

"That's right," I confirmed with a smile. "With long flowing hair the color of amber and eyes that shine like emeralds. I swear, when she sings, it's the sweetest sound you've ever heard."

"Oh my, she sounds divine!" Grandma exclaimed.

Grandpa let out an amused huff. "Our boy does have quite an eye for beauty."

I chuckled. "Anyway, Celeste and I have grown very close. I want to court her properly, as the elves do. So that's why I was hoping you could come out here — to meet her family and make our union official."

Grandma clapped her hands together loud enough for me to hear through the phone. "Of course, we'll come! Anything to help our darling boy win his fair elf maiden."

My heart swelled with gratitude at their support. "You're the best. I can't wait for you to meet her!"

Grandma sounded utterly delighted. "Oh, oh, oh! Our boy! Three beautiful brides! You have been busy out there!"

"He's still got a way to go to catch up with old human legends like King Solomon," Grandpa joked. "Keep him on the frontier a little longer and who knows!"

We all shared a merry laugh before Grandma said sincerely, "We're just pleased as punch you've found so much happiness, sweetheart."

I smiled affectionately at their support. "It means the world to me, and that's why I'm hoping you'll come visit us out here..."

"It's gonna be quite the journey, my boy," Grandpa chimed in. "Now, your Grandma and I are a couple of sprightly old-timers, but don't expect us there by breakfast tomorrow!"

I chuckled. "Don't worry," I said, "The Coalition will provide transportation through a secure teleportation circle to get you here safely."

My grandparents gasped in surprise. "Teleportation?" Grandpa echoed. "Now that's something!"

"Mighty expensive!" Grandma chirped.

"The Coalition pays for it, Grandma," I said. "We don't need to worry about anything."

Grandpa chuckled. "Sounds like you're becoming quite the bigshot! Well, we're thrilled for you, son. Just say when, and your Grandma and I will be there."

"Well, I still have to talk to Celeste's next-of-kin, but I was hoping the day after tomorrow? I'll let you know." After all, I still needed to pick up Celeste in Gladdenfield, too, once we'd settled on a date.

I heard pages flipping as my grandparents checked their calendar. After conferring briefly, Grandpa came back on. "That should work just fine. We can't wait to see you and meet this young Celeste."

"Wonderful!" I said. "I'll make all the arrangements on this end. I will let you know the final date, and the Coalition will send an escort to bring you to the teleportation circle. I'll fill you in on all the details when you get here."

"We'll be ready!" Grandma confirmed eagerly. "Oh, I can hardly wait! Our little David's found love." I could hear the proud tears in her voice.

I chuckled, suddenly feeling a little choked up myself. "Thanks, Grandma. It means a lot that you're willing to do this."

"Of course, sweetheart!" Grandma replied. "Why, your grandfather and I still remember clear as day when your mom and dad first started courting. They had stars in their eyes for each other just like you sound now over this Celeste."

Grandpa jumped in amusedly. "That's right, their meet-the-family dinner was a real hullabaloo if I recall. Your father was so nervous he spilled red wine all over your mother's nice white dress!"

My grandparents shared a fond chuckle over the memory. "But it all worked out in the end, as true love tends to," Grandma said softly. "I just know your Celeste must be very special if she's captured your heart this way."

"She is, Grandma. I can't wait for you to meet her. I think you'll see the same magic between us that you did with Mom and Dad."

We spoke for a while longer, reminiscing about my parents' happy early days and them speculating excitedly about what Celeste would be like and trying to get more details from me. I promised to regale them with the full story of how we met and fell in love when they arrived.

Before long, I bid my grandparents a warm goodbye with promises to see them soon. Setting the receiver down, I took a deep breath, relief and happiness washing over me. It had been good to hear their voices again.

After hanging up with my grandparents, I stepped back out into the luxurious sitting room of the suite where Diane and Leigh were relaxing on a plush sofa. They looked up eagerly when they saw me enter.

"How did the call go?" Diane asked, her blue eyes bright with curiosity. "Were your grandparents excited to hear from you?"

I settled onto the sofa between them, smiling broadly. "They were thrilled. I told them all about life on the frontier and you two lovely ladies." I gave them each an affectionate squeeze. "And of course, about my courtship with Celeste."

"What did they have to say about all of us?" Leigh inquired, sidling closer to nuzzle my shoulder.

"Oh, they were over the moon," I assured her. "My grandpa said I was carrying on the old human legends like King Solomon." We all shared an amused laugh at that.

"They're both eager to meet you two," I said. "And I'm really eager to introduce you to them. They mean a lot to me, and so do you. I'll be having most of my favorite people in a single room."

"Most?" Leigh asked, raising her eyebrow teasingly.

I laughed. "Well, I'm not inviting Darny! No

matter how good his wife's burgers are!"

Diane and Leigh laughed at that, and I squeezed both their thighs. "They're also eager to meet Celeste," I went on. "I explained I wanted to introduce them to Waelin as part of the formal elven courtship ritual. Luckily, they were happy to drop everything and come to the city to make that happen."

Diane smiled warmly. "How wonderful that they're so supportive of you finding love."

I nodded, taking her hand and giving it an affectionate squeeze. "They just want me to be happy. And of course, they can't wait to meet the special women in my life." I winked at Leigh too, making her grin.

Then, Leigh gave me a playful poke. "And what a schemin' man you are, by the way!" she exclaimed, feigning outrage. "You had us come out here bein' all mysterious and whatnot!"

I laughed, giving her a playful nudge back. "Well, let a man have his fun every now and then."

Leigh's eyes turned hazy as she bit her lip for a moment. "Baby, we let you have *plenty* of fun."

I chuckled while Diane's cheeks flushed a little. "Well, I wanted to keep it a surprise," I said, "but *ta-da!* This is it; you're meeting my grandparents. Waelin will be there too, but hopefully a little wine will help him loosen up."

The girls giggled and exchanged excited glances, knowing full well how much my grandparents meant to me.

"Did you settle on a date for them to come?" Leigh asked curiously, absently playing with a strand of her golden hair.

"Not yet," I replied. "First I need to meet with Waelin this afternoon and find out when he can do the introduction ceremony. After that, I'll coordinate my grandparents' arrival."

Diane nodded thoughtfully. "Do you have any idea what the ceremony will entail?"

I considered for a moment before responding. "Brynneth gave me an overview. The families need to meet in a way that allows them both to prepare food for the other. Baked goods are common, but she also told me the ritual is relatively freeform. So, I imagine we'll all share a meal where our families can get to know one another. There will likely be some formal words spoken to signify approval of the match."

"Gosh, it all sounds so official," Leigh said, eyes wide. Then she grinned and elbowed me playfully. "Don't you go gettin' cold feet now, honey."

I laughed. "No chance of that. I intend to do this right. Once I have a date set, I'll go back to Gladdenfield to pick up Celeste, and I intend to host the meeting at the homestead."

"That sounds lovely," Diane hummed. "They could see our home. That's always the best way to get to know someone — by seeing their territory."

"Exactly," I agreed and rose from the plush sofa, stretching a bit. "Well, Waelin should be here soon. I'm going to speak to the innkeeper about reserving a private dining room where we can all share a meal after the ceremony."

"Ooh, smart thinking!" Leigh said approvingly.

Diane nodded her agreement. "Yes! I can't wait to see what kind of food they serve here!"

"Me too," I agreed. I leaned down to give them both a quick kiss. "Wish me luck with Waelin."

"Oh, you'll be fine," Diane assured me sweetly, caressing my cheek.

"You got this, baby," Leigh added with a confident wink. "We'll just be in here explorin' the place. You know there's a Jacuzzi?" She winked at me. "We might try that one out later, too!"

I laughed, heart swelling with gratitude and love for my two amazing women. With their staunch support behind me, I felt ready to take this next big step and unite Celeste and me.

With a final smile, I headed out the door of the lavish suite to go speak with the innkeeper about booking a private dining room.

Chapter 31

I awaited Waelin's arrival with both anticipation and nerves. Though we were already acquainted from working together to save Celeste, I knew her uncle remained wary of humans. In addition, he had that typical elven haughtiness that hampered a deeper connection.

Still, I hoped emphasizing our successful prior cooperation would help sway him. And he must at least trust and appreciate me because he had asked me to check in on Celeste regularly prior to his moving to New Springfield to help the Frontier Division.

For the meeting, the staff had arranged a private room for me, and I was waiting there for him now. Soon enough, a brisk knock heralded the elf's arrival. I opened the door to find Waelin looking much the same — tall and thin with sharp features and long gray hair. His piercing eyes regarded me intently.

"Mr. David Wilson," he said. "Greetings."

"Greetings, Waelin," I said. "Thank you for coming. Please come in." I stepped back and gestured him inside cordially.

Waelin strode past me into the lavish meeting room. "Your message stated you wished to discuss my niece," he said without preamble. His posture was stiff, hands clasped neatly behind his back. "I trust she is well? If she was not, you would've sent a more urgent missive, I hope?"

"She is well," I said. "Better than ever, in fact, so no need to worry."

Some concern fell away from him, but it made place for curiosity and a hint of suspicion. "Indeed? Well, what is this about, then?"

"Please have a seat," I offered as I poured us both a goblet of wine from the fine vintage that the Mestoque had provided. I offered Waelin the drink, and he accepted it, taking a little swig before fixing his eyes on me.

I could tell this wasn't going to be easy.

We both sat facing each other. I met his gaze directly. "Celeste and I have grown quite close since we last spoke. I won't bandy words — I know you're not the type for small talk."

"Indeed," Waelin hummed.

"I am courting Celeste formally," I said, dropping the bomb.

Waelin's eyebrows shot up in evident surprise. "You and Celeste?" he echoed incredulously. "You must be joking?"

"I'm not," I said, repressing the slight pang of anger I felt at his outrage. He was an elf, and one of the old school too, and he would respond this way. "She and I have spent much time together. We have shared an *alath-manae*, and she…"

"An *alath-manae*!" he exclaimed, turning a little red. "What? You just skipped the *tulanei*? What have you done to her! She is a virtuous woman!"

I made a pacifying gesture. "Calm down, Waelin," I said. "She *is* virtuous. We haven't done anything that elven custom prohibits."

"Pah!" he scoffed. "And what do you know — a vagabond of the frontier — of our customs?"

I swallowed that pang of anger again. "Last time I checked, Waelin," I said, voice calm, "you were just as much a 'vagabond of the frontier' as I am. You roam from town to town, selling potions. I, at least, have a home."

His teeth ground together. "I will not be spoken to in such…"

"Now listen," I said, silencing him. "I care deeply for Celeste. We found happiness together. I believe we could build a good life together. I have a home that she will join, loving companions she holds in her heart in friendship. I am a Frontier Summoner, and I have achieved level 9. Few outmatch me now, and soon, none will. In addition, Celeste has advanced by my side as well. Now, before you start spewing anger, you should *think*."

I could see his mind working.

"What do you want for her, Waelin?" I asked. "To be happy with a man she chose herself? Or to live alone in Gladdenfield, waiting for you to return and then joining you on the road? To roam from place to place with no company but you, peddling potions and never staying long enough to grow attached to anything? Is that a life for her?"

He licked his lips, his eyes still shooting fire, but there was more sense in them now.

"You know me, Waelin. I am honorable. And she is full of life, love, and laughter. Even after suffering so horribly at her other uncle's violence, she is still vibrant and full of goodness. I know you see this too. This is why you love her. With me and my other women, that good and happy side of her will flourish. On the road, who knows what will happen? I know you want the best for her."

Waelin looked thoughtful now. My words had

diminished his anger, and he knew they were sensible. At length, he reached for his goblet and took a much less civilized swig of wine before fixing his gaze on me.

"You are not wrong, David Wilson," he muttered. "Even though I want you to be."

I nodded slowly. "You see sense, Waelin. You asked me to look after her, to see to her wellbeing, and I will tell you that she wants to be with me. She wants to stay."

He drew a deep breath. "I promised her mother, my sister, that I would never let anything bad happen to her." His eyes took on a hard light. "I failed that promise once, when her father's brother tried to consume her power and thrust her into a coma from which she barely recovered. I will *not* fail again."

"And you are not failing," I said. "I will make you that very same promise to keep her safe. But you cannot latch onto her and keep her in your shadow for all days to come. She needs to live and to love."

"It... It is difficult for me. My judgment is

clouded by past failures."

"Then let me show you. Come meet my family. See where I come from. See who raised me. You will know what stock I came from, and you will see the happiness Celeste and I share. See with your own eyes how things are."

He looked up at me, and the fierce sternness in his iron gaze was now broken. In its place was left a man who grieved over the loss of his family and clung hard to the one person that remained to him.

I could understand — I had lost people too. From experience, I knew we would find no salvation in clinging desperately to what still remained. The right way goes ever forward.

"Very well," he breathed, his voice almost a whisper. "I shall come."

Chapter 32

The lavish dining room of the Mestoque Hotel glittered around me and my girls as we were seated at an intimate table tucked away in a quiet corner. Crystal chandeliers cast a warm glow over the elegant surroundings.

At first, Diane, Leigh, and I had felt out of place

in all this luxury. We had brought clean sets of clothes, but we had packed them with an eye for activity and travel. So, we weren't exactly in fine attire.

However, the staff solved that problem by simply seating us in a corner behind a divider where we wouldn't feel out of place. Soon enough, we were joking and laughing, actually quite happy that we weren't seated close to the stuffier people that visited an establishment such as the Mestoque.

A smartly dressed waiter arrived with leather-bound menus and offered us a selection of vintage wines to begin our meal. I deferred to Diane and Leigh's tastes, allowing them to select a delicate elven white wine which arrived chilled in a sweating silver bucket.

As the waiter poured our wine, soft strains of classical music from a live string quartet drifted through the opulent space. The conversations of other diners beyond the divider drifted our way in hushed tones, but my focus rested solely on my two lovely companions.

"Well, you two look as pretty as a picture

tonight," I remarked, smiling at Diane and Leigh over my wineglass. Both girls wore pants that hugged their delicious bodies, and Leigh wore a blouse over it — the poor buttons straining to contain the blonde's ample bosom — and Diane wore a shirt that was a little more rugged, befitting the foxkin beauty.

Diane blushed prettily at the compliment while Leigh winked and blew me a kiss. "Not as dashing as you, handsome," Leigh returned with an admiring glance at my physique.

I wore neat jeans and a button-up shirt. We were hardly in formal garb, but we were in good shape, beaming with health.

We clinked our wine glasses together in a wordless toast before sampling the delicate elven vintage. Its crisp minerality complemented the luxurious atmosphere perfectly.

As we awaited our appetizers, soft candlelight played over Diane and Leigh's smiling faces. Their eyes shone with excitement over this small taste of civilization and refinement. It gladdened my heart to give them this experience.

Our conversation meandered pleasantly over shared memories and amusing anecdotes from our time together.

"Y'know, I'll never forget the day you first came into my little shop asking about foxkin courtin' rituals," Leigh said, turning to me with a playful grin.

I chuckled at that, remembering well my early days at the homestead. My relationship with Diane — now a trusted fact, almost a force of nature — had been budding back then, and I had been eager to navigate the cultural maze that separated us.

Diane's eyes widened and a pretty blush graced her cheeks. "Oh, that's right! Tell me again, David." She regarded me tenderly.

I returned her smile. "Well, after we first met, I wanted to learn how to properly court you," I explained to Diane. "But I knew foxkin ways were different, so I asked Leigh for advice."

"And I sure was tickled," Leigh said with a wink at Diane. "I could tell right off this one had fallen head over heels for you." She then smiled at me with her bedroom eyes. "And at the same time, I was hopin' he'd one day be as smitten with me as he was with you."

I grinned and gave her a pat on her shapely thigh. "And I am."

Diane smiled, squeezing my hand. "I appreciate you going to such effort just for me," she said earnestly. "It shows how deeply you cared, even then."

"Of course. You were special from the moment we met," I replied honestly. "I wanted to do things right."

Leigh's eyes twinkled knowingly. "And now you got poor Celeste recitin' poetry by moonlight and all the rest of it!"

We shared a laugh, and I felt warmed knowing my willingness to bridge cultural divides had touched Diane's heart.

When our starters arrived, we temporarily shifted our focus to the culinary delights presented before us. The hotel's chefs certainly lived up to their vaunted reputation. Each artfully plated dish elicited murmurs of appreciation at its refined flavors. I loved good frontier food, but it was nice to change things up a little.

Between indulgent bites, Leigh and Diane pestered me playfully for more hints about my mysterious business with the dwarven jeweler Grimfast. But I remained coyly evasive, assuring them it would be revealed soon. Their persistence left us all laughing.

As the waiter whisked away our empty plates, I reached across the table to take Diane and Leigh's hands in mine. "Have I told you both lately how grateful I am to have you in my life?" I said earnestly.

Diane's eyes misted and she turned her palm up to intertwine her fingers with mine. "Every day we feel how cherished we are," she said softly.

Leigh gave my hand a tender squeeze. "Anyone can see how much you love us, baby," she said, with her honey-sweet drawl. "And the feelin's mutual."

I smiled, emotions welling powerfully within me. With all my heart, I was thankful fate had brought me and my amazing women together. Each day with them was a gift.

The main course arrived shortly after, interrupting the poignant moment. We settled in to feast on braised lamb shanks, butternut squash risotto, and seasonal vegetables prepared to absolute perfection. Rich flavors burst over my tongue with each bite.

As we savored the delectable, braised lamb, talk at our table naturally turned to the impending meeting between my grandparents and Celeste's uncle Waelin.

"So what do y'all reckon?" Leigh asked curiously. "Think your grandparents and that stuffy elf will hit it off?"

I considered for a moment before responding. "Well, they're definitely starting from very different places. But I'm confident they'll find common ground before long."

"I imagine your grandparents are a rather... exuberant duo?" Diane ventured delicately.

I chuckled at that diplomatic phrasing. "You could certainly say that! Especially Grandpa. He's got quite the personality."

Leigh's eyes danced impishly. "Let me guess —

the life of the party type?"

"Pretty much," I confirmed in amusement. "And Grandma's no wilting flower either. She'll talk your ears off once she gets going."

"They sound lovely," Diane remarked sincerely.

"Oh, they're the best," I said fondly. "Only family I've got left. But I know they'll adore you both."

"Won't Waelin find them a bit... overwhelming?" Diane asked.

I considered for a moment. "Perhaps at first. He's rather reserved. But he's got a good heart under all that elf stuffiness. He wants what's right for Celeste, and he will go to great lengths to achieve it."

Leigh nodded thoughtfully while cutting her lamb. "Opposites attract, as they say. I bet by the end of the night they'll be thick as thieves."

"That's what I'm hoping for," I agreed. "Waelin will loosen up with some good food and wine in him. And I know my grandparents will talk enough for the whole table!"

We all shared an amused chuckle at that

prospect. The meeting was sure to be lively, but I felt certain the initial awkwardness would transform into friendship given time.

As the last morsels disappeared from our plates, I ordered a decadent chocolate torte to share for dessert. Its rich sweetness provided the perfect indulgent finale to our meal. Diane and Leigh's expressions were positively rapturous.

At last, replete with sumptuous fare and fine wine, we lingered over fragrant cups of tea brought by our waiter. A deep sense of fulfillment suffused our intimate table. For these precious hours, our stress had melted away entirely.

My eyes drank in every elegant detail, determined to etch this memory forever in my mind — the glittering crystal, the flickering candles, the beautiful women gazing back at me. I wished to seal this exquisite moment in time.

As the hour grew late, other diners gradually drifted out until we had the palatial space nearly to ourselves. We tarried over the remainder of our tea; none of us eager for the night to end.

After our extravagant dinner, Diane, Leigh, and I headed back upstairs, happily stuffed and in a fine mood. Looping their arms through mine, we strolled leisurely down the plushily carpeted hallway.

"Now that was a fancy feast!" Leigh exclaimed. "They sure know how to cook here in the city!"

Diane nodded enthusiastically. "Oh yes, everything was prepared to absolute perfection, don't you think?" She sighed dreamily. "And the music and candlelight made it all so romantic."

I smiled, giving them both an affectionate squeeze. "I'm glad you both enjoyed yourselves. It's not often we get to indulge in that level of refinement out on the frontier."

"You got that right!" Leigh laughed. "I sure would love to meet the chef that cooked up that fancy food and shake their hand. And the fellow who picked the wine — he knew his stuff too.

Smooth as silk, that vintage!"

We continued exchanging lively commentary about the highlights of our luxurious dinner as we strolled upstairs to the lavish penthouse suite that was our temporary abode.

Unlocking the ornately carved wooden door, I held it open gallantly for Leigh and Diane. "After you, ladies," I said with an exaggerated bow and flourish.

They both giggled at my antics, sauntering past into the suite.

"Weeelll, I don't know about y'all," Leigh drawled, "but I'm fixin' to take me a nice long soak in that Jacuzzi tub right this second. Wouldn't that be the perfect conclusion to a perfect day?"

With that, she headed over to the low stairs that led to an elevation in the suite where the Jacuzzi was built. It was a circular hot tub built right into the middle of the floor.

Diane and I watched as Leigh ran the faucets and let the bath fill up. We both smiled as wisps of steam curled invitingly off the gently churning water, which was lit from within by soft-colored lights that shifted hypnotically. It was situated next to a floor-to-ceiling window that overlooked the mountains and the forest.

Diane clasped her hands together, sapphire eyes dancing with excitement. "It does look so lovely!" She turned her luminous gaze my way. "Don't you think so, David?"

I chuckled knowingly, having a strong suspicion about what was coming next. Right on cue, Leigh sidled up next to me, an impish grin playing about her full lips as she began slowly unbuttoning her blouse while the tub filled up.

Then, she gave me a peck on the cheek before she shimmied playfully out of the garment, showcasing her generous cleavage spilling over the cups of a lacy black bra. I felt a familiar stir of desire just from the little preview.

Diane colored prettily as she watched Leigh disrobe without an ounce of self-consciousness. I could tell the idea intrigued her too, but she was hesitant to be the first to suggest it.

"Am I gonna hop in alone?" Leigh teased.

"It *does* look simply blissful," Diane murmured,

her azure gaze fixed longingly on the gently churning water. She unconsciously wet her full lips with the tip of her tongue. "But... is there enough room?"

I hid an amused smile at Diane's half-hearted protest, suspecting Leigh wouldn't be dissuaded that easily once she got an idea in her head. As predicted, the voluptuous blonde was already shimmying out of her pants, clearly eager to slip into the Jacuzzi's steamy embrace.

"Aw, don't be such a stick in the mud," Leigh cajoled, giving her hips an enticing wiggle as she kicked the jeans aside, leaving her clad in just a lacy black bra and a matching thong that cupped her beautiful pussy in a delicious camel-toe that made my mouth water.

"The *whole point* of a Jacuzzi," she continued, "is that there ain't enough room so we all gotta huddle together all nice and cozy-like."

Turning to me, Leigh fixed me with her most pleading doe-eyed expression, all fluttering lashes and pouting rosebud lips. Her freckled cleavage jiggled enticingly as she gave me *that look*.

"C'mon now, baby," she implored sweetly, "won't you join me for a nice steamy soak?" She trailed a finger invitingly down the center of my chest.

I chuckled at her shameless antics, pretending to consider seriously for a moment before replying. Of course, my mind had already been made up from the moment she had suggested it, but I would play along for a bit.

"Well, I suppose a short relaxing dip couldn't hurt..."

Chapter 33

Leigh let out a purr of triumph before nimbly stripping off her bra and panties. I drank in an eyeful of her exquisitely curvy figure as she sank into the Jacuzzi with a long, satisfied sigh, sending the water churning around her.

Now without clothes, she beckoned enticingly

with one finger for me to join her. "The water sure feels real nice and hot! I know I'd enjoy it even more with some handsome company..." She winked playfully.

Turning her pleading gaze on Diane, Leigh implored, "Come on now! It's big enough for all of us!"

Diane hesitated, nibbling her plump lower lip uncertainly even as her fingers toyed with the hem of her blouse. The flirtatious mood was infectious though, and I could tell she didn't want to be left out.

"Oh...alright," she relented at last with a shy smile. "I can't resist either."

Slowly and self-consciously, she began to disrobe for us, the firelight playing lovingly over every inch of her lithe curves as more and more tantalizing flesh was revealed. I felt a surge of desire watching her undress. Leigh let out an approving whistle.

"Atta girl! Now get that cute li'l tail of yours in this water," Leigh encouraged affectionately. "It's pure magic, I promise."

With an uncertain laugh, Diane finished undressing down to her bra and panties — a matching set in a delicate blush pink that complemented her creamy complexion perfectly. Despite her initial shyness, I could tell she was secretly enjoying putting on this little show for us.

After a moment's hesitation while we admired her nearly naked form as she stripped away her final garments, Diane slipped into the Jacuzzi with a contented moan, submerging herself up to her slender shoulders.

"Ooh yes, you were right Leigh," she admitted blissfully, eyes closed. "This feels divine."

"Told ya so!" Leigh said playfully, winking at me. "How about you get comfortable too, hot stuff."

Happy to oblige, I quickly shed my own clothes. There wasn't a shred of self-consciousness about it anymore, as I was utterly comfortable with my women.

Leigh whistled her approval, making an exaggerated show of checking out my physique as I eased into the wonderfully warm, effervescent water alongside my two lovely companions.

"Mm, now this is the life," Leigh sighed, stretching luxuriously, sending ripples across the steaming surface of the frothing tub.

Playfully, she sent a splash my way. "Admit it, don't this just hit the spot after that big fancy dinner?" Her eyes were sparkling impishly.

I laughed, using my hands to send a small splash her way in retaliation, making her yelp. "I have to agree. This Jacuzzi is pretty amazing."

"Just look at that view too," Diane chimed in dreamily, gazing out at the scenic mountains. The moon was peeking out from behind scudding clouds. "It's so beautiful up here."

"Not as beautiful as present company," I replied, drawing a pleased blush from both women.

Leigh preened under the compliment, arching her back to thrust out her generous chest above the waterline. "Aw, ain't you just the sweet talker." She shot me a bold look that made me grin broadly.

Unable to resist, I reached underwater to squeeze her knee teasingly, making her jump.

"Cut that out now," Leigh laughed, swatting playfully at my hand. "You're gonna get me all worked up, baby." She shot me a smoky look. "And you know what happens when I got worked up…"

Diane smiled at our silly antics, shifting position so she leaned comfortably against my shoulder. "This was a lovely idea," she said appreciatively. "I'm so glad we decided to indulge ourselves tonight."

"Me too," I agreed, wrapping an arm around her slender shoulders and dropping a tender kiss on her head, mindful of her fox ears. "You girls deserve to be pampered."

Leigh stretched languorously again, purposefully showcasing her generous curves breaking the waterline. "Pamper away, sugar. We could get used to this kind of high life."

Leigh's flirtatious mood was contagious. As we lounged in the steamy, bubbly water, she and I engaged in some silly splash fights and exchanges of light-hearted banter.

Diane looked on with amusement, contentedly

cuddled against my shoulder. At one point when Leigh deliberately splashed water down the front of my chest, I grabbed the blonde minx around the waist and gave her a playful pull in retaliation, making her slip from her seat and squeal.

"No fair!" Leigh gasped. But her eyes danced with mirth. She attempted to splash me again, but I caught her wrist lightly and used the opportunity to pull her in close.

Keeping my grasp on her wrist, I tipped her chin up and kissed her full on the lips. Leigh readily melted against me, nibbling my lower lip sensuously. We indulged in the deep kiss for several heated moments before finally coming up for air.

"Mm, now that's what I call an apology," Leigh purred approvingly, a little breathless. Her generous chest heaved distractingly with each breath.

"But your apology needs a little more, baby," Leigh said as she shot Diane a wink. The fox girl blushed, while Diane drifted closer to me, obviously up to no good...

The swirling waters of the Jacuzzi caressed my skin as Leigh pressed her delicious and soft body up against mine and kissed me. I reveled in the feeling of her as the heat seeped into my muscles and eased the tension of the day.

Leigh's playful splashing had ended with me pulling her close, our lips meeting in a kiss that sent currents of desire through the steamy water. As we parted, her blue eyes sparkled with mischief, and she turned to give me a view of her ample backside as she got onto hands and knees, her ass peeking out above the water's surface.

It was a sight from heaven, and Diane giggled as Leigh got in her typical naughty mood.

"David, baby," Leigh purred, looking back at me over her shoulder, her voice dripping with sultry power. "Why don't you make it up by playing with me a little, hmm?"

Without needing further encouragement, I slid

closer to her, my hand trailing through the warm water until it found the soft, wet heat between her thighs.

"Hmm," she moaned. "That's the spot, baby. I've been wantin' you all day!"

My cock turned rock-hard at feeling her soft body at my command. I began to stroke her, my fingers slipping easily between her slick folds, finding the rhythm that made her back arch and a moan escape her lips.

Diane, drawn by the erotic display, waded closer, her sapphire eyes locked onto me with hunger that matched my own. She leaned in, pressing her lips to mine even as I fingered her harem sister's tight pussy. Her kiss embodied a mixture of tenderness and raw need that stirred the water around us.

My free hand roamed over Diane's curves, gliding over the smooth skin of her back before coming to rest on the swell of her breasts. I squeezed gently, eliciting a soft gasp from her as she deepened our kiss, her tongue tangling with mine.

But I didn't stop fingering Leigh's tight pussy —
now slipping my finger inside her, then circling her
swollen nub as she trembled beneath me. Leigh's
breathy moans filled the air, mixing with the
sounds of the bubbling Jacuzzi and the distant hum
of the city beyond the window.

"Yes... just like that, David," she purred, her
voice laced with desire. "Make me cum for you,
baby. I want you to feel me unravel under your
touch."

The lust raging within me was overwhelming —
the scent of lavender and the rich aroma of Leigh's
arousal, the sight of Diane's naked body pressed
against mine, and the sound of Leigh's pleasure as
my fingers worked their magic.

I doubled my efforts, my fingers curling inside
Leigh to stroke the spot that made her gasp, her
hips bucking against my hand as she chased the
release that built within her. Diane's breath hitched
against my mouth, her nipples hardening under
my touch as if in sympathy with Leigh's mounting
pleasure.

Leigh's dirty talk spilled forth uninhibited.

"Fuck, David, your fingers feel so damn good...filling me up...don't stop," she moaned, her words punctuated by the splash of water as she moved with my hand.

Diane, caught up in it all, began to mimic my movements on her own body, her hand slipping down to tease her clit as she rode the waves of passion emanating from our trio.

"Keep going, baby," Leigh urged, her voice thick. "I'm so close... I can feel it building... I'm gonna cum all over your hand."

And with a few more skilled strokes, Leigh's body tensed. Her moans reached a crescendo with a high-pitched gasp as her orgasm crashed over her, the waves of pleasure rippling through the water and into my own body, heightening my arousal.

As Leigh's body shuddered with the aftershocks of her climax, Diane's movements grew more frantic, her breathing erratic. "David, please... touch me too," she begged, her voice laced with desperation. "I want it, too!"

With Leigh still panting, I shifted my attention to

Diane, my fingers tracing a path down to her warmth. I found her wet and ready, slipping my fingers into her as she gasped, her body welcoming me eagerly.

Diane's response was immediate, her hips grinding against my hand as I matched the pace that had brought Leigh such ecstasy. Her soft whimpers and sharp intakes of breath told me she was teetering on the edge.

"That's it, my sweet Diane," I murmured against her lips, my voice low and encouraging. "Let go for me. I want to feel you cum for me."

It didn't take much. Poor Diane was aroused beyond imagination. I gave her what she wanted, delighting in how she trembled in my embrace.

Her hands gripped my shoulders as her movements grew more urgent. "David... I'm... oh God, yes!"

A moment later, Diane's climax hit her hard, her body convulsing as waves of pleasure radiated from where we were joined. I took great pleasure in how she convulsed and shook, and how her orgasm shot delicious tremors down her body, making her beloved curves jiggle for me.

When she finally gasped for air, I held them both close, my arms around Diane as she quivered and shook while she recovered from her orgasm, and Leigh as she still struggled to catch her breath, the heat of their releases warming me more than the Jacuzzi ever could.

As the intensity of the moment subsided, we settled back into the water, our ragged breaths slowly evening out. Leigh leaned her head against my shoulder, a satisfied smile playing on her lips.

Diane, still nestled in my lap, looked up at me with eyes that glowed with love and contentment. I kissed her forehead tenderly, overwhelmed with affection for these incredible women in my life.

But they weren't done yet… A moment later, soft fingers were playing with my hard cock, and hazy eyes were looking up at me, full of desire. They were ready for more, and so was I.

I nibbled Diane's neck, unwilling to postpone my own pleasure any longer. "My sweet Diane," I said to her in a low voice, "and ride my cock." She gave me a wide-eyed look; excitement and anticipation clear in her gaze as she moved to straddle me.

Diane's shy hesitation melted away under the steamy spell of the water and her pleasure, and with an encouraging nod from me, she slipped onto my lap, her soft body pressing against mine.

Leigh's sultry voice filled the air, spurring us on with her tantalizing dirty talk. "Ride him just like that, Diane, let him feel how tight and wet you are for him," she coaxed, her gaze fixed on us with a lustful intensity that only magnified the heat of the moment.

My hands found Diane's hips, guiding her as she lifted herself just enough to allow Leigh to reach down and position my aching cock at her slick entrance. The anticipation was a delicious torture, and when Diane finally sank down onto me, the sensation was nothing short of heavenly.

I groaned with delight as my cock slipped into her tight little pussy, and Leigh gave a deep moan of appreciation.

"Look at that," she purred. "It looks so pretty!"

"Hnnnn," Diane moaned. "Oh, David... I feel so full... Gods, I love it!"

"Bounce on him," Leigh urged Diane. "Ride him!"

The water rippled around us as Diane began to do just that, her movements slow and deliberate at first, picking up speed as her confidence grew.

Leigh watched, a delighted glint in her eye, her words a constant stream of encouragement and praise. "That's it, baby, take all of him," she hummed, her voice a melody of arousal that seemed to vibrate through the water.

Diane's breathing grew erratic, her chest heaving against mine as she impaled herself on my hardness again and again. Her arms were around my shoulder as we sloshed in the Jacuzzi, skin slapping together, and she gave a cute yelp every time I bottomed out inside her.

I could feel every contour of Diane's inner walls, so warm and velvety, enveloping me in a rhythm as old as time. Her hands clung to my shoulders, her nails digging in slightly with each thrust, anchoring her as she sought her pleasure upon me.

The sight of Diane's ecstasy, the way she threw her head back, exposing the elegant column of her throat, the soft mewls and gasps that escaped her lips, fueled my desire to new heights. I held her tight, my own grunts of pleasure mingling with hers.

Leigh's hand slipped beneath the water, her fingers finding my full balls and softly kneading them to add to the symphony of sensation. Diane started reaching her summit, her climax building like a storm on the horizon, ready to break.

"Cum for me, Diane," I urged, my voice rough with need. I thrust up into her with renewed vigor, determined to tip her over the edge into blissful oblivion.

Diane's body tensed, her inner muscles clenching around me in a vice-like grip that threatened to undo me then and there. "David... I'm... oh God, David!" she cried out, her orgasm washing over her in waves that crashed against both our shores.

Her climax was a sight to behold, her body

writhing in my lap. I held her through it all, my own pleasure spiraling upward as I reveled in the feel of her coming undone because of me.

Leigh's voice coaxed me closer to my own edge. "Fill her up, David. Give her everything ya got. Make her feel you deep inside."

With Diane still trembling from her orgasm, I gathered my strength and thrust into her with a fervor that matched the passion of the moment. I could feel it, the inevitable surge of my release approaching like a tidal wave. She yelped with delight, hanging from me with her tongue lolling out as she still rode her orgasm.

"I'm gonna cum!" I panted, my movements becoming more erratic as I chased the precipice of my own pleasure.

Leigh leaned in close, her lips brushing against my ear as she whispered, "Do it. Cum in her. Let me see you claim her as yours."

Her words were the final spark that ignited the powder keg within me. With a grunt, I released deep within Diane, my seed spilling into her in hot, pulsing waves.

Diane gasped, feeling the heat of me filling her, her inner walls milking me for more as I emptied myself completely. The connection between us was electric, our gazes locked in a symphony of lust and fulfillment.

As the last tremors of my climax subsided, I held Diane close, our sweat-slicked bodies still joined as we caught our breath.

Leigh's eyes were upon us, dark with desire and something akin to pride. "That was beautiful, you two," she murmured, her voice husky with her own arousal. "But I think it's my turn now, don't you?"

Diane, spent and satisfied, rested against me in the Jacuzzi, her breathing still heavy. I gently lifted her and placed her next to me and turned my hungry gaze to Leigh, who rose to the challenge with a daring glint in her eye.

"Come on then, David," Leigh taunted, her voice full of challenge. "Show me how you're gonna fuck me. I wanna feel your cum in me."

As she spoke, Leigh half-rose out of the water, positioning herself before me. Her voluptuous body glistening with droplets of water, her expression one of pure anticipation.

The sight of her kindled my arousal despite having just given Diane my seed. I was ready to go again and claim my voluptuous blonde.

I grasped Leigh by the hips, pulling her down to me with a possessive strength that matched the hunger in her eyes. Our bodies came together with a splash, the water churning as I placed her on my lap, feeling her delicious ass against my hardening cock as she braced against the side of the tub with her hands.

Leigh's moans filled the air, her body moving with mine in perfect harmony. "That's it, baby," she gasped. "Fuck me. Make me yours. Bend me over and take me."

The warm water surrounded us with a cocoon of delight as Leigh rose, presenting her ample, freckled backside to me. The steam rose around us, veiling her eyes as she looked over her shoulder with a naughty glint in her blue gaze.

"Show me how bad you want me, David," Leigh's voice was thick with lust, "I want to feel that big cock of yours pound me hard."

I stood up behind her, the water cascading off my skin, and with a firm grip, I pulled her hips toward me. Her wet flesh glistened in the low light, and I couldn't resist giving her a playful smack, watching her cheeks ripple with the impact.

She gasped, the sound turning into a sultry moan as I leaned over her, guiding my cock to her waiting heat. "That's it, baby, get me ready for you," she murmured, urging me on.

I slid into her with one smooth, powerful thrust, and her moan was drowned out by the sound of water splashing over the edge. Leigh's warmth enveloped me completely, her inner muscles gripping me tightly, pulling me deeper.

Diane, who had been watching us with wide, sapphire eyes, now blushed a deep shade of red, her gaze fixed on the point where our bodies joined.

"You two are so beautiful together," she whispered, her hand wandering to her own body, her touch light and exploratory.

With each thrust, Leigh's dirty words fueled my

desire even more. "Harder, David, fuck me harder," she begged, "Make me feel it all the way to my core."

I obliged, my hands gripping her hips as I set a punishing pace, the sound of our bodies slapping together mixed with the gasp that came from deep within Leigh every time I drove my cock into her.

Leigh's head tilted back, her hair sticking to her wet skin as she pushed back against me, matching my every move. "Fill me up, baby, let me feel that hot cum inside me," she moaned.

Her words struck a chord within me, my pleasure mounting with each stroke. I could feel her climax building, her body tensing and quivering as she approached the edge. With a growl, I grabbed a full ass cheek, my thumb close to her tight little pucker.

"Oh, yes! Touch me there, David... push it in," Leigh pleaded, her voice barely above a whimper. "I need to feel you everywhere."

I slipped my thumb into the hot, tight ring of her asshole, and she cried out as her softness gave way to me, her entire body shaking with the added sensation.

Diane's voice joined the chorus, her encouragement laced with arousal. "Oh, yes, David!" she called out, her own fingers moving faster over her clit as she watched us.

I reveled in the sight of Diane as I fucked her harem sister and fingered her tight little asshole. I felt my orgasm approaching, my need to fill Leigh up with my cum rising.

Leigh's moans grew louder, her body convulsing as she neared her peak. "I'm gonna cum, David, I'm gonna cum so fucking hard for you!"

Her words spurred me on. I increased my pace with a wordless grunt, driving into her relentlessly, determined to push her over the edge into ecstasy.

And then she was cumming, her orgasm ripping through her with a force that left her gasping and trembling. "David!" she screamed, her inner muscles clenching around me in waves, her tight little pucker almost pushing my thumb out.

Leigh's release triggered my own, the pleasure coiling in my gut before exploding outward. I thrust deep inside her one last time, filling her with a rope of warm cum, my groans mingling with her cries.

"Hnn, yes!" she moaned. "Cum in me, baby! Fill me up!"

Her body continued to shake as she rode out the aftershocks of her orgasm, her breasts swaying with the force of my still-thrusting hips as I spurted rope after rope of seed into her.

Diane, too, reached her peak, her body arching beautifully as she came, her own cries of pleasure echoing off the walls of the suite. As she came, she kept her sapphire eyes on us, watching me fill her harem sister up with warm cum.

I held Leigh tight as she trembled, spent from the intensity of her orgasm. Her skin was flushed with the effort, her breathing ragged as she lay panting. Holding her tight, I pushed for the last time, and she gave a wordless, mindless moan as her pussy overflowed with my cum.

Then, with a grunt, I finally pulled out of Leigh, both of us panting heavily from the exertion. I sat down with a growl, and Diane moved closer, her eyes alight with admiration and a hint of mischief.

"That was incredible, David," Diane sighed, leaning in to kiss me tenderly. "Gods, you gave it to us both so hard."

Leigh chuckled, her arm draping around my shoulder as she settled in my lap and joined the kiss, her lips soft and inviting. "I'll say," she agreed. "You fucked us real good, baby!"

Smiling, I held them close, feeling a profound satisfaction coupled with fatigue after a long and eventful day. We settled back into the Jacuzzi, the girls giggling as they recovered, their laughter and warmth surrounding me like the steamy embrace of the water.

Chapter 34

The next morning, I awoke refreshed, ready to begin the journey back to the homestead. There were preparations to be made before the families could meet, and I was looking forward to getting things underway.

Still basking in the afterglow of last night's

events, we enjoyed a lavish breakfast at the restaurant before heading upstairs to pack up the last of our things.

Using the telephone in the bedroom, I let Caldwell know we would be departing shortly. He wished us well and confirmed he would handle all arrangements to bring Waelin and my grandparents to the homestead the following afternoon.

Before long, we had checked out of the lavish hotel suite and loaded our bags into the Jeep. While we had had our fun in the city, we were folk of the frontier now, and I was looking forward to returning home.

The drive out of New Springfield was slower than the journey in. More travelers crowded the roads heading to market this morning. But we were in no hurry, enjoying the vibrant sights of the awakening city.

At last, we passed beneath the weathered gates and onto the open road. I took a deep breath, savoring the crisp morning air. Though I'd always found refuge in cities, now the lush wilderness soothed my spirit.

Beside me, Leigh rolled down her window, letting the breeze tangle her golden hair as she craned her neck taking in the scenery. In the rearview mirror, I glimpsed Diane's smile as she watched colorful birds flit overhead through the sun-dappled leaves.

Our conversation meandered from idle speculation about the upcoming dinner to funny anecdotes from our trip. Laughter came easily as the miles unwound behind us.

By early afternoon, we had reached the old cottonwood that marked the turn-off toward home. My pulse quickened at the thought of being back at the homestead. Our journey neared its end.

Before long, the winding dirt road delivered us from the shade of the forest. There, nestled amidst the trees and wildflowers beside the glittering thread of the Silverstream River, sat our beloved home.

I parked the Jeep out front and stepped out, inhaling the familiar mingled scents of pine and freshly worked wood that meant home. It felt sweeter than ever, knowing that I would soon bring Celeste to the threshold of my house and carry her in.

While I unloaded our bags, Leigh was already fussing over the snorting larroling as it greeted her. After it had greeted her fondly, it happily ambled off to patrol its territory.

Diane smiled softly, taking in the cozy cabin. "It's so good to be back," she sighed. I slipped an arm around her shoulders, giving her a welcoming squeeze.

"I've missed this place," I admitted. Though our trip had been full of splendor, our simple home was where my heart resided.

Eager to settle back in, we carried our bags inside. The domesticants zipped over to greet us, chattering excitedly. Their enthusiasm brought smiles to our faces.

After unpacking, we enjoyed a simple lunch together at the wooden table. The familiar setting was comforting after our travels, and we were all eager to get to work making the place in order for the big event.

As we ate, our conversation turned to preparations for the upcoming dinner. It would be no easy feat to ready the place and provide a meal for our esteemed guests, as well as a place where they could present their own baked goods.

"Where do we even start?" Diane wondered.

"Cleaning every inch top to bottom's first on the list," Leigh said decisively. "Gotta make sure this place is spick and span. Reckon the domesticants kept it clean enough, but it might need some extra work!"

I nodded my agreement. "The place could definitely use a thorough scrubbing. And we'll need to prepare a nice bedroom for my grandparents and for Waelin."

"I can tidy things up and make it all inviting," Diane offered brightly. Her artistic eye for detail would work wonders.

"And I'll head into town to buy what we still need," Leigh said confidently. "Just leave the food to me."

"That's perfect," I said. "You can also hand Celeste a letter from me to invite her for tomorrow.

She knows the ceremony is coming, but she'll need a little heads-up that I'll be picking her up tomorrow."

"You got it, baby," Leigh hummed. "I'll take Colonel and be back before nightfall."

Our path forward was decided. After eating, the domesticants cleared up the dishes while the rest of us got started. Soon, we were all hard at work making the homestead presentable for our important guests.

The hours passed swiftly. While I made minor repairs and furniture upgrades, Diane cleaned every corner until the entire place shone and made everything look extra cozy and comfy. By evening, Leigh returned, reporting that Celeste would be ready, and she filled up our pantry and larder with the supplies she had brought from Gladdenfield.

By nightfall, noticeable progress had been made, though there was still much to do. Luckily, we still had tomorrow morning. Weary but satisfied, we fixed a humble supper before enjoying a quiet evening of music and reading by the fire.

Tomorrow would be a busy day preparing the

meal and final touches, but tonight was for rest. As we ascended the creaking stairs to bed, I felt confident that our efforts would ensure the dinner's success.

Chapter 35

I awoke eager for the trip into Gladdenfield today to pick up the shimmerstone rings from Grimfast. I was keen to see what the dwarven craftsman had made of them, and I was also looking forward to seeing Celeste again.

If all went well, I would present the rings after

the ceremony today. And I would ask all three of them to marry me. It would be a grand step in the progression of our relationship, and I would be lying if I claimed I wasn't a little nervous for it...

After breakfast with Leigh and Diane, I soon departed down the forest trail leading to town. The girls promised to make the rest of the homestead in order so everything would be perfect once the guests would arrive.

The journey passed pleasantly before Gladdenfield's gates appeared ahead. The guards recognized me and waved as I entered the lively frontier settlement. I drove slowly down the bustling main thoroughfare.

Parking near Grimfast's modest jewelry shop, I stepped onto the packed dirt street. Townsfolk smiled and tipped their hats in greeting as they passed by on errands. My pulse quickened, aware of the purpose for my visit today.

Entering the shop, the bell over the door jingled merrily. Behind the counter sat Grimfast, inspecting a jewel through an eyepiece. He looked up and grinned broadly beneath his fiery braided beard upon seeing me.

"Right on time, laddie!" Grimfast rumbled jovially. He retrieved a polished wooden box from below the counter and slid it reverently toward me.

This was the moment I had been waiting for. Taking a deep breath, I unlatched the metal clasp and opened the hinged lid.

My jaw dropped.

Nestled inside gleamed three spectacular, golden rings, each set with a large, flawless prism-cut gemstone that seemed to glow from within with spectral fire. My breath caught at the incredible sight.

"Shimmerstone, the rarest gems about," Grimfast pronounced proudly. "From that troll cave vein."

Speechless for the moment, I carefully lifted one jewel, turning it to admire the dazzling play of rainbow hues in the crystalline depths. The delicate golden band was beautifully engraved with elven designs.

"These are true masterpieces, Grimfast," I said sincerely when I found my voice again. "You have exceeded my expectations... greatly."

The dwarf accepted my effusive awe with characteristic modesty, though pleasure shone in his eyes. "Happy ye like 'em, lad!" he said.

I took time to properly admire each exquisite ring, picturing presenting these tokens of love to Diane, Leigh, and Celeste. So much care and skill had gone into crafting the flawless gems and delicate bands. The rings were utterly breathtaking.

"The gems are purest shimmerstone, lad," Grimfast told me. "Had to dig deep to reach the vein, but it was well worth the effort! You'll not find better specimens anywhere around these parts." He looked immensely satisfied with the end result.

"Or a finer jeweler than you to cut them so expertly," I added sincerely, lifting one ring again to appreciate how he had maximized the dazzling flashes of spectral color. Grimfast flushed with pleasure at my words, waving away the praise even as he stood a bit taller.

After I had thoroughly inspected each of the three stunning rings, I carefully closed the polished wooden box and reverently placed it inside my jacket, keeping it secure near my heart for safekeeping. The treasure these rings symbolized was beyond measure.

Grimfast beamed with satisfaction at the obvious delight I took in his handiwork. "I'll not have ye pay, laddie. Bringin' joy to young lovebirds is reward enough for me," the kindly dwarf demurred gruffly. Yet I could tell my appreciation of his skill meant much.

"They will bring joy," I assured him. "This means very much for me, Grimfast."

"Ah, make no mention, laddie! Take 'em! And know ye I can make more if the need arises, aye? I owe ye that much!"

"Thank you, my friend," I said, giving him an appreciative nod before looking around at the shop. Things were looking better with more supplies and stock. It seemed Grimfast had used my investment well.

"So how are things shaping up here in your new shop?" I asked.

Grimfast launched eagerly into an update about his steadily growing inventory and clientele, made possible thanks to my investment. "Aye, business is booming now," he said happily. "Word is spreading quick about quality dwarven craftsmanship in humble Gladdenfield. Mark my words, one day my jewelry will adorn the finest folk in these parts!"

I heartily approved of my friend's ambition. "You have orders from some of the townsfolk?"

"Aye, aye," he said. "Mayor Wilhelm was the first. Baubles for the wifey, eh!" He grinned broadly. "More followed, and I have no doubt the name Grimfast will spread."

We conversed a while longer, and I was in no hurry, enjoying this opportunity to catch up with the kindly dwarf. To have a dwarven gem cutter and jeweler among my friends was valuable, but his company was enjoyable for its own sake as well.

However, I knew I couldn't linger in his shop forever, no matter how pleasant the company. The day was getting on, and I was very eager to pick up Celeste and finally show her my homestead. And after that, the ceremony would follow.

I bid the fine jeweler a temporary farewell, sincerely thanking him again for crafting such exceptional betrothal rings. Grimfast clasped my hand warmly in his rough grip before I turned to leave.

It was time to go pick up Celeste...

I made my way down the dusty street toward the familiar facade of the Wild Outrider Inn. My heart beat faster, knowing Celeste awaited me within. Soon I would bring her home with me to meet my family. And if all went well, she would become a part of that family.

Entering the cozy taproom, I immediately spotted Celeste seated alone at a corner table nursing a mug of tea. She looked up, and her delicate features lit up with a radiant smile. Rising gracefully, she crossed the room to meet me.

"David, you've arrived!" Celeste exclaimed. Before I could react, she had thrown her arms around me in an enthusiastic embrace.

I chuckled and returned the hug, breathing in her sweet floral scent. It had been only a few days, but I had missed her dearly. I wanted nothing more than to have her at my house and never miss her again.

"It's good to see you too," I said sincerely as we parted. Up close, she looked as beautiful as ever, eyes luminous and skin dewy. The inn's lantern light cast a warm glow over her fine features.

"Please, come sit," Celeste invited, taking my hand and leading me to her table.

I followed readily, unable to take my eyes off her graceful form. We settled across from one another and a barmaid brought me an ale.

"Did everything go well in the city?" Celeste asked eagerly. "Were you able to arrange the meeting between our families like we hoped?"

I smiled and nodded. "I was.. I spoke with your uncle Waelin, and he has agreed to participate in the ceremony."

Celeste's eyes lit up with joy. "Truly? Oh, I can hardly believe it! I know how difficult it must be for him to accept our relationship." She clasped my hands happily across the table. "You have made me so very happy, my love."

I squeezed her hands gently, warmed by her obvious delight. "All I want is your happiness, Celeste. I'm relieved Waelin was willing to meet my family."

"As am I!" Celeste agreed fervently. "He can be stubborn when it comes to change, but deep down, he is a caring and loving man. Life has just... been unkind to him. I'm sure he'll come to see how right we are for each other."

We smiled softly at one another, still clasping hands. Celeste's obvious excitement over the impending ceremony was a pleasure to see, and I shared it deeply. Our future would be bright — I knew it would be.

After a moment, Celeste gave my hands a final grateful squeeze before releasing them. "Well, shall we be off soon?" she asked, barely contained eagerness creeping into her dulcet voice. "I'm so excited to finally see your homestead and meet your grandparents!"

"Absolutely," I agreed readily. I quickly downed the last of my ale as Celeste tidied away her half-finished tea. We were both eager to reach our destination.

Together, we stood and made our way outside into the bustling frontier town. Celeste slipped her arm through mine as we strolled down the dusty thoroughfare towards where I had parked.

Reaching the Jeep, I stowed Celeste's travel bag and opened the passenger door for her. She leaned up on her tiptoes to kiss my cheek tenderly before climbing in. I grinned and went around to the driver's side.

Soon we were on our way, leaving Gladdenfield behind. As the vibrant forest scrolled by, Celeste chattered happily. "I can't wait for the ceremony," she confessed. "It means the world that Uncle Waelin is willing to give us his blessing."

I smiled at her. "Well, we still have to take this final hurdle and get him to get along with my grandparents. If I understand elven culture well enough, this whole thing might still end in bloodshed."

It was a joke, of course, but one with a seed of truth. According to elven custom, the whole thing could go wrong if the families did not approve of one another.

She chuckled. "Perhaps," she hummed. "But I have a good feeling, David. It will be alright. And it will be special."

I reached over to squeeze her hand, navigating the winding trail one-handed. "It'll be a special moment for sure." Up ahead, the cottonwood tree marking the turnoff to home came into view. We were close now.

Celeste fell silent, watching the forest go by. But her eyes were bright with anticipation. At the turnoff, I steered onto the narrow path leading the last stretch to the homestead.

Dappled sunlight filtered down through the leafy canopy shrouding the path as we neared the homestead. The aromatic scent of pine filled the air. My pulse quickened knowing our destination was near.

Then suddenly, there through the trees, the sunlit log walls of home emerged. Celeste gasped softly. We had arrived.

Bringing the Jeep to a halt by the front walkway, I switched off the rumbling engine and turned to my lovely passenger. "Welcome home," I said warmly.

Celeste's answering smile outshone the sun. In that moment, with joy lighting her exquisite features, she had never looked more beautiful. This remarkable woman would soon be mine. The future brimmed with promise.

Together, we stepped out of the Jeep, and I retrieved Celeste's bag. As we started up the walkway, the front door burst open.

Diane and Leigh spilled out, joyful smiles on their friendly faces. "You're here!" Diane exclaimed happily.

Celeste hurried forward to embrace them. The sound of their laughter carried on the crisp air, and by the looks of Celeste, it seemed like she was finally coming home...

Chapter 36

Arm in arm with Leigh and Diane, Celeste turned to me with an expression of pure delight as we approached the front steps of the homestead. "Oh, it's absolutely wonderful!" she exclaimed, gazing at the cozy log cabin nestled amidst the vibrant trees. "You've created such a peaceful sanctuary here!"

"We're so happy you could come see it at last," Diane said warmly, giving Celeste's hand an affectionate squeeze.

Leigh grinned and nodded her agreement. "We've been fixin' the place up real nice, just for you!" She then grinned. "Well, and for the ceremony, of course. But mainly for you!"

I laughed, and the other girls joined in. It was great how Leigh always made someone else feel right at home with a joke and a little levity. I could tell Celeste appreciated it too as we all headed toward the house.

Ascending the creaking front steps, I held the door open gallantly. "Welcome to home," I said as Celeste stepped over the threshold.

Her emerald eyes shone as she drank in every detail of the cozy interior. "It's incredible," she breathed. "I can feel so much love in these walls already." She looked at me full of awe. "You built all of this yourself!?"

"Most of it, yeah," I said. "The large living room is actually the cabin that was already on the property. Everything else, we added ourselves."

While Celeste acquainted herself with the living room, Diane hurried to the kitchen. "Come see where I work my magic making meals for this crew," she invited Celeste eagerly.

In the spacious farmhouse kitchen, delicious aromas filled the air from the meal preparations underway. Celeste admired the butcher block countertops and the rack hanging with seasoned cast-iron pans. She turned slowly, smiling. "What a wonderful space. I can't wait to cook with you here, Diane."

Leigh laughed good-naturedly. "You ladies and your fancy food! Now come on, let me show you where the *real fun* happens."

Taking Celeste by the hand, she led the way through the back door and outside. There, she proudly demonstrated the smokehouse and showed off the plots for our crops.

I laughed at that, having fully expected Leigh to show her the bedroom instead. Leigh understood well enough why I was laughing, and she playfully stuck out her tongue at me.

As Leigh elaborated on the crops, Celeste listened attentively, amber hair lifting in the breeze. I stood watching them from the porch, and Diane joined me, leaning her pretty head on my shoulder as her harem sister initiated Celeste into the family. I was profoundly thankful — for their acceptance of each other *and* for their love. I couldn't have found better women.

When we returned indoors, I gave Celeste a tour of the workshop where I practiced my alchemy. Her fingers trailed reverently over the leather-bound tomes as I told her of the hours spent honing my skill.

Upstairs, she admired the spacious bathroom before I showed her the master bedroom. "It's so wonderful knowing I'll share this space with you and Diane and Leigh," she said softly, cheeks coloring. The emotion in her voice spoke volumes.

"We can't wait to have you here," I told her.

Back downstairs, we rejoined Leigh and Diane just as the tea kettle on the stove began whistling shrilly.

"Perfect timing!" Diane said brightly, moving to

take the kettle off the heat.

Leigh fetched some mugs from the cabinet. "I hope y'all are in the mood for some tea," she said. "Diane here bakes up the best tea cookies this side of the Shimmering Peaks."

Diane blushed modestly. "Oh, I don't know about that."

"Hush now, no need for false modesty," I teased lightly. I turned to Celeste with a grin. "Just wait until you try them — you're in for a real treat."

Celeste's eyes lit up. "I can't wait! I love a good tea cookie."

Diane carefully arranged some plump, perfectly golden cookies on a plate and set them on the table just as Leigh finished pouring steaming tea into each of our mugs. The delicious aroma of black tea mingled tantalizingly with the cookies' vanilla and cinnamon scent.

"Do your people have customs around sharing tea?" Diane asked Celeste curiously as we all settled in around the worn wooden table.

Celeste nodded, cradling her mug appreciatively to warm her hands. "Oh yes, tea-drinking ceremonies are very important in elven culture. Everything is done mindfully and with great ceremony. The teas are always exquisite blends and pairings."

"Well, our tea tradition here on the homestead is probably a mite more casual," Leigh said with a grin and a saucy wink. "We just brew up whatever tea bags we got lyin' around and chat over a hot mug."

Celeste laughed, a clear, musical sound. "That sounds lovely and cozy! I'm happy to take part in your way."

Her obvious delight to share in this everyday custom of ours brought a smile to my face. I raised my mug. "To new friends and new traditions," I proclaimed.

"Hear, hear!" Leigh readily agreed, raising her own mug. We all clinked our cups together and took grateful sips of the fragrant, perfectly brewed tea.

As we enjoyed our tea and cookies, conversation flowed comfortably. Celeste's peals of laughter soon filled the cozy farmhouse kitchen as Leigh and Diane regaled her with humorous anecdotes of homestead life. In that cozy farmhouse kitchen, surrounded by the happy chatter and laughter of those most dear to me in the world, I felt truly blessed.

When the tea had been drained and the last cookie devoured, Leigh stretched and shot me a playful look. "Why don't you take Celeste out for a nice stroll, show her the grounds?" she suggested with a wink.

I chuckled, reading her intent expression easily. "Good idea. I know Celeste is eager to see more of the homestead." Taking Celeste's hand, I led her toward the door. "Shall we continue the tour?"

Her answering smile outshone the sun. "I'd love nothing more."

Outside, we strolled hand in hand along winding forest paths, listening to birdsong overhead. Sunlight filtered through the crimson and gold canopy. Celeste smiled serenely; face upturned to the sky.

By a babbling brook, we paused. I slipped my arms around Celeste's slender waist, drawing her close. Tilting her chin up, I captured her lips in a tender kiss that conveyed all the love and promise harbored in my heart. She melted against me with a contented sigh.

When at last we parted, Celeste's eyes shone like stars in the twilit woods. "How I've longed to see your home, the place you've poured so much dedication into," she told me earnestly. "It's everything I imagined and more. You've created such a welcoming sanctuary."

I smiled, lightly caressing her cheek. "Only made possible by those who share it with me. Our home is yours now too, for as long as you'll have us."

Emotion swam in Celeste's luminous gaze. She opened her mouth to reply when suddenly a distant rumble sounded. We exchanged a rueful smile.

"Come on, let's head back," I said, taking her hand again. "Sounds like our guests are arriving."

Emerging from the trees, we saw two vehicles pulling up the drive, no doubt containing Waelin and my grandparents. Squeezing Celeste's hand, I felt ready to take this momentous next step on our journey together.

Side by side, we started up the gravel path to greet our kin and unite our families as one.

Chapter 37

Celeste and I approached the two vehicles pulling up the driveway containing Waelin and my grandparents. As we walked, Leigh and Diane emerged from the house as well, exchanging excited looks. As the four of us neared the vehicles, my pulse quickened, knowing this introduction would be critical for our future together.

I wasn't very concerned about my grandparents. I knew they loved me, and I knew they would do anything they could to help me achieve my happiness. Waelin, however, was a bit more of an uncertain factor. I knew he wanted the best for Celeste, but I was not sure if he would be able to overcome his own haughtiness.

The first car, a sleek black SUV bearing the Coalition's insignia, parked. The rear door opened, and Waelin stepped out, dressed impeccably in a formal robe bearing the sigil of the magical academy he had attended in Thilduirne.

Great... He had come in full attire.

Waelin's stern features were set in their usual dour expression as he waited there, and he showed no trace of the sensitivity he had displayed when we had spoken earlier. His sharp grey eyes scanned the homestead surroundings critically before settling on me.

Just then, the second vehicle, an identical black SUV, came rumbling up behind the town car in a cloud of dust. It skidded to a halt at an angle across the drive. The doors flung open, and out popped my grandparents — Grandpa in his best suit — which was a far cry from a fine suit — and Grandma in her Sunday dress.

"Well, here we are!" Grandpa hollered enthusiastically, looking around. Spotting me, his weathered face split into a huge grin.

"David, my boy!" Grandma cooed, hurrying over as fast as her arthritic knees allowed to sweep me into a big hug. I hugged her tightly back, a little choked up seeing her again after all this time. Back when I lived in New Springfield, I barely saw my grandparents since they lived in Louisville, and I saw them even less since moving to the frontier.

Releasing me from the hug, Grandma stepped back, looking me over fondly. "Let me get a good look at you," she fussed, patting my cheek with wrinkled hands. "My, how you've grown into such a handsome, strong young man!"

As she spoke, her gaze drifted past me to the three lovely women waiting patiently on the porch steps. Grandma's eyes widened in delighted surprise. "Oh, my word! Are these your lovely ladies?" she exclaimed.

Bustling over despite her arthritic knees, Grandma warmly embraced Diane first. "What a pretty young thing!" she declared. "David is so lucky to have found you." She then looked over Diane's foxkin features, but she didn't care a bit. "So cute!" she just hummed again.

Diane flushed prettily at the praise. "Diane Whikksie, ma'am," she said. "A pleasure to meet you."

"And polite, too!" Grandma beamed, shooting me a wink. "Just call me Grandma, dear!" Turning, Grandma then engulfed Leigh in an effusive hug. "And you, my dear! Aren't you just the prettiest."

Leigh laughed good-naturedly as she hugged Grandma back. "Pleasure to make your acquaintance!" she said, then grinned as she shook Grandpa's hand. "I see where David gets his looks," she joked.

"Now this here's a keeper!" Grandpa exclaimed, immediately charmed by my bubbly blonde.

Finally, Grandma came to Celeste, visibly awed by her delicate beauty. "You must be Celeste," she breathed, taking the elf maiden's hands in hers. "Why, you are fairer than any poem could describe!"

Celeste dipped her head graciously. "Thank you, madam. It is a pleasure to meet you. David has told me much about you and how much you mean to him."

Meanwhile, Grandpa laughed heartily and slapped me on the shoulder. "You've got yourself quite the bevy of beauties here, my boy!" He winked knowingly. "Come on now, introduce us proper."

With pride swelling in my chest, I formally introduced each of the ladies in turn. They exchanged warm handshakes and enthusiastic greetings, all smiles and laughter.

As my grandparents got acquainted with my women, I glanced back toward the driveway. Waelin still waited stiffly by the sleek town car, looking decidedly out of place and impatient. Celeste headed over to him with a warm smile to greet her uncle.

They spoke a few words as I reveled in my

grandparents' joy at meeting my women. Then, Celeste and Waelin came over, but the elder elf's expression was not particularly warm...

Grandpa turned toward the driveway, spotting Waelin observing aloofly. "Say, who's this fancy fella?" he said.

Waelin's lip curled slightly in distaste at my grandparents' exuberance. Stepping forward with Celeste at his side, he executed a perfunctory bow. "I am Waelin, uncle and caretaker to Celeste," he introduced himself formally.

Grandma blinked uncertainly at the reserved elf before pasting on a friendly smile. "Well, hello there! Aren't you dressed to the nines? We're David's grandparents, come to meet our future granddaughter-in-law!"

Waelin's eyebrows rose at Grandma's presumption. "Indeed," was his only clipped response.

An awkward beat of silence followed, but Celeste quickly intervened. "I'm happy you're here, Uncle," she said. "It is an important day for me."

He nodded, and Grandpa was the next to speak. "Say, I could sure use a drink after being cooped up in that car and getting teleported around. You got anything wet around here, David?"

Before I could respond, Grandma shot Grandpa a stern look. "Albert, mind your manners," she admonished under her breath. Turning back to Waelin with an apologetic smile, she added, "Please excuse my husband's bluster. It was a long drive out."

Waelin gave a curt nod. "I, as well, have traveled far. Perhaps we could continue indoors?" His tone made it clear he considered their simple ways rather uncouth.

Biting back a frustrated sigh, I gestured toward the house. "Yes, let's head inside and get comfortable."

As we started walking, I gave Celeste's hand a reassuring squeeze. Our families were certainly off to a rocky start, but we had a whole night ahead to make things better.

Entering the cozy living room, Grandma let out an appreciative gasp. "Oh my, just look at this place! You've done so well for yourself out here, sweetheart." She turned to Diane and Leigh with a warm smile. "You girls must be so proud of him!"

"We sure are," Leigh readily agreed, giving me a playful wink. "David's built most of the place himself, too. He's a real frontier man and a good homesteader."

I smiled at her, certainly noticing how my grandparents beamed with pride at that. "Just like his parents," Grandma hummed, a wistful touch to her voice.

Waelin's sharp eyes cataloged the modest surroundings dispassionately. If he was impressed, he did not show it outwardly. "The ceremony requires tea before we may engage in casual conversation," he pronounced. "It should be *vaethalam* or *winsumiel*. Properly brewed, in the elven fashion."

Before I could respond, Grandpa snorted in amusement. "*Vay-tell-'em*, you say? Elven tea? That's some fancy stuff right there." He shot Waelin a challenging look. "Just English Breakfast tea is fine for us simple folks."

I suppressed another sigh. This was one thing I had feared. Grandpa wore his heart on his sleeve, and he didn't care for fanciness. Waelin was at the other end of the spectrum.

"Albert," Grandma pleaded, giving him a pointed look that told me they had discussed this behavior prior to their arrival.

Waelin drew himself up, bristling visibly. I jumped in before he could respond. "I'll brew some tea for everyone," I said diplomatically, then added for Waelin's benefit, "With care for elven custom. I have *winsumiel*." His approving nod relaxed me slightly.

While I prepared the tea in the kitchen, I could hear my grandparents' lively barrage of questions, directed mainly at poor Celeste, whose soft replies were largely drowned out. Waelin sat rigidly, looking decidedly out of place amidst all the chaotic warmth.

Bringing the tea tray out to the living room, I poured carefully prepared cups for each person. Waelin accepted his with a gracious nod. Grandpa took a long slurp of his steaming cup, winning another annoyed look from Waelin.

I glanced at Diane and Leigh, whose expressions betrayed that they, too, were not really under the impression that this was going very well. Celeste, her cheeks already flustered, threw me a look that practically begged me to force everyone to get along.

Too bad I could do no such thing.

However, Grandma shot Grandpa a quelling look. "Mind your manners, Albert," she said pointedly. To me, she added, "Everything is just lovely, David. Now come sit with us and tell us more about your life here!"

Settling onto the sofa between Celeste and Grandma, I began recounting the tale of my coming to the homestead, telling it for Waelin's benefit as well. He seemed at least interested when alchemy came into play. When I came to my courtship of Celeste, she gazed at me tenderly as I described our deepening bond and the formal elven courtship rituals we had undertaken.

But my words seemed lost on dour Waelin, who showed little interest in any participation beyond simply attending. This was not going as smoothly as I had hoped. But the night was still young. I prayed that over a meal, our families might find some common ground.

After I had finished recounting my courtship with Celeste, an awkward silence descended over the room. Waelin sat ramrod straight in the armchair, occasionally taking small, precise sips of his tea. He looked decidedly out of place amidst the rustic surroundings.

My grandparents, seated together on the sofa, kept exchanging uncertain glances, as if unsure how to bridge the gap with the aloof elf. Grandma smoothed her floral dress over her knees while Grandpa tugged at his collar and cleared his throat.

Eager to break the uneasy tension, I decided to bring up the traditional baked goods each family was meant to contribute to the ceremony.

"So, if I understand elven custom correctly, both

families should prepare a dish to share, is that right?" I began.

Waelin inclined his head slightly in confirmation. "That is correct," he replied briskly. "For the ceremony, I shall prepare *thalos* — a traditional elven tea cake made with honey and edible rose petals. The recipe has been passed down through generations of our family." He shot Celeste the first warm look of the evening.

Grandma's eyes lit up at his description. "My, that sounds just lovely!" she exclaimed. Turning to Grandpa, she prompted brightly, "Doesn't that sound delightful, Albert?"

"Hm, I suppose so," Grandpa grunted noncommittally into his teacup. I suspected the dainty elven delicacies were not to his taste.

Undeterred by his lackluster response, Grandma flashed an encouraging smile at Waelin. "Well, for our part, I'll be baking my famous snickerdoodles!" she informed him. "It's an old family recipe too, you know. The cinnamon sugar coating perfectly complements a nice hot cup of tea."

Despite Grandma's friendly tone, Waelin

remained impassive, merely inclining his head slightly again. His lack of enthusiasm was palpable.

"Well, proper tea cakes are *very* important," Grandpa suddenly declared in an overloud voice, and I was pretty sure that he didn't care about 'proper tea cakes' in the slightest. He was clearly trying to be loud and present, probably because Waelin made him uncomfortable. If it were any other occasion, I would have found it very funny.

Grandpa took another noisy slurp of tea before continuing. "Can't say I have much taste for those fancy elf cakes with the flower petals and whatnot. A good old-fashioned snickerdoodle cookie suits me just fine."

"Albert, mind your manners," Grandma admonished again in an urgent undertone, casting an apologetic glance at Waelin.

I tried to smooth over the sudden spike in tension, forcing an upbeat tone. "I'm sure both the *thalos* and snickerdoodles will be absolutely delicious," I said diplomatically. Under the table, Celeste squeezed my hand gratefully.

Waelin merely arched one thin eyebrow, looking decidedly unimpressed with my grandparents' humble offering of homey cookies. "Indeed," was his only flat response.

Desperate to change the subject to something less contentious, I turned to Celeste, hoping she could provide a positive redirection.

"Celeste, why don't you tell everyone more about your singing at the Wild Outrider tavern?" I suggested encouragingly. "I'm sure they would all love to hear more about it."

At my prompting, a pretty blush colored Celeste's fair cheeks. She smiled shyly. "Oh, it is merely a small pastime of mine," she demurred modestly. Before she could continue, Grandma jumped in eagerly.

"Oh yes, do tell us more about your singing!" she exclaimed. "David mentioned your lovely voice in his letters. You and Diane must put on quite the musical show!"

Diane flushed slightly, shaking her head. "We just try to liven things up a bit, is all," she explained humbly from her perch on the nearby armchair. "Celeste is the real talent!"

"Oh, shush!" Celeste hummed, turning red. "I have never heard a voice quite like Diane's."

"You're both great!" Leigh interjected with a good-natured grin. "Once word got out about Celeste's heavenly singing at the Wild Outrider, we started getting folks traveling from all over the area just to have a listen."

Celeste colored further, staring down at her lap. "You are all too kind with your praise," she murmured, clearly self-conscious. "Music is simply a passion of mine which brings me joy."

"Well, I for one would just love a private concert," Grandma declared warmly. Turning her hopeful gaze to Celeste, she added, "Maybe we can convince you two songbirds to sing us all something a little later on?"

Celeste managed another shy smile. "If you wish it, I would be more than happy to oblige."

At that moment, Waelin pointedly cleared his throat. "Perhaps we might return the conversation to the matter of the ceremony itself?" he suggested crisply.

Though framed as a polite request, his tone brooked no argument.

"Of course," I said, wanting to satisfy him. "Let's get to the baking, shall we?"

Chapter 38

Standing decisively, I suggested to everyone gathered, "Why don't we start preparing our traditional dishes for the ceremony? I'm happy to offer the use of my kitchen to both parties."

I forced an upbeat, rallying tone because I wasn't going to let Waelin's dour attitude ruin this. I would try my best to win him over. Failing that, I would convince him that — even though he had his reservations about me and my family — Celeste and I were a good match.

Waelin considered for a moment before inclining his head in consent. "Yes," he pronounced judiciously. "Let us move on."

"Excellent idea, David!" Grandma chimed in, though she kept darting uncertain glances at dour Waelin. With some effort, she struggled to her feet, leaning on her cane. "Come along then, Albert. Time's a wastin' - let's get bakin'!"

As we all filed solemnly into the farmhouse kitchen, I exchanged an anxious look with Celeste. Though tensions still simmered right beneath the surface, perhaps sharing the workspace to prepare our ceremonial dishes would help thaw relations.

At least, I prayed fervently that having a task to focus on and channel their energies into might bring our disparate families a bit closer together. Only time would tell if my hopes bore fruit.

Upon entering the warm, inviting kitchen, Grandma made an approving sound. "What a wonderful space!" she exclaimed, hobbling over to inspect the butcher block countertops and racks of pots and pans appreciatively. "You've done so well for yourself out here, sweetheart."

"All thanks to David," Diane chimed in sincerely as she helped lay out ingredients and kitchen implements. "He works so hard to make this place everything we could need." I flushed slightly under her effusive praise.

Waelin remained silent, keen eyes cataloguing the kitchen's dimensions and layout with an inscrutable expression. I wondered if he was comparing the humble farmhouse kitchen unfavorably to the lavish accommodations elves maintained back on Tannoris. If so, he kept such opinions to himself for now.

Turning to our grandparents and Waelin, I invited them graciously, "Please make use of any equipment or space you need. And let me know if I can provide anything else." I tried to play the proper host.

Waelin responded with a nod before he removed his ornate outer robes, fastidiously draping them over a chair. Underneath, he wore a simple but impeccably tailored tunic and trousers.

Moving with precision, he began laying out ingredients — honey, some Tannorian breed of rose petals, flour, sugars — and selected specific measuring tools. I recognized the items as those needed to craft the elven tea cakes he had mentioned.

Meanwhile, Grandma tied an apron around her waist before pulling her timeworn recipe card out of her handbag. "Get the oven ready for me, would you please, Albert?" she requested over her shoulder. Without a word, Grandpa got to work getting the oven ready.

As our families set about their tasks, the kitchen soon filled with purposeful activity and the mingling scents of baking. Grandma started measuring out flour, sugar, butter, eggs, cinnamon, and other ingredients into a large bowl. I recalled helping her make snickerdoodles as a child, bringing her measuring cups and stealing scraps of tasty dough.

With practiced motions, she worked the butter

into the dry ingredients, then beat in the eggs and vanilla extract. As she mixed the cookie dough, the sweet scent of cinnamon wafted through the air. Beside her, Grandpa greased a baking sheet without being asked. They worked in easy tandem born of decades together.

At the other counter, Waelin worked with meticulous precision, combining the ingredients for the elven thalos cakes — honey, rose water, eggs, and more. Using an intricate copper measuring spoon, he carefully leveled off exact amounts of sugar and flour on the scale.

Moving gracefully between workspaces, he combined the ingredients in a glass mixing bowl, whisking smoothly without letting a single drop spill over the rim. The heady aroma of roses mingled with the vanilla and cinnamon smells as he folded in edible rose petals by hand. I could see the meticulous skills of an alchemist even in his cooking.

As our families set to work, the tension filling the warm kitchen air remained stubbornly intact. Waelin and my grandparents continued occupying their separate culinary islands, the only conversation terse requests to pass ingredients. In fact, it seemed to be turning into a competition more than anything else…

Measuring and mixing occupied all attention. The industrious sounds of wooden spoons beating batter and knives chopping nuts filled the silence between them. Watching anxiously, I clung to the frail, flickering hope that sharing this baking ritual might yet kindle some familial camaraderie.

Celeste stepped closer, slipping her hand quietly into mine and giving a supportive squeeze. I knew she shared my hopes for accord between our kin. The success of this ceremony held sway over our future together. We could only wait and pray the relations might gradually thaw.

Once her ingredients were thoroughly incorporated, Grandma scooped mounds of tan cookie dough onto the baking sheet in neat rows. Beside her, Grandpa opened the oven, releasing a puff of hot air, and slid the tray onto the center rack.

As the first batch baked, the cinnamon scent

intensified until my mouth watered. It reminded me viscerally of childhood visits to their home, when the kitchen always smelled deliciously of baking. Grandma hummed tunelessly to herself as she portioned out more dough balls, and that simple act also kindled many childhood memories.

At his station, Waelin carefully spooned the thin rosewater batter into intricate tin molds etched with elven designs. The elegant shapes would imprint the cakes with flowers and leaves. His brow furrowed in concentration as he filled each mold, taking care not to spill a single drop.

Once finished, he opened the upper oven and slid the molds onto the rack with steady hands. The sweet floral aroma grew stronger as the small cakes started baking, mingling with the nostalgic scents of cinnamon and vanilla in an aromatic dance.

Despite the industriousness, both parties maintained their separation, interacting only when briefly required by the confines of the kitchen. But perhaps time and shared purpose might gradually chip away at the icy divide.

I could only hope.

Before long, the kitchen was filled with the warm, delicious scents of freshly baked goods. Grandma's snickerdoodles emerged from the oven golden brown and liberally coated with fragrant cinnamon sugar. She transferred them onto a pretty floral platter to cool.

At the same time, Waelin carefully removed the ornate tin molds from the upper oven, revealing a tray of perfectly formed elven tea cakes. Their flowery shapes had imprinted flawlessly. As the cakes cooled, their sweet rose perfume perfumed the air.

"The snickerdoodles sure smell divine," Grandpa remarked, eyeing the platter hungrily. Turning to Waelin, he added bluntly, "Can't say much for the scent of them fancy elf cakes though."

"Albert!" Grandma admonished, mortified.

But Waelin merely arched an eyebrow. "Yes,

edible roses can be an... acquired taste," he acknowledged mildly.

I blinked at that — it had been the first somewhat human admission from his side, and I was more than pleased to hear it. Perhaps Waelin was warming up a little?

An awkward beat of silence followed before I jumped in. "Why don't we adjourn to the dining room to sample everything?" I suggested briskly.

There were murmurs of assent, and our odd assortment filed into the cozy farmhouse dining area. I set out plates, napkins, and teacups while Grandma arranged the platter of snickerdoodles in the center of the table.

With great pomp, Waelin bore in the tray of ornate little rose cakes, setting it down beside the homey cookies with a gracious dip of his head. The contrast was almost comical.

Once everyone was settled, I poured fresh tea all around from the *winsumiel* blend that Waelin had insisted upon. Steam rose fragrantly from our cups as we each took a small plate and prepared to sample the ceremonial confections.

Grandma beamed happily as everyone took one of her snickerdoodles first, biting into the fragrant, cinnamon-coated cookies.

"Mm! Delicious as always, dear," Grandpa mumbled through a mouthful, powdered sugar dusting his lapels.

The cookies proved light and buttery, contrasted by the zing of cinnamon and sugar. I made an approving sound, transported back to childhood by the familiar taste. Even Waelin muttered that the cookies were "acceptable."

Next, we each took one of the ornate little rose cakes crafted by Waelin. Beside me, Celeste took a small, cautious bite of her cake and forced a polite smile that told little good of the taste.

Next to her, Diane and Leigh also gave polite smiles and nods that told me enough. I knew them well, and I could tell when they were just being polite. This was going to taste... well, *not good*.

I bit into the petite confection hesitantly, discovering an odd sweet-tangy flavor underneath the flowery aroma.

But to say they were *nice*... That would be a

gross overstatement. If anything, the taste of these *thalos* reminded me of….

"*Potpourri!*" Grandpa snapped after taking one large, unrestrained bite of the cake.

He pulled a disgusted face. "Yeugh! This tastes like I'm eating potpourri!" he restated through the mouthful before he could stop himself.

"Albert David Donahue Wilson! You mind your manners this instant!" Grandma scolded, utterly aghast at his lack of decorum before their elven guest.

Waelin eyed Grandpa with what I could only describe as cold fire.

At that moment, a million things went through my mind, each focused on saving this situation and trying to find a way for Celeste and I to be together despite this fiasco.

But then, the look of icy fire in Waelin's eyes melted away.

And instead of taking offense, Waelin let out an abrupt, barking laugh — the first unrestrained sound of mirth he had made all evening.

We all stared at him in surprise as his thin

shoulders shook with genuine amusement. For a long moment, we were all just bewildered as Waelin laughed.

"You are not wrong, sir," Waelin said at last, an unwonted twinkle in his eye. "In truth, I am a miserable baker. This ancient recipe has been passed down for generations, yet despite my alchemical expertise, I seem unable to reproduce it correctly. And even so…" He raised a finger. "I remember my dear mother making these *thalos*, and by Ilmanaria, I hated them back then, too!"

At that, we all broke out laughing. The tension in my shoulders finally fell away, and I could sense the same elation in Celeste, Diane, and Leigh.

Finally, Waelin smiled ruefully down at the cakes. "Forgive me — I desired to prepare something worthy of tradition, but I fear this attempt was rather pitiful." He then looked up at Grandpa. "I appreciate candor," he said. "Too long have I lived among politicians and conniving mages. Truthfulness is something I appreciate, sir."

Grandpa gave a nod. "Well, I'm happy to hear that. And I appreciate a man who can handle some… uh, *constructive* criticism."

Grandma clapped her hands, beaming ecstatically now the ice had been broken. "Still, it was a lovely gesture," she assured Waelin. Turning to Grandpa with a playful glare, she added pointedly, "Wasn't it, Albert?"

"Er, yes! Of course!" Grandpa sputtered, looking properly chastised but also relieved the tension had melted. He took a conciliatory bite of snickerdoodle as if to cleanse his palate.

Casting his inedible cakes one final self-deprecating look, Waelin selected a snickerdoodle for himself instead. "Perhaps we shall simply let this be our little secret, and only the cookies need be eaten moving forward."

His tentative, conciliatory tone heartened me. Perhaps there was hope of accord between our families after all.

"It shall be our secret," Grandma agreed conspiratorially before leaning in to speak quietly to Waelin. "Truth be told, not all old family recipes stand the test of time. Why, I've got one for a terrible aspic that looks simply ghastly!"

Waelin let out another surprised bark of laughter as Grandma launched into a colorful account of the offending aspic's origins, punctuated by Grandpa's intermittent guffaws as he described the terrible appearance with his honest words. The mood around the table warmed exponentially now the rigid formality had cracked.

My fingers intertwined happily with Celeste's under the table. Her answering radiant smile outshone the sun, speaking volumes. Laughter and lively chatter filled the cozy dining room, binding our families closer together bite by bite. Though differences remained, kindness and humor would smooth the path ahead.

In this moment, sharing humble cookies instead of fussy tea cakes, I glimpsed the real possibility of accord between us all. The future shone brightly.

Chapter 39

As we finished the last of the snickerdoodles, a much more relaxed mood had settled around the table. The initial awkwardness and formality had melted away, replaced by animated conversation and frequent laughter.

"My boy, you've built yourself quite the life out

here," Grandpa said proudly, giving my shoulder an affectionate pat. "Your father would be so pleased to see the skilled frontiersman you've become."

I flushed with gratitude. "It's been a lot of hard work, but very rewarding. And I couldn't have done it without Leigh and Diane's help." I smiled at my amazing women, and they beamed back.

"They seem like perfectly lovely young ladies," Grandma remarked warmly. Turning her kindly gaze to Celeste, she added, "And you, my dear, are just as lovely as David described. We're so pleased he found you."

Celeste flushed prettily. "You are too kind. I feel very blessed as well to have found David." She smiled tenderly at me, and my heart swelled.

"If I may say so, Celeste has been a ray of light chasing away the melancholy that plagued my household since we lost her parents," Waelin spoke up sincerely. "And I can see that David's affection — while relationships between our kind and humans are rare — has brought such joy to her countenance."

I nodded gratefully at him. "All I want is to make her as happy as she's made me."

Waelin inclined his head in acknowledgment, some of the earlier wariness fading from his eyes. "I know. Your intentions are good."

Buoyed by the thawing relations, Grandma turned eagerly to Waelin. "Why don't you tell us a little more about yourself? What was it like living among the elves back in… Thilduirne, you said?"

Looking slightly self-conscious, Waelin took a careful sip of tea before beginning. "Well, in my youth, I studied alchemy at the academy in Thilduirne. I had some skill with potions, so I was soon recruited by the academy itself to teach."

As Waelin spoke of studying alongside other promising elven mages and alchemists, I listened raptly, fascinated to learn more of his past and culture so different from my own humble human roots. Occasionally Celeste would chime in with a clarification or colorful anecdote about living with him.

"It all sounds so refined," Grandma said in wonder when Waelin had finished.

Waelin smiled. "Well, it was... until the Upheaval tore away the world of the elves. But let us not dwell on such unpleasant things. Pray tell, how was life for you? I do not often speak to humans in... well, a *setting* like this — one that is not transactional in nature. I would like to learn some more."

Grandma smiled, doing her best to step over Waelin's expensive words and somewhat haughty demeanor. They were trying hard, and I loved them for it.

"Well," she began, "David's grandfather and I both grew up on small farms in rural Kentucky. My papa used to make the best apple butter every fall." Her eyes took on a nostalgic, faraway look.

"Life was simple back then — never had much use for fanciness," Grandpa added. "But we worked hard and got by alright. Had some good times too — bonfires, barn dances, pie contests at the county fair." He chuckled at the memories. "At one such country fair, I met this pretty lady right here." He smiled warmly at Grandma. "And I've been walking with my head in the clouds ever

413

since."

"Oh, Albert, you charmer, you!" Grandma purred with a delighted chuckle.

Waelin listened with interest, perhaps comparing their humble lives to the lavish privilege he enjoyed as one of the elite elves. But I could see flickers of wistfulness in his expression as my grandparents described their wholesome, common experiences he likely did not share.

Eager to bridge the cultural gap still lingering between them, I suggested lightly, "We should have a nice big bonfire tonight and share stories under the stars. The weather is still good, and we can enjoy the dinner Diane and Leigh will prepare by the banks of the river. Would you like that, Waelin?"

Waelin blinked, looking startled but not displeased at the friendly moniker. At length, he nodded. "I believe I would enjoy such an experience," he allowed graciously. "Although I am used to eating at a table, it could be... educational."

Grandma beamed and clapped her hands. "Oh,

how wonderful! We'll make it a real bonfire celebration."

Grandpa rubbed his hands together eagerly. "Should we see about roasting some marshmallows too? Can't have a proper bonfire without marshmallows!"

I laughed. "I'm sure we've got the fixings for s'mores around here somewhere." Rising from the table, I called for the domesticants.

At once, they began clearing empty cups and plates, zipping about and working with great speed and skill.

"Oh my!" Grandma gasped. "I'd love to have some of those little fellows around the house."

"I'll summon you one," I said, "and I can bind it as a familiar and instruct it to listen to you."

Grandma placed her hands on her cheeks in astonishment. "Oh, David! That would be wonderful."

"Ah, that's great! Lil' guy can grab me a beer, and I won't have to get up!" Grandpa put in.

I chuckled at that. Giving them a domesticant would cost me a slot, but I believed that was worth it. Here were two people who had cared for me with all the love in their hearts after my parents had passed — and plenty of times before that, too. And they were getting older; a little magical help around the house would do them well.

"Alright," I said. "Let's get things ready for a nice night by the bonfire!"

Our guests and Celeste readily agreed, and soon we were all bustling about in pleasant activity. Diane and Leigh got to work preparing a meal, made wholly of ingredients from the farm and fish from the Silverthread. Meanwhile, Celeste helped me light a fire with her burgeoning survival skill, while my grandparents continued chatting amiably. In the meantime, the domesticants zoomed about, cleaning up.

Before long, we had a cheerful blaze crackling in the firepit outdoors. The sun was just starting to sink below the trees, bathing the homestead in warm amber light. Our family gathered around the flickering glow, reflecting in silence for a moment.

Celeste and I exchanged a warm look, and we both knew that things were boding well.

As dusk settled over the homestead, we gathered around the crackling bonfire in a spirit of friendship. The dancing flames cast flickering shadows over our faces as we settled atop scattered logs, drawn close to share warmth and companionship. Overhead, the first twinkling stars of evening were emerging in the dusky sky.

Our odd yet intimate assembly was colored by a profound sense of contentment. Surrounded by the people I held most dear, I felt a powerful swell of gratitude. The ice dividing Waelin and my grandparents had thawed, kindled by compassion, humor, and patience on all sides. Our families were blending before my eyes.

The sounds of sizzling meat soon drifted from the grill Leigh and Diane had set up at a prudent distance from the lively flames. My mouth watered at the savory aroma of seasoned trout along with roasted new potatoes fresh from our garden. A perfect frontier feast.

While we awaited the meal, Celeste serenaded us with a haunting yet hopeful elven ballad, plucking her traveling harp's strings to coax forth exquisite melodies. Her lyrical voice soared and fluttered, rising and falling like a nightingale's on the evening breeze.

Enraptured, none of us spoke a word, scarcely daring to breathe lest we disturb a single note of her song.

"O Nightingale, your song so pure,
Lifts my spirit, calms my heart.
Your melody, a mystic cure.
Soothes the soul, and balm imparts.

Your silv'ry voice both fierce and frail,
Heals the hurt, dispels the cold.
Rising, falling, song regales,
Brave and bright, yet soft and bold.

Sing out, let your music fill the night,
Rise up, like the dawn after darkest night.
Ring out, voice so clear, by lantern's light,
Hope lives on, though day fades out of sight.

Nightingale, perched in yon tree,

Tireless, trilling out your tune.
Let your song set my spirit free,
Chase away the shadows' gloom.

Lift your voice up to the moon,
Flooding meadow, moor and fen.
Singing lest the darkness swoon,
Bringing joy to elf and man.

Sing out, let your music fill the night,
Rise up, like the dawn after darkest night.
Ring out, voice so clear, by lantern's light,
Hope lives on, though day fades out of sight.

Nightingale, your burning song,
Kindles courage, fans the flames.
Stay with me, nocturnal siren,
While the long night remains.

Sing out, let your music fill the night,
Rise up, like the dawn after darkest night.
Ring out, voice so clear, by lantern's light,
Hope lives on, though day fades out of sight."

When at last the final ethereal strains faded, we broke into hearty applause.

Celeste dipped her head graciously, cheeks endearingly flushed from the attention. Yet her emerald eyes glimmered, betraying her inward delight to perform for an appreciative audience.

"Why, your voice is even more angelic than David said!" Grandma gushed. "You must sing something else for us again after dinner."

Celeste smiled warmly. "It would be my pleasure. Music has a way of binding souls together." Her eyes met mine, ripe with affection. My pulse quickened, counting the moments until we would be bound in marriage.

Just then, Leigh stepped forward carrying a heaping platter of sizzling trout. "Music ain't the only thing that binds souls," she joked with a playful wink. "Dig in, y'all!"

Our gathering wasted no time loading up plates and tucking in. For several moments, the only sounds were those of contented chewing and wordless sounds of gustatory delight. The fresh trout's smoky richness paired perfectly with the roasted potatoes.

As we ate, conversation resumed, meandering pleasantly from fond reminiscences to amusing anecdotes. Laughter flowed as freely as the food and drink. Traces still remained of our different backgrounds, but kindness and humor had smoothed the path between us.

Lost in our lively fellowship, no one noticed the emerging stars marching steadily across the heavens until Grandpa paused to comment on them apropos of nothing. "Would ya look at that sky!" he exclaimed. "I ain't seen stars shine so bright since the Upheaval, and we had to go to Louisville." He shook his head, eyes full of wonder.

We followed his gaze upward, conversation trailing off for a moment. The velvet firmament sprawled above us, strewn with innumerable glittering pinpricks of light. I slipped an arm around Celeste, drawing her close as we marveled silently together at infinity's majesty.

"It reminds me of home," Waelin spoke up unexpectedly. His sharp features had gone distant, almost wistful. "Of walking beneath the forest's fragrant boughs with my sister, when Celeste was just a babe." A melancholy smile ghosted his lips. "How she adored gazing at the stars."

Celeste reached out to gently take her uncle's hand in a tender gesture of support. Though grief shadowed his heart, solace and purpose were yet to be found under starry skies.

After a moment of contemplative silence, Grandma ventured warmly to Waelin, "Your sister sounds like she was a wonderful woman. We'd be so pleased if you'd share some memories of her with us."

Waelin hesitated, unaccustomed to such openness with relative strangers. But at last, he gave a gracious nod. "I would be happy to enlighten you about my dear sister." As we listened, spellbound, he began spinning colorful tales of mischief and mayhem with his sister when they were youths. Laughter once again wove an enchantment around us.

The supply of food dwindled, and our appetites along with it. At last, comfortably full, we settled back replete, gazing into the hypnotic flames as they danced and popped. Somewhere out in the surrounding woods, a great horned owl began its plaintive hooting solo. The homey serenade only added to the peaceful atmosphere.

Before long, Leigh brought out the supplies for s'mores, eliciting eager sounds all around. "Come and get 'em!" she proclaimed, spearing a marshmallow onto a stick and extending it toward the fire. She showed Waelin how to roast the white puffs to a perfect golden brown.

Soon we were all crowded around the bonfire. Sticky fingers and lips testified to our success replicating the fireside classic.

Around mouthfuls, Celeste explained the significance of the stars in elven culture to my grandparents, who listened raptly. They soaked up her lyrical descriptions of the elaborate midnight solstice rituals and poetic verse written in honor of Namenas, the elves' most sacred constellation.

As the fire gradually died down, so too did our lively discourse, lapsing into a comfortable silence filled by the symphony of the surrounding woods at night. No one seemed inclined to stir from this peaceful scene just yet. I slipped my arm around Celeste again, and she nestled against my shoulder contentedly.

"This is perfect," she said softly so that I alone could hear.

I smiled and nodded. "It really is," I replied. "I was a little afraid things wouldn't turn out that well at first, but it seems everything has turned around."

"It has," she confirmed, and when I looked at her, a blaze of desire burned in her green eyes. "I think it's time, David."

"Time?" I asked.

"Time for you to speak to Uncle Waelin," she said. "To ask his approval. And while you do so, I shall ask approval of your grandparents and your wives."

"That is... That is elven custom, too?" I asked. Brynneth hadn't told me about it, but then again, it made sense that some approval was needed be stated outright.

She giggled. "It is, my love. And if all approve, you may speak the words. Do you know them?"

I nodded, recalling the beautiful words that Brynneth had taught me. With that, Celeste kissed me on the cheek, and I smiled at her and rose, approaching Waelin.

The elf looked up at me as I drew near, and I could see in his stern gaze that he knew also that the time had come.

"Waelin," I began, "may I have a moment?"

Chapter 40

Waelin regarded me solemnly, the firelight glinting in his gray eyes. "You may have a moment, David," he replied.

By his tone, I could tell he understood we were about to talk about what this was all about. Before he rose, his gaze flickered briefly to where Celeste was speaking animatedly with my grandparents.

Together, we walked to the edge of the fire, out of earshot of the others. Compared to when he had arrived, Waelin seemed more accepting and calm, and I hoped this was a good sign.

I took a steadying breath. This was a pivotal moment. "I wanted to speak with you privately about Celeste," I continued. "Our courtship has progressed, as you know, and my feelings for her have only grown stronger."

Waelin said nothing, merely arching one thin brow expectantly. His expression remained unreadable. He wasn't necessarily going to make it easy. But I knew he appreciated candor, and so I spoke plainly.

"I wish to ask Celeste to marry me," I said. "But I know that in elven tradition, it is customary to seek formal consent from her guardian first." I met Waelin's piercing eyes. "So, I ask for your permission to wed Celeste."

For several taut heartbeats, Waelin was silent, his sharp features cast in an impassive mask. Out of the corner of my eye, I could see Celeste speaking earnestly with my grandparents and Diane and Leigh.

At last, Waelin spoke, his tone carefully measured. "You must understand, David — Celeste is very dear to me. As you know, I have counted her safety and happiness as my solemn charge since her parents passed."

I nodded gravely. "I know, and I assure you Celeste's well-being will always be paramount to me."

Waelin studied me a moment before continuing. "Perhaps so. But you are still young, with the impulsiveness of youth." He paused. "And we remain divided by more than culture alone. You may think your feelings fixed, yet human hearts are... fickle."

Stifling a flare of indignation, I kept my tone polite and composed. "My feelings for Celeste are true. They have been tested through hardship and adventure and emerged only stronger." I met his skepticism steadily. "And while your experiences with human emotions may not be positive, they are also very limited."

He perked an eyebrow and pursed his lips. "*Limited*, you say?"

"What do you really know about us, Waelin?" I asked. "You admitted at the start of all this that you rarely talk to humans beyond a transactional level. I've done my best to learn your ways, and I only scratched the surface. You have done nothing, and you know nothing."

The words were somewhat frightening to speak. After all, I risked blowing up the whole endeavor.

But by now, I understood what kind of man Waelin was. He was someone you spoke frankly to, no matter the disdain in his expression. He appreciated that, and I would not let him down in that aspect.

Conflict warred openly on Waelin's features as he weighed his response. At length, he spoke again, reluctantly. "Were the circumstances different, I would refuse you without hesitation. But Celeste..." His eyes softened sadly. "The light has returned to her spirit since you came into her life. Her laughter and songs, so long missed, ring out again."

Heart lifting hopefully, I remained silent, allowing Waelin space to gather his thoughts and voice them uninterrupted. Around us, the bonfire crackled, casting wavering shadows over our solemn exchange.

"For that alone, I find myself inclined to grant consent," Waelin admitted heavily. He scrubbed a hand over his face. "Can you swear to me that you will guard her with your life? Especially considering the nature of her Class, which is outlawed among elves?"

"I give you my solemn oath that I will," I vowed fervently.

Waelin searched my face a long moment as if gauging my sincerity. Finally, he gave a single slow nod and exhaled sharply. "Then you have my permission to wed Celeste, if she will accept you." His voice was low but lacked any real bitterness now. "Speak the words to her, and she will be your wife if she wishes it."

Relief broke over me in an exhilarating wave. My face nearly split with the force of my answering grin. "Thank you, Waelin," I said earnestly, offering my hand.

He clasped it in acceptance. "Honor her," he said. "Honor her in the spirit of my family and her mother, who was my sister, and without whom my world has become bleak. Give her life, laughter, and return the colors to her world. Paint again that which is drab and take her on your journeys through life. Make it so that she shall not suffer my fate and end up dour, alone, and full of regret."

"I will."

The briefest of smiles flickered over Waelin's usually stoic features. "See that you do." He took a bracing swig from his cup. "Now, off with you! Make merry and speak your words of promise."

I offered him a final nod before I turned to look at Celeste. She stood by Diane and Leigh now, conversing softly and giggling as if they were discussing a secret of sorts. My grandparents stood a few steps away, arms around each other and smiles on their faces.

My eyes met Celeste's, and her conversation with Diane and Leigh fell silent. The blonde and the foxkin took a step back, exchanging meaningful looks and smiling.

"Go on," Waelin said again. "She is waiting."

Chapter 41

Heart pounding, I slowly approached Celeste where she stood by the glowing bonfire. Her emerald eyes were luminous as she watched me draw near, a soft smile curving her rosebud lips.

The dancing flames cast a warm glow over her fair features, heightening her ethereal beauty. This was the moment we had waited for.

As I came to stand before her, the chatter around the fire quieted. Though she said nothing, worlds of meaning and emotion passed between us in our joined gaze. Reaching out, I took both of Celeste's delicate hands in mine, marveling as always at their soft warmth.

"My beloved Celeste," I began tenderly. "From the first moment I saw you, I felt as though I beheld the fairest vision my eyes had ever known. Your beauty dazzled me, but even more than that, I found myself captivated by your spirit — your kindness, your courage, and your musical gifts that I feel blessed to have witnessed."

Celeste's eyes misted over with emotion as she listened. Her hands tightened gently around mine. Buoyed by her reaction, I pressed on.

"During our travels and trials together, my feelings for you have only deepened, like roots spreading unseen over time. I can no longer imagine my life without you."

Celeste let out a soft gasp, visibly hanging on my every word. Nearby, Diane and Leigh were smiling broadly.

Sinking slowly to one knee — my left, as Brynneth had told me — on the forest floor, I still clasped her hands in mine as I gazed up at her. The crackling bonfire framed her in a soft radiance as tears of joy slipped down her fair cheeks. This was the moment.

I took one of the rings of shimmerstone from my pocket, winning gasps of delight from those assembled.

"Dearest Celeste," I began, "I kneel before you without disguise or pretense. If you will have me, I offer you my heart, my home, my hearth, and my hand in marriage from now unto eternity."

Celeste let out a joyful sob, emerald eyes luminous.

Then, I spoke the words that Brynneth had taught me. *"Kel-amon,"* I said, *"nan-aieseth tara, aes ylmar antara aieser. Vel-ona a vel-mata — ylmë a ylamas faluin."* And before she could answer, I added my own words in English, since this was a marriage for my culture as well. "My dearest Celeste, will you do me the honor of becoming my wife?"

For a breathless instant Celeste simply gazed down at me, features alight with wonder and elation. Then she cried, "Yes! Of course, I shall marry you, my love! *Tara uin! Tara uin!*" she added in her native tongue.

Scarcely daring to believe the rapturous words I had longed to hear, I leapt to my feet and swept Celeste into my arms. She clung to me as joyful laughter mingled with euphoric tears. Spinning her in an exultant circle, I felt I could take flight, so airy and light were my spirits.

Setting her back on her feet at last, I tenderly framed Celeste's lovely face between my hands. Our gazes locked with profound understanding, and slowly, I drew her to me in a kiss that sang of promises and tremulous joy.

Her lips were impossibly soft and gentle against mine. We lingered blissfully in that tender kiss beneath the approving stars while our families watched with smiles on their faces.

Finally drawing back to behold my radiant bride-to-be, I put the ring around her finger, much to the delight of Leigh, Diane, my grandparents, and even Waelin.

She beamed a smile as she admired the ring. "David," she hummed, "it is so beautiful!" Clasping one of my hands tightly, Celeste turned to my grandparents. Eyes shining, she said, "Your grandson has spoken his heart, and I have accepted. With your blessing, we shall be wed."

My grandparents beamed, immediately rushing over to embrace us both. "Bless you both!" Grandma cried joyfully. Grandpa beamed with pride and gave the nod of respect that passed between men.

But then, I turned to Leigh and Diane and beckoned them close. Their expressions turned into ones of surprise, then to gasps as I went to my knee for them, too.

"Leigh, Diane," I said.

"Oh my!" Leigh purred, unable to contain herself. "Yes! Yes! I do! We do!"

Diane laughed and gave her harem sister a nudge. "Let him finish!"

I smiled broadly, taking one of their hands in

each mind as Celeste stood behind me. "No one shall be first among my wives," I said. "You are each special to me, and nothing on this world would make me happier than forging this bond with you, as I would forge it with Celeste."

Then, I turned to Diane. "Diane, my love. You are the foundation of who I am, my brave woman of the frontier. Living with you has made me happier than I could have ever imagined I would be. You have been at my side always, cautioned me when I was rash, urged me on when I hesitated, and you have completed me." My gaze dipped to her stomach. "You carry my child, my future, and my hope. Please, Diane, will you marry me?"

With that, even as my grandparents gasped at the revelation that Diane was with my child, I presented Diane the second of the shimmerstone rings. She made a happy hop that sent her tail and fox ears bobbing before she fell to her knees herself and embraced me.

"Yes!" she cried out. "Oh, David, yes!"

We kissed deeply, still kneeling on the ground, and when we finally separated, I placed the ring on her finger. She extended her hand and admired the lustrous piece of jewelry before giving me another kiss.

Then, I turned to Leigh, who was practically hopping in place with excitement.

"Leigh..."

But she couldn't contain herself. Within a breath, she was on the forest floor with me, having pushed me down and showering me with kisses, muttering 'yes, yes, yes' in between — so fast and intense I was afraid for a moment she might lose her breath.

I kissed her back with fiery passion as the others laughed full of happiness and joy at her exuberant display of affection. When finally, our kiss came to an end, she fixed me with those hazy eyes of hers that I loved so much.

"No words are needed between us, David," she whispered. "I will marry you, and I will follow you to the end of the Earth."

I smiled and took her hand, pushing the ring around her dainty finger. "Then you, too, will be my wife," I whispered to her.

Leigh nodded, tears clouding her eyes, and

threw her arms around me once again, and we lost ourselves in another kiss.

Chapter 42

As Leigh and I finally separated, breathless and beaming, a joyful cheer went up from our assembled friends and family. My grandparents rushed over to offer hearty congratulations and embrace each of us brides-to-be in turn. Even stoic Waelin allowed himself an approving nod, visibly touched by the outpouring of emotion.

"Oh, what a wonderful night this is!" Grandma cried, dabbing happy tears from her eyes as she admired our glittering betrothal rings. "Three beautiful brides! And a little baby soon! Oh, I can't wait to hold him! Or her! I always knew you were destined for great love, David."

Grandpa laughed heartily, clapping me on the back. "You've done very well, my boy! We're so happy for all of you." He smiled warmly around at Diane, Leigh, and Celeste. "Welcome to the Wilson family, girls!"

Leigh looped her arms around Grandma and Grandpa's shoulders. "Thanks! I promise I'll eat all the snickerdoodles you bring us!" she joked merrily.

Diane slipped her arm through Celeste's, smiling tenderly. "Sisters," she said simply.

Celeste's answering smile glowed brighter than the bonfire as she squeezed Diane's hand. Their display of affection as harem sisters touched me deeply.

As we basked in the circle of warmth and light

cast by the lively flames, I drew all my amazing women close. "I'm the luckiest man alive," I told them earnestly. Their answering smiles lit up the night brighter than any star.

Waelin watched our celebratory embrace, his sharp features softening almost wistfully. Perhaps memories of his own sister, Celeste's mother, stirred bittersweetly within him. But the cheer around the fire remained undimmed.

Leigh nudged Waelin playfully. "C'mon now, don't be a stick in the mud! You're part of this family now too." Laughing, she pushed a fresh mug of mead into his hand. After a moment's hesitation, the trace of a smile lifted Waelin's lips as he accepted the drink.

Together with Waelin, we shared jokes and stories around the crackling bonfire as the inky night sky wheeled slowly overhead. For these precious hours, the world consisted only of our circle of fellowship and light amidst the ancient woods. Diane and Leigh brought out more food, ensuring none went hungry or thirsty during the impromptu betrothal celebration.

At one point amidst the merriment, Celeste drew me aside. Looping her arms around my neck, she smiled up at me tenderly. "My husband-to-be," she murmured dreamily, as though trying out the words. Happiness suffused her every feature. "I can scarcely believe this bliss is real."

I encircled her slender waist, smiling down at her radiance. "Believe it, my love," I whispered before capturing her lips in a deep kiss.

Celeste melted against me with a contented sigh. For long moments, we lingered blissfully in each other's embrace under the benevolent stars, our future bright before us.

When at last we reluctantly parted, Celeste kept her arms draped loosely around my neck. An impish smile played about her rosebud lips as her emerald eyes probed mine. "Tell me, my beloved — do humans have any customs to mark a betrothal?" Mischief danced in her luminous gaze.

I grinned at her playful query. "Well, except for the ring, no." I chuckled.

"We do," she said, a green fire blazing in her eyes. "My kin, the wood elves, go on moonlit strolls in the woods. Would you come on one with me?"

"A moonlit walk sounds perfect," I agreed readily. By the blaze in her eyes, I could tell there was a little plan going on there, but I decided not to ruin the fun.

Delight sparked in Celeste's expression. "Perfect," she hummed before looking at the others. My grandparents, Waelin, and Leigh and Diane were conversing. "As per custom," Celeste announced, "David and I shall go for a walk in the forest."

My grandparents waved, and Waelin touched his forehead in greeting. "Be careful," he said.

"Oh, the larroling and Mr. Drizzles patrol the grounds," Leigh said. "They're safe!"

As Waelin gave a confused frown and Leigh began explaining who Mr. Drizzles was and why we had our own larroling, Celeste smiled and took my hand. She began to guide me away from the fire's cheerful glow into the surrounding woods now swathed in silvery moonlight.

As we slipped away, Leigh shot Diane a

mischievous grin and the two dissolved into giggles. I wondered at their sly behavior but had no time to ponder it before Celeste drew me deeper under the shadowy boughs.

Alone amidst the hushed forests, Celeste slipped her arms around me once more. Tilting her face up to the pale moonlight, she waited expectantly, eyes drifting closed. Heart swelling, I leaned down to meet her waiting lips in a tender kiss underneath the starry sky.

For a blissful interval, we lingered in each other's arms, the rest of the world receding. But she was driving me crazy by pushing herself up against me. Her body was exquisite and curvy and soft, and I felt myself turning heady with desire before she loosened herself and shot me a meaningful look.

We strolled on together through the moon-washed woods, and Celeste looked up at me with radiant green eyes, pools of mystery that seemed to harbor a little secret. "What are you thinking about, my love?" she asked.

I smiled down at my radiant bride-to-be. "That I'm happy here with you. And, well... to speak the truth, I'm looking forward to our wedding night as well."

"Wedding night?" Celeste hummed, her green eyes big.

"Yeah," I said. "You know, when the ceremony is complete, and man and wife finally get to enjoy each other."

"What a strange custom!" she exclaimed.

I blinked. "You... You do things differently?"

But then, her hand loosened itself from mine, and she shot me a coy smile and ran off, giggling.

"Wait!" I called out.

"Come!" she just replied, laughing and dancing through the moonlit forest as only an elf can. Light seemed to shine from her, and there was nothing I could do but follow her, caught up in her beauty.

I followed her, breaking from the tree line and stood blinking as I watched a secluded forest pond I had never noticed before. Moonlight shimmered on its glassy surface. Celeste let out a delighted gasp at the sight, and she stood half-turned toward me, framed in the glow of the moon.

"David," she said, a fire kindling in our eyes, "to

elven custom, we *are* married. There will be a celebration, but the words bound us, David. You are already my husband; I am already your wife. We may finally enjoy each other."

As she spoke, Leigh and Diane emerged from behind the trees, eyes dancing impishly. They were like little faeries of the forest themselves, clothed in moonlight and the light and spotless white dresses they had worn for the occasion.

"Leigh?" I muttered. "Diane?"

Celeste gifted me with a tender smile as her harem sisters came to stand beside her. "Another elven custom," Celeste said. "One you will enjoy more than the poetry and the formal visitation, I don't doubt."

With that, she turned fully to me, her beautiful breasts heaving with passion. Leigh and Diane stood beside her, their eyes blazing as they watched me.

"A new wife must be initiated in the presence of her harem sisters," Celeste spoke, her voice like a song in my heart. "Make me your wife, David. Fill my cup with your love, and let us never be apart again in this life or the next."

My heart hammered in my throat as I stepped forward finally — to claim my elven maiden.

Chapter 43

I stepped closer to Celeste, the silver light of the moon casting her in an ethereal glow that seemed almost otherworldly. Her amber hair shimmered in that magical light, the soft strands falling in a delicate cascade over her shoulders as she waited with bated breath.

My heart felt like a drumbeat, loud and insistent, as I leaned down and pressed my lips to hers. The kiss was gentle at first, a tender exploration that grew deeper, more insistent as the connection between us sparked to life.

Celeste's lips were soft and yielding, sweet as the nectar of the rarest flower. Her shy hesitance gave way to a growing passion, her arms winding around my neck to pull me closer, her body melding to mine as if we were two halves of a whole.

My hands roamed over the delicate curves of her body, feeling the warmth of her skin through the fabric of her dress. The pleasure of the kiss deepened into a slow burn that ignited every nerve ending and sent a rush of desire coursing through my veins.

Diane and Leigh watched with wide eyes, their expressions a mix of amazement and delight as they watched me initiate their new harem sister.

At last, Celeste pulled back slightly, her cheeks flushed with the heat of the moment. "It is elven custom for newlyweds to undress one another," she whispered, her voice laced with desire.

"Then let us honor your customs," I replied, my voice husky with need.

She smiled and spread her arms for me. I reached out and carefully began to unbutton her dress, each tiny loop slipping free under my fingers with a soft, teasing sound.

Celeste's breath hitched as I peeled back the fabric, revealing the pale, flawless skin beneath. Her dress fell away in a whisper of silk, pooling at her feet like liquid moonlight. She stood before me, a vision of elven perfection, her body curvy and divine.

My gaze drank in the sight of her, from the gentle swell of her breasts to the delicate curve of her hips. Her skin glowed in the moonlight, a canvas of ivory that begged to be touched, kissed, worshipped — claimed.

It was now her turn, and I stepped back, allowing her to undress me. She reached up to trace the contours of my chest, her fingers light and exploratory. She fumbled slightly with the buttons of my shirt, her movements betraying her nervous anticipation.

I helped guide her hands, our fingers entwining as we undid each button together. My shirt fell open, and she pushed it off my shoulders, her eyes wide as she took in the expanse of my torso.

Her hands were warm on my skin, hesitant at first but growing bolder as she traced the lines of my abs and the definition of my chest. There was a reverence in her touch, a silent promise of the passion to come.

With a shared, breathless laughter, we worked to free me from the rest of my clothing. My pants and undergarments joined the pile of discarded fabric, and I stood naked before her, fully revealed.

Celeste's eyes roamed over me, taking in the sight of my arousal. Her blush deepened, a rosy hue that spread down her neck and across her chest. She looked up at me through long lashes, her green eyes shimmering with desire.

"Come here," I said, opening my arms to embrace her.

Our naked bodies pressed together, skin against skin, finally united. The heat of her body was like a living flame against mine, igniting a deeper hunger that had nothing to do with the chill of the night air.

I kissed her again, more fiercely this time, our lips and tongues tangling in a passionate embrace that left us both breathless. Our bodies moved together; a seamless rhythm that spoke of the connection that thrummed between us. The press of her soft breasts with their hard little nipples against my chest drove me wild, and I couldn't wait to fully have her.

Celeste's hands traced the lines of my back, her nails scraping lightly over my skin in a way that sent shivers down my spine. I groaned into the kiss, my hands roaming over her, exploring every inch of her beautiful form.

Her skin was like velvet under my touch, smooth and soft, the curves of her body fitting perfectly against mine. The press of her breasts, the softness of her belly, the roundness of her hips — every part of her called to me, a siren's song of desire.

We moved together in the moonlit clearing by the pond, our bodies entwined in an intimate dance that felt both sacred and profane. The night wrapped around us, the stars and the moon our only witnesses to the passion that burned so bright.

Celeste's breath came in short gasps, her body arching against mine as the heat of our desire built to an almost unbearable pitch. Her fingers tangled in my hair, pulling me closer, her lips leaving a trail of kisses along my neck.

I could feel the press of her against me, the warmth of her skin, the softness of her curves enveloping me. The world fell away until there was nothing but us, our bodies moving together in a perfect harmony that spoke of love and longing.

The kiss deepened, grew more urgent, as if we were both trying to consume the other. My hands gripped her hips, holding her to me as if I could merge our bodies into one.

Celeste's nails dug into my back, her movements growing more frantic as the need between us built to a crescendo. I could feel her heat, her desire, a mirror of my own.

Our bodies pressed together, skin on skin, the connection between us undeniable. Celeste's breath was hot against my face, her lips brushing mine as she whispered, "Please, David, I need you."

I answered her plea with a fierce kiss, our lips and tongues tangling in a dance of pure passion. I was consumed by the need to possess her, to claim her as mine.

"Please me, David," she begged softly. "Please me as I saw you please your other women — my harem sisters. Give me the love you gave them."

With the moon casting its silvery glow over the secluded pond, I gently guided Celeste to the soft grass by the water's edge. The night was ours, a private world where the only sounds were the gentle lapping of the water and the rustling leaves in the gentle breeze.

Diane and Leigh stood a little distance away, their giggles floating in the air like the music of the night. They watched us with eyes full of mirth and encouragement, their hands already beginning to explore their own curves as they slowly undressed themselves in the moonlight.

I knelt beside Celeste, my gaze locked with hers, full of love and desire. Her breath came in soft gasps as I leaned down to press my lips against the tender skin of her neck, evoking a sweet sigh from her lips.

The warmth of her skin was intoxicating, and I kissed her slowly, savoring the taste of her. My lips moved over her collarbone, trailing kisses down to the swell of her breasts, where I lingered, teasing her nipples into hard peaks with my tongue.

Celeste's hands found their way into my hair, holding me to her as her back arched slightly, pushing her breasts closer to my eager mouth. Her moans grew louder, a symphony of pleasure that spurred me on.

"Yes, David," she moaned. "Show me the pleasures... Please..."

My kisses traveled lower, over the soft plane of her stomach, where I could feel her muscles quiver under my touch. Celeste's hips rose to meet me, an unconscious invitation that I accepted with fervor.

As I reached the juncture of her thighs, I took my time, planting soft kisses along the insides, feeling her tremble with each touch. My hands caressed her legs, parting them gently as I made my way to the center of her desire.

The scent of her arousal mingled with the fresh forest air, and I inhaled deeply, intoxicated by her essence. I moved down, my lips grazing her cute tuft of amber pubic hair. Finally, my lips found her pussy, warm and wet, waiting for me.

I kissed her there softly at first, eliciting a sharp gasp from Celeste. Her fingers tightened in my hair, urging me closer, silently begging for more.

My tongue flicked out to taste her, drawing a long, slow path up her slit before circling her clit. Celeste's moans filled the clearing, and she began to move her hips in time with my tongue's explorations.

"David... oh, please..." she whispered, her voice laced with need. I could feel her body tensing, her pleasure building as I continued to lavish attention on her.

Diane and Leigh, lost in their own world of

pleasure, had sunk to the ground, their fingers working between their own thighs as they watched us. Their soft moans of pleasure echoed Celeste's, a chorus of arousal that filled the night.

Celeste's breaths came faster now, and I could feel her pussy clenching and unclenching as her orgasm approached. I doubled my efforts, determined to push her over the edge.

Her hands gripped my head, her legs wrapped around my shoulders as she rode the waves of pleasure my mouth and tongue provided.

"Yes, David... just like that... I'm so close..." Celeste moaned, her voice rising in pitch as she neared her climax.

I sucked her clit into my mouth, flicking it with my tongue, and that was all it took. Celeste's body arched off the ground, a strangled cry of ecstasy escaping her as her orgasm washed over her. She gasped and shook with pleasure, her beautiful cheeks colored red.

And even as she came, Diane and Leigh, too, aroused beyond themselves, came hard while watching us. Their delicious bodies quivered, the moonlight playing on their curves, and my cock nearly burst with a need for release as I turned my eyes back to Celeste, squirming before me in all her delights.

The sight of her coming undone under my ministrations, the taste of her climax, drove me wild with desire. My cock ached with the need to claim her, to be one with her.

As Celeste's tremors subsided, I raised my head to look at her, her face flushed with the afterglow of her release, her eyes heavy-lidded and full of love.

"David," she hummed, her voice small. "I have wanted this for so long."

I smiled, my heart echoing that same sensation. "So have I," I said, my voice hoarse with desire.

And as we watched each other in the moonlight, Diane and Leigh, still recovering from their orgasms, crawled closer to us, their expressions full of awe and admiration for the love they had witnessed.

"Come here," Leigh hummed to Celeste. "Lay your head on my lap."

"Hm-hm," Diane purred. "It's time."

Celeste giggled — equal parts arousal and anticipation — as Leigh gently scooped Celeste's head into her lap, cradling her new harem sister as she looked up at me with those big blue eyes, inviting me to finalize my claim to Celeste.

Diane lay beside them, her hand resting softly on Celeste's thigh, as if beckoning me to claim the prize it led to. There was a soft smile on her lips as she watched me with expectation.

Celeste, now nestled in Leigh's embrace, turned her gaze to me, her eyes still burning with the fire of her climax.

"David," she breathed, "take me... claim me as yours."

Celeste lay naked before me, her head sweetly nestled in Leigh's lap while Diane stroked her amber locks. She was ready and eager for me to claim her maidenhood and consummate our marriage, and there was nothing more I wanted in this world.

"Come," she hummed, her green eyes dreamy and soft.

Her eyes beckoned me closer, her body a siren's call that I could no longer resist. I positioned myself before her, my arousal flawlessly demonstrating the depth of my desire. The head of my cock pressed against her slick entrance, eager to enter her.

She gave a cute gasp at feeling the tip of my weapon about to penetrate her. She bit her lip as she looked up at me with eyes full of desire.

"Yes," she mewled. "Do it, David. Please."

"Take her, David," Leigh whispered. "Make her part of our family."

"Love her and fill her with your seed," Diane echoed.

I looked down at Celeste, at the love and trust shining in her eyes, and I knew this was where I belonged. With a gentle thrust, I entered her, finally making her mine.

As I filled her, Celeste let out a soft cry of

pleasure. I began to move gently within her, our bodies joining in a rhythm of love and lust. Leigh and Diane inched closer; their eyes locked on us as they witnessed the sealing of our bond.

The moment was deep within her; the world around us ceased to exist. There was only the sensation of her warmth enveloping me, her tightness gripping me in a way that was both an embrace and a welcome.

Celeste gasped, her hands gripping my shoulders as she adjusted to the new sensation. Her eyes fluttered closed, a soft moan escaping her lips as I began to move within her.

I started gently, allowing her time to become accustomed to the feel of me. But as her breaths grew deeper and her moans more insistent, I knew she wanted more — needed more.

"Faster, David," Celeste breathed, her voice a whisper that carried the weight of her need. I obliged, quickening my pace, each thrust bringing a new cry of delight from her lips.

Diane and Leigh, their own pleasure evident, urged us on, their voices a chorus of encouragement that spurred me to greater heights. "Yes, David, claim her, love her," they sang out, their words wrapping around us like the night air.

And I did. We made love like the free heirs of the earth, born to live in the open and love with no shame or bounds. Under the soft spell of moonlight, we shared each other, and a spiritual union formed between the four of us as we melded into one.

Celeste's body began to tremble, her climax approaching like a storm on the horizon. Her fingers dug into my back, her movements growing more frantic as she sought release.

"I'm close, David... so close," she panted, her voice breaking with the intensity of her pleasure.

I felt her pussy clamp down on me. Her inner walls pulsed as she reached the pinnacle of her desire. The sight of her in the throes of ecstasy, the feel of her body surrendering to the waves of her climax, pushed me to the brink.

Leigh and Diane's hands were gentle on Celeste's shoulders and stroking her amber locks as if displaying the elven beauty for me, inviting me to fill her with my seed.

With a final, deep thrust, I released inside Celeste, my orgasm crashing over me with a force that left me breathless. My body shuddered with the intensity of my release, every nerve ending singing with pleasure.

Celeste cried out, her voice mingling with the night sounds as she felt the heat of me filling her. Her body clung to mine, her orgasm rolling through her in waves that seemed to touch the very stars above.

We were silent, all of us, at the beauty. There was something deeply natural and spiritual about this union, and I reveled in it as Celeste's shapely legs wrapped around me to keep me inside her, wanting every drop of my essence that I had to give.

As our climaxes subsided, I held Celeste close, our bodies still joined in the most intimate of embraces. Diane and Leigh were with us, wrapping their arms around us both as they murmured soft words of beauty, love, and appreciation.

After that, the night grew quiet once more, the wind whispering softly in the background as the brook babbled. Celeste rested against me, her body sated and content, her eyes telling me without words how much she had enjoyed our union.

I kissed her forehead, feeling a sense of peace settle over me. This was what it meant to be truly alive, to love and be loved in return. Diane and Leigh nestled with us, their bodies a comforting warmth as they shared in our happiness.

As we lay like that, the moon continued its silent vigil overhead, its light a blessing upon our love. The pond mirrored the sky above, a perfect reflection of the beauty that surrounded us.

Finally, Celeste turned to me with a smile that outshone the moon itself.

"David, this was so special," she murmured. "I enjoyed it more than words can say."

I nodded in agreement. "It will be like this for the rest of our lives," I said, keeping my women in a tight embrace.

Chapter 44

The first light of dawn crept over the horizon, painting the sky in strokes of pink and orange. I rose before the others, slipping out of bed and leaving the warmth of my women's embrace.

The first night with Celeste in our bed had been perfect, and we had hardly slept at all. We had celebrated and enjoyed each other's bodies until deep in the night, and it had been all I had hoped it would be.

I dressed quietly, pulling on a simple shirt and pants, and made my way down the stairs. The homestead was still, a serene calm only the early morning could bring. The air was cool and crisp, a gentle reminder that autumn was on its way.

I was in the mood for a walk — just to breathe the fresh air and clear my head a little. So much had happened.

Stepping outside, I took a deep breath, filling my lungs with the fresh, pine-scented air. My land was quiet, save for the soft chirping of birds greeting the new day. I cherished these moments of solitude, a chance to reflect on the whirlwind of events that had transpired.

The domesticants, ever diligent, noticed my presence and floated over, their spectral forms darting around me playfully. I greeted them with a smile, their antics bringing a lightness to my heart.

"Good morning, little guys," I said, chuckling as they zipped back and forth.

I began my walk, strolling along the well-worn paths that crisscrossed the property. The dew-covered grass glistened under the awakening sun, each drop a tiny prism reflecting the growing light. It was moments like these that I felt a profound connection to my land.

I passed the garden plots, where the magical crops were thriving under the care of my companions. The magebread flowers swayed gently in the morning breeze, their petals unfurling to catch the first rays of sunlight. It was a sight to behold, nature and magic intertwined.

My path led me to the banks of the Silverthread River next, its waters a silvery ribbon winding through the forest. The river had greatly grown on me, and it provided many things to our little corner of the Earth. I watched it for a while, lost in thought.

As I walked, I pondered the days ahead. The wedding celebration would soon come, a day that would mark the beginning of a new chapter. I imagined the joy it would bring, the union of our hearts and lives declared before family and friends.

According to elven custom, it was just a formality, but my grandparents would love it, and so would I.

Then there was Diane, her pregnancy a miracle that filled me with both excitement and a protective fervor. The thought of becoming a father, of holding a new life in my arms, was both exhilarating and daunting.

But amidst the joy, there was also the shadow that loomed on the horizon. The dragon Father's coming was an inevitability that I could not ignore. No word had come from Ironfast to announce its coming yet, but the thought of the elder dragon's arrival cast a chill over me, despite the morning's growing warmth.

I knew that whatever threats lay ahead, I would face them with the strength and determination that had carried me this far. The safety of my family was paramount, and I would do whatever it took to protect them.

The domesticants fluttered around me, their presence a reminder of the mystical forces at my command. I felt a surge of confidence, knowing I was not alone in my endeavors. Magic and might were on my side.

With a determined stride, I turned back toward the homestead, ready to embrace the day's tasks. There was much to do, preparations for the celebration and ensuring our defenses were strong against any threat.

As I walked, my thoughts turned to my women, their love a fortress against any darkness. The bond we shared was unbreakable, a beacon that would guide us through whatever trials we faced. The homestead was our sanctuary — a place of love and life that we had created together. It was here that we would stand against whatever came our way.

The domesticants followed at my heels as I approached the house, their forms glowing softly in the morning light. As I approached the door, the scent of breakfast began to drift from the kitchen, a sign that the others were stirring.

The thought of the warm, cozy atmosphere inside, filled with the laughter and chatter of my loved ones, quickened my pace. Waelin and my grandparents were still here, having spent the night. I was looking forward to spending a morning with them, especially now that Waelin had warmed up a little.

I reached the porch, the wooden boards creaking under my feet as I ascended the steps. Pausing at the doorway, I took one last look at the tranquil land stretching out before me.

With a contented sigh, I made ready to step inside, ready to join my family and share the news of the coming day. But as I reached for the doorknob to rejoin my family, a sudden sense of foreboding washed over me.

I couldn't explain it, but something told me that someone was coming. On the threshold, I turned to look back once more, my eyes scanning the horizon.

And that's when I saw her — a lone figure approaching the property.

A tall and lithe woman in a hooded cloak.

I frowned, wondering how this visitor had managed to escape Mr. Drizzles' notice. And just as I was about to call for my rifle — it was best to err on the side of caution — the figure saw me.

She stopped and threw the hood back, revealing cat ears. A cat tail billowed out from under the cloak.

A catkin...

"Who goes there?" I shouted.

She stood silent for a moment. Then came her voice, carried to me on the wind.

"I am Yeska of the Wildclaws," she announced. "A Bloodmage, and I answer your summons!"

Finished and eager for early access to my next book? Check out my Patreon: patreon.com/jackbryce

THANK YOU FOR READING!

If you enjoyed this book, please check out my other work on Amazon.

Be sure to **leave me a review on Amazon** to let me know if you liked this book! Like most independent authors, I use the feedback from your review to improve my work and to decide what to focus on next, so your review can make a difference.

If you want early access to my work, consider joining my Patreon (https://patreon.com/jackbryce)!

If you want to stay up-to-date on my releases, you can join my newsletter by entering the following link into any web browser: https://fierce-thinker-305.ck.page/45f709af30. You can also join my Discord, where the madness never ends... Join by entering the following invite manually in your browser or Discord app: https://discord.gg/uqXaTMQQhr.

Jack Bryce's Books

Below you'll find a list of my work, all available through Amazon.

Frontier Summoner (ongoing series)

Frontier Summoner 1

Frontier Summoner 2

Frontier Summoner 3

Frontier Summoner 4

Frontier Summoner 5

Country Mage (completed series)

Country Mage 1

Country Mage 2

Country Mage 3

Country Mage 4

Country Mage 5

Country Mage 6

Country Mage 7

Country Mage 8

Country Mage 9

Country Mage 10

Warped Earth (completed series)

Apocalypse Cultivator 1

Apocalypse Cultivator 2

Apocalypse Cultivator 3

Apocalypse Cultivator 4

Apocalypse Cultivator 5

Aerda Online (completed series)

Phylomancer

Demon Tamer

Clanfather

Highway Hero (ongoing series)

Highway Hero 1

Highway Hero 2

A SPECIAL THANKS TO...

My patron in the Godlike tier: Lynderyn!
My patrons in the High Mage tier: Christian Smith, Eddie Fields, Michael Sroufe, and Christopher Eichman!

All of my other patrons at patreon.com/jackbryce!

Stoham Baginbott, Louis Wu, and Scott D. for beta reading. You guys are absolute kings.

If you're interested in beta reading for me, hit me up on discord (JauntyHavoc#8836) or send an e-mail to lordjackbryce@gmail.com. The list is currently full, but spots might open up in the future.

Made in the USA
Monee, IL
14 April 2024

56938694R00277